# AZRAEL

# William L. DeAndrea

# AZRAEL

**THE MYSTERIOUS PRESS**

New York • London

Printed in the United States of America
First Printing: August 1987
10  9  8  7  6  5  4  3  2  1

**Library of Congress Cataloging-in-Publication Data**

DeAndrea, William L.
  Azrael.

  I. Title.
PS3554.E174A99  1987        813'.54        86-31127
ISBN 0-89296-203-8

*For Meredith*

# AUTHOR'S NOTE

This is the third book in my series of mythologically titled spy stories. All the characters, incidents, and institutions are fictitious, except for the FBI and the KGB, which are used fictitiously. The Northside Church is intended to represent no actual religious denomination. The town of Kirkester and its neighboring towns are invented as well.

The only factual element of the story is the running catalog of Soviet atrocities, which are well documented, though you wouldn't think so if all you see are regular American media.

As in *Cronus* and *Snark*, the previous books in this series, I want to stress that while there is a Congressional committee that oversees American intelligence operations, and it has a chairman, the character called the Congressman is in no way intended to represent anyone who has ever held that office.

Finally, I wish to thank Richard Meyers, for help on some technical details, and Barbara Gonzo, without whom Azrael would never have flown at all.

—WLD

# PROLOGUE

*Kirkester, New York, May*

He held the boy's head under until the bubbles stopped, then gently lowered it through the last few inches of cold, clear stream water until it rested on the bottom.

He was—had been—a fine-looking boy, *Saturday Evening Post* material, sandy hair, bright hazel eyes, freckles. He had just landed a sunny when Roger spoke to him for the first time.

"Nice fish," Roger said.

"Not bad for a sunny," the boy conceded. His name, Roger knew, was Keith Smith. He was three weeks short of his tenth birthday.

"I didn't expect anyone to be out here," Roger said.

"Usually isn't," the boy told him. He finished unhooking the fish and put it in a water-filled plastic bucket. Then he reached into a plastic bag that sat beside him on the rock, took out a slice of white balloon bread, tore off a piece, wadded it into a ball, stuck it on a hook, and tossed his line back into the stream.

"The trouble with sunnies is that they're too easy to catch. Nobody usually comes here, because the water's too calm. All you

1

get here is sunnies, and little ones, at that. All the real fishermen are upstream, where the water is faster and the good fish are. Except, every once in a while, I see a couple of colored guys on the other bank fishing for eels. Did you ever eat an eel?"

"Sure," Roger said.

Keith looked at him skeptically. "Okay, well, I never have. Sounds gross to me. Still, the black guys swear by them."

"Are they here today?"

"Naw, never on a weekday. They used to. They're pressmen. When they worked the night shift, they were here a lot, but they got rotated onto days, so they can only come on Saturday and Sunday."

"Sounds like you're here a lot," Roger said.

"Sometimes. I like to go where the bigger fish are, but my dad has to take me. I was going to go there today with him—he's on vacation—but he got called in special because of that thing in the Middle East."

"Is your father a diplomat?" Roger asked, though he already knew what Frederick Smith did for a living.

"No," the boy said. "He's associate managing editor of *Worldwatch* magazine. He's on call all the time." Keith's voice held a mixture of pride and a sort of wistful resentment.

"But what brings you out here?" Keith asked. "Not fishing."

Roger grinned at him. If he let himself, he could get to like this boy. Of course, there wouldn't be time. "That was easy enough to figure out," he said. "No gear."

Keith grinned back; Roger went on. "No, I just like to walk in the woods, by the stream. I'm new around here, so I try to take a different direction every day. Except when it rains, of course. Didn't expect to find anyone to talk to. My name's Roger."

"Mine's Keith," the boy said. "I don't mind talking." He slid over to make more room, but Roger never joined him. Instead, taking care to walk only on the rocks (it wouldn't do to leave footprints), he circled around to the side of the boulder the boy sat on. At one point he lost his balance and went down. One knee and one hand landed in the water.

"Are you okay?" Keith asked.

"Fine, fine. Just slipped. The sun will dry me out in no time." He rose again. In his hand, he could feel the weight of a moss-covered stone. He showed it to Keith. "I think this is the one that got me."

The boy nodded. "The moss makes it slippery. You could break your head."

Roger came closer, then hit Keith in the temple with the mossy side of the rock, a short, straight blow that did the job with

2

merciful efficiency. Keith slumped over sideways without making a sound. Roger lifted the boy's body carefully and brought him down to the stream, to the place where he'd slipped and picked up the rock. He put the stone back in its place, mossy side up, then took Keith's head between his hands and held it under the surface. Roger's lips moved.

When it was done, Roger looked around for traces of his presence. He had walked where he'd leave no footprints, and the rough natural surfaces of the rocks and trees would take no fingerprints.

Someone, some uneducated person, might wonder about the serene expression on the boy's face, might say that if he'd slipped and fallen and hurt his head, there should be a surprised look there.

Someone *might* say that, until someone of superior knowledge informed him that there was no scientific basis for that kind of assumption.

Roger wasn't worried about it. There was a good chance that there would be no recognizable expression on the face by the time the boy's clay was found.

Besides, Roger had no intention of changing the boy's expression, even if he could. Keith had done no one any harm. He deserved the peace.

Roger looked down at him for a long moment, then took a deep breath and walked away. He was careful to step only on stones, to leave no traces of his having been there.

## August

The heat and humidity had steamed the neighborhood clean. There was a patch of shimmer above the sidewalk, and swing sets and tricycles sat gleaming and abandoned in small front yards behind low privet hedges.

This was the Flats, the lower-middle-class section of Kirkester (there were no poor), but life was pleasant here all the same. All the men of the neighborhood, and most of the women, were out working in air-conditioned offices or printing plants or stores or restaurants or at the new Quality Inn near the Hudson complex. Those who didn't work would be lying down in air-conditioned bedrooms after a tough morning's housework or with their children at the James Hudson, Sr., Memorial Pool.

No one would see him, Roger was sure, and if someone did, no one would recognize him. He looked like an exhausted door-to-door salesman. Kirkester was a town that still got door-to-door salesmen; the police kept them away from the fancier neighborhoods.

Roger had a sweat-stained hat on his head, a pair of lavender-beige summer suit pants on his legs. He carried the jacket. His shirt sleeves were rolled up, his tie was loose and his collar was open. He was carrying a sample case that was obviously heavy. He was trying very hard to look like a man who was just hoping to make it to where his car was parked on the next block.

He was, in fact, headed away from his car. Well, not his car. It had been provided for him by his employers. Untraceable. They were good at things like that.

He followed the sound. As his groundwork had shown him, it was very likely to be the only sound in the neighborhood, aside from the hum of air conditioners. This sound was the clang of metal on metal to a rock beat. Roger was close enough to hear the lyrics of the song now. It seemed the singer (presumably, but not demonstrably, a male) wanted to make love to a girl during a nuclear holocaust. Roger shook his head and followed the music up a driveway.

Louis Symczyk was lying on his back under a wheelless sports car supported by blocks. Every once in a while an oily hand would appear and grab one of the wrenches arrayed just in reach. From under the car came alternating grunts, first of effort, then of, Roger supposed, musical ecstasy.

The song—it was coming from a tape player—was very loud, and Roger walked quietly.

He stood and watched the young man for a minute. He never went more than ten seconds without changing wrenches, and he never touched more than one wrench each time he reached for one. It was a pleasure to watch someone at work who knew what he was doing.

Roger sometimes wished someone would appreciate what he did. But his employers judged him only by results; technique didn't come into it. And of course, Roger didn't dare breathe a word about purpose. Not theirs, and *definitely* not his.

And that left only the work to be done.

"Hello," Roger said.

Casters rolled on concrete, and Lou's face appeared from under the car.

"Oh, hi," he said. "Didn't hear you come up." Even with sweat-soaked hair and oil marks on his face, he was a handsome young man.

"Sorry to bother you," Roger said. The idea was to sound a little breathless, which wasn't difficult, considering the weight of the briefcase. "It's just that it's so hot, I feel like I'm burning up. I

**4**

think I'm going to have a stroke in a second if I don't splash some water on my face."

"Geez," the young man said. He pointed over Roger's shoulder at a sink Roger already knew was there. "Help yourself," he said. "You want a beer or something? Soda? Ice water?"

To make it look good, Roger had already put down the case and made for the sink. He was splashing water over his face. It was part of the plan, but it felt good all the same.

He paused between double handfuls of water to tell Lou no thanks. When he was finished, he turned back to the young man and thanked him. "You probably saved my life."

Lou smiled at him. "You're still dripping," he said.

"It feels good," Roger told him. "A man has to be crazy to go door-to-door on a day like this. Nobody's home, anyway. I don't know what you were doing out, but thank God you're here."

The young man's smile took on a slightly wicked gleam. "Heavy date tonight. Have to make sure the mechanical phallus is in perfect shape. Believe me, when I'm done here, I'm standing under a cold shower until it's time to get dressed, then I'm hitting an air-conditioned movie."

Roger said it sounded like a good idea to him. "Well," he said, "better get going. Thanks again." He bent to pick up his sample case, then straightened suddenly, swinging the case in a wide arc into the side of Louis Symczyk's head.

The young man dropped to the floor like a pile of laundry. Roger put the brick-loaded case down again and bent over the young man. No moans. No detectable breathing. Roger brought his hands up close to his chest and carefully flicked them dry. Tiny drops of water beaded up on the skin of the young man's face.

Carefully, Roger placed Louis Symczyk back on his mechanic's dolly and rolled him back under the car. He made certain that the young man's shoes stayed clear of the cement floor. This was not likely to be investigated too thoroughly, but if by any chance it should be, Roger was too professional to leave drag marks on clothes or shoes.

When he had the body positioned, he spent a few seconds taking stock. The head was under a suspension spring. Right. He'd put the bricks back at the construction site and burn the briefcase tonight. Right.

Mission accomplished. Or it would be, in just a second. Roger kicked out the left front block, and the car came down. Tendrils of red began to trace their way across the black grease on the floor.

Roger turned and left before any could reach him.

## September

In some ways this would be the easiest job yet, in some ways the hardest. Easiest because it demanded no guile, no deception. The victim didn't need to be lulled. Hardest because it involved breaking into a house, with others home. Breaking in was simple enough—a butter knife could move a window latch, and the rattle of raindrops and the banging of thunder from the late-summer storm tonight would cover any noise *he* happened to make.

But there was always a chance someone would walk in on him, wanting to "check on the baby" or something, and if that happened, everyone in the house had to die. That would be bad for two reasons: it would dilute the message his employers were trying to send, and it would force him to use fire. He didn't like to use fire. Fire diluted the message *Roger* was sending.

Still, he had his mission. Window latch slipped, sash slid up during a crash of thunder. A roll of dry plastic taken out from under his jacket, spread out on the floor to save wet footprints on the rug. A few soft, crackling footsteps across the plastic to the crib.

He could hear voices from another room. He held his breath to hear better. Someone said, "Blake." Television. Roger let his breath go.

The baby was asleep, which was good. Quieter. The wadded towel in one hand, the kid's head in the other. It was over in seconds.

Now, a few quiet steps back to the window, pull the plastic out behind him and relatch with a piece of waxed dental floss. In the morning, or whenever, they would discover the tragic crib death. The water on the sheet, on the baby's head, from Roger's rain-wet hands, would have dried. And no one would ever know.

Except, of course, the one who was supposed to know. That, however, wasn't Roger's department. All he had to do now was go back to his other life and await further orders.

# PART ONE

## CHAPTER ONE

She would have had more fun if she'd gone to the funeral.

Not, of course, that the funeral wouldn't have been gruesome enough. God knew the other ones had. Weeping mothers. And fathers. Regina had been shocked and disappointed in herself to discover that a weeping man upset her much more than a weeping woman. A minister of God telling the mourners, as if he thought they didn't already know, what a tragedy it was for a life to be snuffed out so young, with so much ahead of it. Back in May, the minister at the service for Keith Smith had told everyone to take comfort in the knowledge that God knows what he's doing but that it is not always given to man to understand. He also assured them that God Never Tries Us Beyond Our Strength, and that Faith Would See Us Through. The priest at the services for Lou Symczyk had been much simpler about it—Lou was in heaven, and for that we should be happy.

Maybe so, Regina thought. It was hard, though, to be happy for someone whose head had been crushed by a '77 Firebird slipping off a jack onto his head. Heaven had also been problematical, considering the number of speeding tickets and public scalps Lou had managed to accumulate with a succession of faster and faster cars in the three years between his reaching driving age and his death. He had even had the nerve to ask Regina to "go for a ride" with him once. She had, of course, refused. It would have been ridiculous. Regina was aware, though, that if she had been Lou's age or younger, instead of four and a half years older, she might have been tempted.

Regina had spent an August morning sweltering in black at the side of Lou's soon-to-be grave, hating every minute of it, as she had hated the glorious late-spring day she'd spent with the box containing little Keith Smith. She'd gone because, as her mother said, the Hudson Group was more than just a publishing concern. To the millions of people its two-hundred-odd local newspapers, radio and TV stations and cable systems reached, it was a spokesman, a teacher, and a goad. It informed them, spoke up for them, challenged them. To the readers of *Worldwatch* it was a fresh and different look at each week's national and international news.

To the people of Kirkester, especially to those who had given up Manhattan or Chicago to come work here in the boonies at the home office, the Hudson Group was family.

Regina grinned. Speaking about the billion-dollar business Father and she (mostly she) had built, Mother had a tendency to sound like a rough draft of the introduction to the annual report.

But she meant every word of it, including the business about family. When tragedy struck, the Hudsons had to be there. It made no difference if the employee involved was top management, like Fred Smith, or a janitor, like Kasimir Symczyk. Duty called; Regina went.

But not today. Today they were burying a baby.

Clara Bloyd, age nine months, daughter of Tina Bloyd, typesetter. Sudden infant death syndrome. Crib death. Parents awoke to find perfectly healthy infants dead. Regina remembered it had been one of the first *Worldwatch* cover stories.

Regina had decided enough was enough. Yes, a journalist should be inured to all sorts of suffering and tragedy, and yes, Regina was going to be a first-rate journalist in spite of her name and connections. But she was damned if she was going to spend a beautiful, cool, October Thursday, with the sky bright blue and the trees trying to make up in a week for a year of single-color drabness, listening to sermons and lamentations over a small white wooden box. She'd stay in the office instead. Go over circulation reports. Relay her mother's instructions to writers and artists and researchers. Wait for late-breaking stories.

Feel guilty.

And petty, and cowardly, and like a phony. Mother was at the funeral. Jimmy was at the funeral. Regina's brother seemed to like nothing about the family business except the people who worked for it. He probably thought of, supervised and carried out more community and charity work than any nineteen-year-old in the world, with the possible exception of European royalty. Regina loved him, but she didn't understand him very well.

She did understand that her mother and Jimmy were right about noblesse oblige. The way Old Man Symczyk had carried on, you might have thought it was a privilege for him to have his grandson die, if only as an occasion of proof of the respect in which he and his were held by the first family of the community.

Regina felt guilty about that, too, and guilty at the thought that at the age of twenty-four, when most of her friends were already disillusioned or divorced, she was still worried about her right to avoid an unpleasant experience versus her obligation to help other people get over theirs. Maybe she should suggest a Lifestyles piece on it—the Me Decade Meets the Old Guilt.

She was about half ready to start taking herself seriously when the phone on her mother's desk buzzed.

And kept buzzing. Her mother's secretary should have picked up, but he was probably in the bathroom or something. Regina sighed, punched a button, and picked up the phone.

"Petra Hudson's office," she said. She had always loved the idea of somebody's office answering the phone. One of Regina's small triumphs at the Kirkester *Chronicle*, the hometown paper her mother had given her to run the way other mothers give their children the wooden spoon to lick, was to forbid the practice of sending memos attributed to your desk. Some of the old-liners, the I-was-working-here-before-anybody'd-ever-heard-of-your-father crowd, had grown very protective of the authority of their desks, but Regina was in charge, Regina had made a decision and Regina had made it stick. Desks did not send memos, people did. If a newspaper couldn't say what it meant, what good was it?

Regina's mother had watched the memo war with a sort of absent amusement. Petra Hudson could have settled the matter by fiat at any time, but Regina would be damned if she was going to ask, and Mother, to her credit, did not volunteer. It was one of the things Regina admired about her mother—she didn't meddle.

Regina admired a lot of things about her mother, and respected her, and even loved her, but it was a distant kind of love, communicated through the media of nannies' reports and letters to and from boarding schools here and abroad, while Mother fought the good fight to keep the Hudson Group in Hudson hands after the death of James Hudson, Sr.

Sometimes it seemed to Regina that she was not so much a

daughter as she was a Chosen Successor. The feeling had been stronger over the last few years, since it had become obvious that Jimmy had no interest in the family business, but it had always been there. Why else had they named her Regina, for God's sake, if they didn't expect that someday she would reign?

Thank God she loved the business.

Now Regina sat (temporarily) on her mother's throne, holding her mother's electronic scepter to her ear.

"Western Union calling," a voice of indeterminate sex announced.

Regina smiled. It was appropriate that somebody's office should pick up the phone to find an entire corporation on the other end of the line.

"We have a message for Ms. Hudson."

"I'll take it."

"Ms. Hudson?"

Regina wondered when Western Union had gotten so picky. "I'm Ms. Hudson," she said truthfully. Her mother was going to be in no mood to chase down messages after she got home.

"Deepest condolences for your loss," the voice began.

"What?" It took a split second for Regina to realize this was the beginning of the message, rather than some kind of gentle insult, but it was still bewildering. Petra Hudson hadn't suffered any loss her daughter knew about.

"Deepest condolences on your loss," the voice said again. "It is well known how you feel about your family. Tragedy can strike at any time, but strength and wisdom can see us through. Best personal regards."

There was a silence. Regina doubted it was a pause for effect, since the whole thing had been read in the mechanical singsong of a court stenographer.

"Is that it?" she asked.

"There is a signature."

"Okay," Regina said. "Whose?"

"It's signed, Cronus."

There'd been some expression in the voice that time, and there could be no doubt that the pause had been intentional. Regina was losing her patience.

"Cronus," she said.

"You heard me correctly," the voice said. It was less Western Union-like all the time.

"And who the hell," she said, "is Cronus?"

But even if she'd been expecting an answer, she wasn't going to get one. The owner of the voice had hung up before she'd even gotten to "hell."

# CHAPTER TWO

The people may have come to the child's funeral to mourn, but they stayed to gossip. Petra Hudson had good ears, better ears than the gossipers thought she did. They kept choking off their sentences or lowering their voices a split second too late. Petra heard the fragments of insult and insinuation all the way from the gravesite to the car.

". . . her 'driver.' Too democratic to say 'chauffeur' . . ." This with a finger pointed through the crook of an elbow at Wes Charles, who held his cap in one gloved hand and his employer's elbow in the other, helping her over the muddy spots.

". . . sleeping with him?" another voice said.

". . . never needed a driver before this year. Drove herself. Said she liked it that . . ." Petra recognized that last voice, one of the photo editors on *Worldwatch*. She was ready to whirl on the man and fire him on the spot, but that would have been madness. A child had just been laid to rest here, an infant. A young mother was facing the greatest grief imaginable. This was no time to make a scene.

And, she decided, there never would be a good time to fire the man. Not for gossiping about her, at least. It was, she reminded herself, a free country, and this was part of the price you paid for being the boss.

They reached the car. Charles let go of her elbow and attended to the door. Petra Hudson sat on soft white leather and let her breath go with an undignified *whoosh*. She unpinned the hat and shook her hair loose, thick black hair that halfway through her fifties needed no touch-ups. Which was something else they gossiped about.

When journalists wrote about Petra Hudson (and they frequently did, the only thing journalists like to write about more than crooked politicians being other journalists), two words never failed to appear—*statuesque* and *handsome*. She had no complaints, even when they managed to work in the information that the late James Hudson, Sr., had been a mere five feet five inches tall. As if there were something perverted about a small man marrying a large woman.

11

To hell with them. James might have been attracted to her because she was big. She had, in fact, counted on that before she ever met him. But anyone who thought that was what their marriage was based on was pathetically wrong.

James Hudson had a small body, a moderate amount of capital, and a genius for the communications business. He took joy in it, and he shared every bit of that joy with his wife, so much so that when he died, she was able to take over and to build on his plans without missing a beat. Her happiness in the growth of the Hudson Group was doubled by the knowledge that she was carrying on for the man who'd changed her life.

Had changed her life so profoundly, in fact, that until late February of this year, she had almost managed to put her old life from her memory.

In February there had been a letter for her that reminded her of what her life had been before. That same day, she had the new security system put in at her home. She began to pressure her daughter subtly, relentlessly, but so far unsuccessfully, to give up her apartment in town and move back home. From the security company, she got the name of a very special employment agency, and they sent Weston Charles.

Charles was an excellent driver—actually better than excellent, since he was a master of antiattack maneuvers. The employment agency had insisted on bringing her out to some deserted roads and having Charles demonstrate his skills. That, Petra was grateful, had been the only time he'd needed to use those particular skills, or his black-belt karate skills, or his world-class pistol marksmanship.

With all that it was an undeserved bonus that he was such a nice man. He was polite without being subservient. Both her children liked him, and he them, and the dogs adored him. He was well educated and well spoken, and he had a sense of humor. He could even, in a pinch, cook. She wouldn't go so far as to say that finding someone like Charles had made facing the threat worthwhile—nothing could do that. But he did make things easier to face.

Charles blotted out a large percentage of the October sunlight as he got into the car. He was large enough to make the statuesque Petra Hudson seem petite. He had short, wavy blond hair and a florid complexion. He wasn't handsome, but he had a nice smile. He never talked about himself, which was, of course, the quickest way to get anybody remotely connected with journalism fascinated with you. Aside from his name, age (forty), and previous employer (a European businessman who'd died of natural causes), Petra knew nothing about him. Except she liked him as a person and valued him as an employee.

"Back to the office, Mrs. Hudson?" Charles asked.

"Yes, Charles. Regina's watching the office for me." She tried to keep her irritation at her daughter's refusal to come to the funeral from her voice.

"Very good, Mrs. Hudson."

Petra Hudson opened a compartment and brought out a pile of computer printout, circulation reports from around the chain. There was a whole group of papers in eastern Kansas that wasn't earning as well as it should, and she was going to find out why.

But not now. She looked at the neat figures on the neat little stripes of pale green and paler green, and all she could see was the senseless death of a little baby. Nothing she told herself about journalistic toughness, or about being a "good soldier" (one of her husband's favorite phrases), could get her mind off the tears and the sobbing from little Clara Bloyd's mother and grandmother. Petra Hudson would have cried with them, but no one would allow her to be the kind of woman who wept. No one would *believe* it.

Instead, she had to be the kind of woman who patted arms and said calm, soothing words, insisted she be notified if there was anything she could do.

The kind of woman so smooth and in control that strangers had to wonder what (or who) she spent her passion on.

"I'm sorry, Charles," she said.

"About what, Mrs. Hudson?"

"You must have heard. As we were leaving."

"Oh, that. Don't concern yourself. At least on my account. There's always talk like that."

"Really?" Petra was interested. This concerned her, and the part of her brain that was always working suggested that there might be a back-of-the-book article for the magazine in the life of someone like Charles.

"Yes, ma'am," Charles said. "Apparently, so many people can drive cars, they can't conceive of someone doing it for a living, so a driver is always sized up for what other services he might be providing."

"Like bodyguarding."

"Most people's imaginations run to other things. Even when the employer is so old the idea approaches science fiction."

"That must be embarrassing."

"You get used to it. Not that you have to."

"Have to what?"

"Get used to it. I can make people stop if you'd like. At least in your hearing."

"No, Charles. That would make people believe it, wouldn't it?"

The driver chuckled. "I doubt it, ma'am. Lovely, successful woman like you could do a lot better than a beat-up old bodyguard."

Petra Hudson smiled for the first time all day. She was still smiling when she walked into the office.

"Hello, Regina," she said.

"Hello, Mother. Where's Jimmy?"

"He went off with Mr. Polacek from the hospital. Something about a blood analysis machine or something. Any messages?"

"Yes," Regina said, and scowled.

"What's the matter, trouble with the computers again?"

Regina shook her head, picked up a sheet of paper from the desk, and handed it to her mother as the older woman stepped around to reclaim her seat.

She slipped on her glasses and read the words Regina had taken down.

She went numb. It had to be wrong. *Cronus.* She read the note again.

"Cronus," she whispered.

"Mom? What's wrong? You're white as a glass of milk. Mother?"

Petra Hudson didn't answer. Couldn't. Her last thought before she fainted was that she was glad she'd sat down before she read the note.

# CHAPTER THREE

The receptionist smiled brightly. She looked maybe fifteen years old. That indicated a young dentist. Dentists had a tendency to hire receptionists when they set up their offices and keep them there till death did them part.

"Have we done work for you before, Mr. . . . ?"

"Trotter," he said. He was calling himself Trotter these days. It seemed appropriate, since he was no longer so wholeheartedly on the run. "Allan Trotter."

The receptionist smiled again, as though those were the most beautiful sounds she'd ever heard. It was a nice smile. A good advertisement for her boss.

"No," Trotter went on. "I just moved to Oregon a little while ago."

"Oh," she said. "Do you like it?"

"It's beautiful," he said. It was the truth, but it wasn't the answer to the question. As far as Trotter was concerned, there was nothing out here but scenery. Scenery was fine in its place— on postcards. Still, it wasn't too far from Portland, which was a city, in spite of the fact that a snowcapped mountain was visible from every point in town.

"It is lovely, isn't it?" Trotter had found that Oregonians, especially new ones, behaved as if they planted every single pine tree personally. They were fairly normal otherwise.

The receptionist told him to have a seat and handed him a clipboard with a green mimeographed form on it. It had all the same questions in all the same places as the other forms he'd filled out across the country. He answered them with all the same lies. Nobody was going to trace him through dental work, or health records, or drug allergies. Spies got sick (ex-spies, Trotter reminded himself), and spies lost fillings, but spies who went to the same doctor or the same dentist more than once were liable to wind up dead. Or even worse, back on a payroll in Washington.

If Trotter stayed smart, he could stay fairly happy. As happy, at least, as it was possible for someone who'd been twisted from birth to fit snugly into a crooked world of lies and killing. Trotter's father was the king of that jungle, and like most kings, he planned a dynasty. He perpetrated a son with the (temporary) cooperation of a beautiful young woman who happened to be a particularly successful Soviet spy. The young woman eventually caught on to what the General (as he was then—he was the Congressman now) had in mind and, after a lot of trouble and effort, managed to beat her brains out against a metal bed frame.

But the Congressman, as he usually did, had the last laugh, arriving in time to see his son delivered by cesarean section and delivered into his care. Into training and conditioning that honed a natural talent for the work that was so strong, the boy had been doing it for twelve years before he realized he hated it.

The young man who called himself Allan Trotter had run, but his father had played him like a prize salmon, letting him run, then hauling him back when he needed him.

Finally, with the aid of an FBI man named Fenton Rines, Trotter had been able to acquire enough leverage to force his father to leave him alone. Not that the old man gave up that easily. But Trotter could choose his operations now.

He chose damned few. He had money, in the form of diamonds—portable, inflation-proof, and redeemable for cash anywhere in the world. He had a new name, a new identity, a new town every five months or so. Before he was Trotter, he'd been Bellman; before that, Dekker; and before that, Driscoll. And most important, he had a literal lifetime—his own lifetime—of training and experience in survival.

The doctor would see him now. The receptionist pointed the way for him down a narrow hall. Trotter was pleased to see that he'd been right about the dentist's age. The dentist was a tall blond guy who'd been born about the same time Trotter had. He filled Trotter's mouth with cotton, then treated him to a monologue made up of equal parts of the wonders of modern dental surgery and the fortunes of the Portland Trail Blazers.

When the drilling was done, the dentist told him he was about due for a cleaning and led him through into another office where Miss Petrello, the hygienist, was as delighted to see him as the receptionist had been. Miss Petrello was plump and pretty, with dark curly hair and black eyes her glasses made seem even larger than they were. She asked Trotter to sit in an astronaut-type couch built low to the floor, sat behind his right shoulder, grabbed an implement, and started to work.

Trotter found himself staring up at Miss Petrello's full, dark-pink, gloss-free lips. Then he became aware that the warmth on the side of his neck was Miss Petrello's decorously covered but ample bosom. He felt the tingle in his loins that told him he was about to become the owner of a determined and unbelievably embarrassing hard-on.

He killed it with willpower, then told himself how pathetic he was. Here he was in a parody of Victorian intimacy, with his head (for all intents) in a woman's lap, and she gazing intently at his face, and his body responds with a longing that almost hurts.

He had his father to thank for this. He had read all the books; he had studied normality, which he defined as the kind of life led by people who can reasonably expect to get through the next year without having to murder or torture anybody or fight for their own lives, but he had never experienced it.

In moments like this he realized how badly he wanted it. The knowledge that he could never have it burned with a pain that was almost incandescent. He'd conquered his penis; now he had to fight tears.

"I want you to show me how you floss," Miss Petrello announced.

Trotter laughed. Miss Petrello asked him what was so funny.

"Nothing," he said. "I was just thinking of something."

"I'm out of floss. I'll be right back."

Trotter told her it was no problem. He lay back and looked at the ceiling. Maybe he should ask Miss Petrello for a date. That would be a big step toward normality. He had never had a date or any kind of relationship with a woman, without a professional reason, in his life.

They'd have things to talk about. He could tell her how to garrote someone with dental floss or tie someone up with eight inches of the stuff in such a way that they'd never escape unless they were cut loose. She, on the other hand, could—

"Mr. Trotter?" A man's voice.

Trotter was out of the chair and on his feet instantly. He had been taught how to react when someone took him by surprise: 1. Decide whether you want to cripple or kill. 2. Do what you have decided. All this should take half a second or less. Trotter saw no gun; he'd disable his opponent, killing him only if he failed.

The rest was automatic, decided by the size of the room, the location of obstacles, the lights, dozens of things he didn't have to think about. He didn't want to go for the eyes or the groin, since injuries to those organs tended to make interrogation difficult afterward. All they wanted to talk about was their eyes or their testicles, and Trotter couldn't afford that if he wanted to get a few quick answers before he got out of there.

The soles of Trotter's shoes were soft rubber, no good for breaking a kneecap. Trotter grabbed a handful of stiff white cotton jacket and drew the man toward him. You can break a man's foot by smashing your heel down hard enough into the top of it, even if you aren't wearing shoes.

Stiff white cotton.

Trotter stopped his foot one inch from the dentist's. He decided he wasn't quite ready to ask Miss Petrello out.

"Sorry."

"*Sorry*! What's the matter with you? You could have crippled me! What the hell are you trying to do?"

Trotter thought of telling him it was his old fraternity handshake, but that would only have made him angrier. He tried a sheepish grin instead. "I really am sorry," he said. "I-I've been very jumpy lately. I'm thinking of seeing a doctor about it."

The dentist was smoothing finger marks out of his lab coat. "That might be a good idea. Doesn't have to be a psychiatrist, you know. Jumpy doesn't mean crazy. There are plenty of organic causes that might be behind this. Something as simple as diet could—"

"Where's Miss Petrello?" Trotter asked the question gently, but the dentist jumped as if he'd stepped on a jellyfish.

"Ah . . . she was done with you. I came in because there was a gentleman outside who wanted to see you."

Trotter raised an eyebrow.

"He . . . he says he's from the FBI."

"Ah," Trotter said. "Did he say anything else?"

Trotter suppressed a smile. He could see why the dentist was so upset. To have an FBI man come and ask for a patient, then to have the patient wheel on you like a homicidal maniac. . .

"Just that you're not in any trouble and that he would wait for you."

Trotter let the smile out. It felt odd, lopsided through the novocaine. "I won't keep him waiting any longer," he said. "How much do I owe you?"

The other man's mouth worked, and for a second Trotter thought the dentist was going to tell him, forget it, it's on the house. When the man got it together enough to say, "Eighty dollars. For the filling. And the cleaning," he told himself he should have known better. "On the house" was not the way these guys wound up driving BMWs.

The dentist flinched again when Trotter went to his pocket. He pulled out a wallet that contained about a thousand dollars in currency and better than four times that much in Grade A phony ID.

He pulled out two fifties and handed them over, apologized again, and told him to buy something nice for Miss Petrello with the change.

Trotter was tingling as he turned his back on the dentist and walked out to the waiting room, and not just from the novocaine. He was excited, and he knew it, and he hated himself for it. An FBI man, here to find him, could only have been sent by Fenton Rines. Rines was the only one Trotter kept in touch with, therefore the only one who knew where to find him.

And Trotter had given Rines specific instructions about the reasons he wanted someone to be able to find him. Rines had not taken the instructions lightly.

Cronus. The Russians were pulling another Cronus operation. Trotter wanted to be in on it. Had to be.

Because Cronus was the reason he'd been born. Fighting it was the only thing that could make his life worthwhile.

# CHAPTER FOUR

"Wake up," Trotter said. "We're landing."

"I'm not asleep," Joe Albright told him.

"I know, you were watching me through slitted eyes, waiting for me to make my move. Whatever the hell that might be."

"Listen, Trotter. This started out as a routine day. They told me to find you and escort you to Washington. That's *all* they told me. I don't know who you are, except that you're not wanted for anything, and I don't want to know who you are. And I really don't need you pulling my chain."

That last sentence, at least, was one hundred percent true. Joe Albright was thirty years old. He was smart, honest, educated and good-looking. He dressed conservatively. He did not smoke, drink, use drugs, or mess inordinately with women. He was an expert shot, and he was an expert in Caribbean languages and cultures.

He had, as far as he could tell, a great future with the FBI, especially since he was black. He didn't want to be favored because of his race; he was sure he didn't need any favoritism. He just wanted to be *noticed*. And that was fairly certain. Black guys were still thin on the ground in the Bureau.

Trotter could represent an opportunity or a problem, Albright wasn't sure which. Because despite what he'd told his—what? Companion? Prisoner?—the message from Washington had contained considerably more information than just a statement of the job. They told him to identify himself to Trotter *very clearly,* not, for example, to drop a hand on his shoulder and say, "Hey, buddy, come with me." That, it turned out, had been good advice. Albright should have passed the advice along to the dentist. He'd heard the man telling the receptionist how poorly Trotter had taken a sudden surprise.

But Washington had told him something else—not to tell anybody else at his regional office.

That's where the problem/opportunity business came in. Because the only reason Albright could see to keep this secret from his boss was that it was something the boss shouldn't be allowed to know. Did that mean trouble at the office? Was this Trotter a witness or something? Or was this all a scam? Maybe

Trotter was escorting *him* to D.C., and the interrogations were going to start with him.

On the other hand, maybe the powers had decided Joe was the clean man in a world of dirt and were going to give him a central role in the housecleaning.

Trotter was no help at all. For a guy who'd been pulled out of a dentist's chair and brought three thousand miles to see a top federal law-enforcement official, Trotter was something beyond calm. He acted like a man starting off on a fishing trip. For a guy who was goosey enough to come near to breaking a man's bones for startling him, Trotter was a surprisingly serene traveler.

Joe tried to figure out what it was about Trotter that had gotten things moving so quietly on such a high level. He was about Joe's age, tall, about six-one, and in good shape without getting militant about it. That was another thing. They had given him nineteen descriptions for the guy when they sent Albright out to look for him. The only thing that didn't vary was the height. His hair was listed as anything from sandy to black. He might weigh anything from 175 to 240 pounds. He wore glasses, or he didn't. His eyes were blue, or they were green or gray, but most likely they were brown. If he was wearing glasses, as he was now, they'd most likely be brown. As they were now. He might be brash or timid, living well or poorly, alone or with a woman.

So, Joe wondered, if this guy was such a chameleon, how did the Bureau in Washington have his address? Joe was tempted to ask him, but it was against procedure. Besides, all it would probably get him was one of those irritatingly charming smiles Trotter was currently using on the stewardesses.

Joe didn't dare go to sleep, even after they'd changed planes in Chicago and there was nowhere Trotter could go before they got to Dulles, short of hijacking the plane. Trouble was, if Joe went to sleep, Trotter probably *would* hijack the plane. Just to show Joe he could do it. So, tired as he was, Joe stayed awake, watching Trotter through slitted eyes, only to get twitted about it as the plane was coming down.

As soon as they were in the terminal, Trotter said, "Call the office."

The guy really *was* a chameleon. To look at Trotter now, you would never believe the owner of that face was capable of smiling and bantering with stewardesses. Giving orders, though, seemed perfectly natural. Joe irritated himself by starting to move his head to look around for a phone, then said, "Nobody said anything about you giving orders."

Trotter looked bored and, for the first time, as tired as Joe was. "Right," Trotter said. "*Please* call your office, okay?"

"There was nothing about that, either."

"What did they tell you to do, bring me right in?" Joe said nothing, but it didn't matter, since Trotter didn't wait for an answer. "Sure, they had a good night's sleep, probably in their own beds. Guys like us have to be Superman."

"Guys like us?"

"Oh, for God's sake," Trotter said. "Who are you supposed to report to?"

Joe looked at him.

Trotter started to laugh. "No, it's not a test, and I'm sorry to bring it up with all these people walking by." He lowered his voice. "Rines, right? No, don't tell me, I'll tell you something. They told you to find me and bring me, but not a word why, and now you don't know whether, as my daddy frequently says, to shit or go blind.

"So I'll help you. I'm supposed to be briefed on something, but I'm too tired to take it in. Also, my teeth hurt."

"Your teeth hurt."

"Right. So let's go to a phone. You call in and tell them if they swear to God that it can't wait until—what is it now, six-thirty A.M.?—you tell them that if it can't wait until three this afternoon, I will come in, but I won't like it, and I won't be good for much. If they won't swear to that but insist I come in, I am going to disappear, find some aspirin and a bed, and see them at three o'clock, anyway."

"Unless I stop you," Joe suggested.

"Unless you stop me, of course. You'll have to shoot me to do it, the way I feel now. I know you guys always shoot to kill."

"You sound like you're daring me to."

"Joe—can I call you Joe? I just don't care."

Joe looked into the man's eyes and saw only truth. Trotter was no older than Joe was, but his eyes were ancient.

"Where's a phone?" Joe said. Trotter pointed, and they made their way through morning shuttle commuters to a pay phone on the wall.

A half hour later Joe was checking them into a Holiday Inn. The last thing Joe heard before he got into bed was Trotter shooting the bolt on the connecting doors. He had a flash of alarm, then remembered Rines's voice on the phone. "Sorry, Albright, we should have told you. You can trust Trotter. Do whatever he wants. We'll see you this afternoon."

Amazing. This guy had some kind of juju on the brass. Not only does he get carte blanche, but he gets one of the Bureau's top men apologizing to lowly field hand Joe Albright.

Joe didn't know what he'd gotten into, but it promised to be educational. In the meantime, they told him not to worry, so he didn't worry. He went to sleep.

# CHAPTER FIVE

Trotter walked into a fifties-vintage glass-and-turquoise-fronted building in Silver Spring, Maryland. It was as anonymous a place as you could find, one of two dozen or so interspersed among the fast-food places along the first two miles outside the D.C. line. They housed government contractors (Washington, D.C., being the nation's ultimate one-industry town, Detroit notwithstanding) and companies that sold office furniture and stationery to government contractors. This particular building, Trotter learned from the directory, also housed a couple of low-budget lobbying groups (like the National Wooden Utensil Foundation) and the Greek-American Information Service, one of the dozens of special-interest journalistic enterprises that swarmed about the area.

The Agency was not in the directory. Trotter was willing to bet, however, that the Agency owned the building.

The Agency's budget did not appear in that mound of telephone-directory-sized volumes the President submits to Congress every year. The Agency was not supposed to exist. It got its money in two ways—nickel-and-diming the budgets of dozens of different government departments, programs and agencies (Trotter's father called this "spillage"); and from investments. Anonymous little office buildings in Silver Spring, for instance, and maybe one or more of the burger and chicken places across the street. No *big* earners, nothing to grab attention, but steady. And a lot of them. By the time Trotter had stopped working full-time for his old man, the Agency had been a whisker away from being self-supporting; by now, it was probably showing a profit.

It had taken a certain amount of insistence to get Albright to drop him off here, once he'd seen the place. He couldn't believe that the Bureau, with all the space it could want over at Justice, would waste its time with a building like this. He finally faced the fact that this was indeed the address he'd been given, with suitable authorization codes, over the phone, and let Trotter go without further fuss.

The FBI had the huge establishment, marble pillars to lean on and everything. The Agency, on the other hand, traveled light, without a building, recognition, or even a name to its name.

It was just the Agency, founded after World War II by an OSS general who knew that there were going to be times when a Central Intelligence Agency would be too big, too procedure-bound, and too scrupulous to do what had to be done. He fought for, and got, a hyper-secret organization with no official jurisdiction and, therefore, no limits on what it could concern itself with. There would be no chain of command—each Agent would answer solely to him, and he only to the President.

That cozy setup lasted until Watergate. The press got a taste for blood, and the "National Interest" had been invoked so many times to cover embarrassing petty political bullshit that nobody would listen to it anymore. Congress was going to take a hand; Congress was going to oversee *all* American intelligence operations, and the President might not have the juice to resist.

So the General became the Congressman. He found a district in his home state and persuaded the good old boys of the local Democratic Committee to nominate him (he was a War Hero, after all) in a place where, once the nomination was in hand, the election was an afterthought.

Then he pulled strings until Washington looked like a spider-web, only nobody could find the spider. When it was over, the Congressman was the chairman of the House Intelligence Oversight Committee. He did a hell of a job, too. Every spy outfit anyone had ever heard of had to admit that the Congressman was tough but fair. And the one nobody had ever heard of continued to operate as it always had.

Trotter followed the fallout-shelter signs, the ones that had been put up in the early sixties when, if people looked up, it was even money whether they were checking for rain or for Russian ICBMs. Nobody'd needed the shelters (they were inadequate from the start, anyway), and nobody checked on them or maintained them, but nobody ever got around to taking the signs down, either. They'd become invisible, unless you looked for them.

Trotter looked at them now, yellow-and-black signs streaked with red-brown rust, following the forgotten arrows to the basement, to a dirty, white-painted fire door. Around the thick edge of the door was a small button. There always was. Trotter pushed it, three shorts and a long. Trotter knew it was ridiculous, since it was certain he was being monitored by a hidden camera at this very second, but as his father frequently told him, a big

part of the reason anybody was in this business was because of
the game.

Or rather, The Game. Prisoner's Base with real prisoners.
Capture the Flag with real flags. The Game his father assured him
was in his blood, no matter how loudly he claimed he hated it.
The one he'd never be able to turn his back on, no matter how
hard he tried.

Trotter preferred not to think about it. But then, here he was.

The door slid open. Trotter stepped in. Fenton Rines was there
to greet him, offering a handshake but no smile.

Looking at him, Trotter doubted Rines ever smiled anymore.
He was like one of the people in fairy tales whose wish coming
true was the worst thing that ever happened to them.

Rines was a veteran FBI man, ex-Marine, legal and business
education. Trotter had always thought he resembled the president of a small-town bank. He still did, but in a town that the
economic recovery had passed by. He had always been a skilled
and dedicated agent, but now his rugged, handsome face was
harried, and his steel-gray hair was going white along the sides of
his head.

He met Trotter with his jacket off, another first. His tie was
loose and his sleeves were rolled up. This was a man with more
on his mind than a dress code.

Because Rines had made a wish. Over the course of years, he
had become aware of strange happenings in areas the FBI had
some interest in. Convenient appearances and disappearances.
Unlooked-for luck in the counterespionage business. Crimes and
other sorts of mysterious operations that were obviously the
work of top pros but made no sense. Phenomena, in short, his
instinct told him were intelligence operations but which his
connections showed to be attributable to no known intelligence
agency.

Then, two years before, a young girl had been kidnapped and a
truckload of dead bodies had been stolen. These events turned
out to be tied together, as part of a Russian operation known as
Cronus, and Trotter's (successful) attempt to stop it.

And that led to Trotter—or Driscoll, as he was calling himself
then. Trotter/Driscoll was the Congressman's son, and suddenly,
Rines's wish had come true. He knew now about the Agency. But
he wasn't through with it. Rines had been caught between the
Congressman and his son—he was the only person Trotter would
trust with knowledge of his whereabouts.

Trotter supposed it wasn't fair. The old man was as persuasive
as Satan; it was inevitable he'd be using Rines as another
operative, this one with access to, and a certain amount of
control over, the facilities of the FBI.

"Anything to stretch the budget," Trotter said.

Rines thought he meant the sparse furnishings. The place still looked like a fallout shelter, albeit one with a couple of desks, a telephone and fluorescent lighting. "Oh, he's practically all moved out, here. The canned water will be back in by tomorrow."

"I figured that was what was going on. I had Albright bring me to the door."

Rines nodded. The Agency didn't have much use for a fancy physical plant—a secure switchboard, storage for various electronic equipment, some filing cabinets and a comfortable chair for the Congressman to sit on and think, on those rare occasions he wasn't sitting and thinking in his apartment or in his office on the Hill. The Agency parasited (the Congressman's word) more than money from other government agencies. Computer time, background reports, satellite photographs, statistics. If anyone anywhere in the government knew something, the Congressman could get hold of the information without leaving a trace. If no one knew, and learning it was a matter of routine, he could have someone find out. Not the least of his resources was the staff of the Library of Congress, sort of a fringe benefit of his new cover.

Not having much to move, the Agency moved frequently. Granted, nobody in this particular building might check into the "fallout shelter" for another ten years, but why be there when they felt the urge to look if you owned another dozen buildings just like it in the Greater Washington area?

"What do you think of Albright?" Rines asked.

"Going to be a good one, I think. He's tense because he doesn't know what to make of me, and that makes him overcautious. And apprehensive, when I talk him out of it. If I were in his place, I'd be quietly checking out the building."

"He is," Rines assured him. "Electronic security is the last thing to be moved."

"Yeah," Trotter said. "I know how the old man works. Is he here?"

"Of course he is." For a second it looked as if Rines was going to say something else—"he misses you," Trotter thought absurdly—but he closed his mouth before anything got out.

"What should we do about Albright?" Rines asked.

"What the hell, he's your man. Make up a story for him. Tell him the truth."

"You sure you want him to know the truth?"

"If I decide I don't like it, I can always kill him."

Rines looked at him. "I never know when you're kidding."

"That's right. I'm here to be briefed. Something about Cronus."

"Yeah," Rines said. "Let's go talk to your father."

# CHAPTER SIX

The Congressman was sitting in a half-darkened room watching television. He seemed absorbed, half hypnotized, like a man watching a fireplace, but Trotter knew better. When the old man looked most detached was when his brain was working the fastest.

"Hello, Congressman," Trotter said.

" 'Lo, son," his father murmured. So much for the fatted calf.

"Well," Trotter said, "if that's what you flew me three thousand miles to tell me, I'll be off."

"Don't be foolish, son." The Congressman's eyes never left the set. "What are you calling yourself these days?"

As if he didn't know. As if he didn't know everything. It was a test. If Trotter made an issue of it, the old man would draw this out until his son wanted to scream. Trotter had outgrown that kind of foolishness. Maybe someday the old man would too.

"Trotter. Allan Trotter."

"I liked Clifford Driscoll better." Trotter said nothing. "All right," the old man said, "all right. Allan, come over here and take a look at this tape, would you?"

Trotter complied. A plump man in a dark blue suit was preaching. He had been taught how to use his voice. He was immaculately groomed. He was flanked by a cross and an American flag.

"You ever seen this boy before?" the old man asked.

"Nobody who owns a TV set can avoid him. What about him?"

"Well, son, this has nothin' to do with what you're interested in, but as long as you're here, I thought I'd get the benefit of your opinion."

"I think you're wasting my time."

"Maybe not, son. I've been watchin' a lot of these boys lately—"

"If you tell me you've been born again, I'm going to throw up."

"No, son. These boys have got me worried. They got it right about Russia, or mostly right. The thing wrong with Godless Communism isn't that it's Godless. But they got it wrong about America. What's the sense of fightin' the Russians when you want to tell people what to think and how to dress and how to act?"

It didn't seem strange to Trotter that his father, who, to his

26

certain knowledge, had ordered the deaths of hundreds of people, Americans and foreigners, who had been convicted of no crimes, would come out so staunchly for the Constitution. The Congressman loved America, and the Constitution was the soul of the country. But the Congressman had proclaimed one Truth that let him—forced him, really—to do what he did. "Anybody who is not willing to get down in the mud and fight dirty is at the mercy of anybody who is."

"You trust yourself messing around with the Bill of Rights, but you don't trust these guys," Trotter said.

"You say you don't like me, boy, but by God, you know me. Have I ever stopped anybody from doin' somethin' he had a right to do?"

"Go to trial? Die a natural death?"

"Besides that."

"No. Of course, these guys have a right to preach."

"I know that. That's what has me worried. They're tellin' everybody that if you can convince yourself you found it in the Bible, you can force other people to do it, or not do it, or whatever. They have a right to feel that way, but the Bible ain't what runs the country. That's the goddam Ayatollah's kind of talk."

The old man switched off the TV and turned to face his son. "That's what's got me worried, boy. I sit here and get to thinkin' they ought to be stopped. One of those boys is talking about running for president. Then I think I'm doing the same kind of thing they're doing."

"Yeah," Trotter said, suddenly impatient. "What are you trying to pull, Father?"

"What do you mean, son?"

"I mean you have never, ever admitted to anybody, least of all me, that you were worried about anything. Let alone whether a doubt could cross your mind to stop you from doing something you thought ought to be done."

"Maybe I'm getting old, son."

Trotter looked at him. He did look older, more sag, more wrinkles. But the eyes still burned.

"Or maybe," Trotter said, "you're trying to soften me up."

The old man's look got hard. "You'll have to decide that for yourself, then." A lot of the Congressman's Southern accent had dropped away, a sign that they were getting down to business.

•    •    •

Rines pulled the evangelists from a VCR on the shelf below the TV set and replaced it with another cassette.

"You're about to see a young woman named Regina Hudson," Rines said. "She's the daughter—"

"I know who she is," Trotter said. The Congressman made everyone in the Agency learn to recognize the faces of the most powerful people in the media and their families. This was not only in the interest of knowing whom to avoid, but also to be on the lookout for things these people might not want the public to exercise its famous Right to Know on. In trying to run an effective operation in a (mostly) free country, leverage with the press was vital.

"Good," Rines said. He pressed a button. The screen showed five seconds of electric confetti, then came in with a picture of a young woman in basic black and pearls. The outfit seemed too old for her, but she wore it with confidence.

The camera had a fish-eye lens and was placed at what has come to be known as the ABSCAM angle, above the top of everybody's head. The last time he had committed Regina Hudson's picture to memory, she'd been a pretty teenager, but the angle and the distortion made it impossible to tell.

The scene, judging from the nice carpets and the antique walnut desk, was Rines's official FBI office. It was certainly Rines who was talking to her.

"You realize how unusual this is, Miss Hudson."

"I wouldn't think it would be unusual for people in trouble to come to you."

"People in trouble in Upstate New York tend to go to our office there. They don't make up a story to slip away to Washington."

"And talk to someone at your level, I suppose." She was trying to sound like nothing more than a member of a powerful family taking advantage of one of the perks of power, but Trotter could hear the tension in her voice, see it in the way she held her head.

"I came to see you, Mr. Rines, because I wanted to talk to someone honest—"

Trotter shot a look at Rines, but the FBI man had his eyes firmly on the screen.

"—and I also wanted someone better than competent, with enough imagination to understand what I'm talking about. I asked around, and every reporter and source I spoke to told me that was you."

The Rines on tape grunted noncommittally.

"Of course, I've heard of you on my own, too. I used to know Liz Fane slightly. We were at the same school for a while, and I know that when she was kidnapped, you were the one who got her back."

This time the Rines in the room grunted. Rines had gotten the credit for that one, and as far as Trotter was concerned, he was welcome to it. It might not have been modesty, acknowledging that Trotter and some other of his father's agents had done most of the work in that case, that had caused Rines to make the noise. It might have been the knowledge that if he hadn't been assigned to the Liz Fane case and learned everything there had been to learn, he might not now be in the Congressman's clutches.

The tape rolled on. Regina Hudson told of the series of deaths in her town and how the phone call had come at the end of the third one. The telegram read over the line, signed Cronus.

# CHAPTER SEVEN

Trotter said, "Ah."

"Ah is right," Rines said. "You can't see it on the tape, and she didn't notice, but I have just turned purple."

"I can imagine. But tell me later, she's still talking."

"Of course," the young woman went on, "when I saw how Mother took it, I checked with Western Union, trying to see who this Cronus was. They had no record of any such telegram."

"Anybody can pick up a phone and say they're from Western Union," the recorded Rines said. He did sound a bit distracted.

Regina Hudson was nodding. "That's why I checked."

"Well," Rines told her. "It seems as if someone has pulled a hoax on you, or on your mother through you. What makes you think it's a matter for the FBI?"

"The way my mother has taken this. I mean, she started acting strange about seven months or so ago, hiring a bodyguard, trying to get me to move back home. Now she's positively paranoid. One night I thought I was followed home from work and later saw someone watching the house. I called the police, and the man turned out to be a private detective hired by my mother to 'watch out' for me."

"Your mother is afraid."

She leaned forward in her chair, dropping for a second the pose of sophistication. "She's *petrified*, Mr. Rines. No pun intended. I think that fake telegram was a threat—and not the first one, either—something only my mother would understand."

"It would be stretching things to look into this even if your mother came to us herself. . . ."

Trotter said, "What are you, nuts?"

Rines said, "I was playing her, Trotter. Did you think I'd chase a lead to Cronus off?"

Damn well better not, Trotter thought, but said nothing.

Regina Hudson was frankly pleading now. "There must be *some* way you could look into this. Judging from my mother's actions, the threat has to be directed, at least part of it, at my brother and me. For an official report, I could make it a blatant kidnapping threat."

"I wouldn't have you lie, even if there were to be an official report."

Regina Hudson sat up straight in her chair, and for the first time Trotter got a good look at her face. Cold, angry, and lovely. And, if what he was thinking was right, she was, in a way more fundamental than biology, his sister. He'd made a promise to himself to help them, the other children of Cronus, whenever he had a chance. His father's testing him had been a waste of time. There was no way to keep Trotter out of this one.

There was more to the tape. Miss Hudson said, "I see," and started to get to her feet. "Sorry to have wasted your time."

Rines's voice was very quiet. "I didn't say we couldn't help you."

She sat back down and looked at him.

"I just said there would be no official report."

"I don't understand," she said. She was interested, though.

"No," Rines conceded, "and you won't, for a while. I *might* be able to help you. Just might. I can't make any promises, but you have to make me some."

"Such as?" Trotter was glad to see that scared as she was, she had brains enough not to give the store away. Most people at this point would say, "Anything," and mean it.

"The big one is this: No matter what happens, no matter if we can help you or not, none of this is to go any further. It won't appear in a Hudson newspaper, or anybody else's. No media of any kind. You won't tell anybody privately. Without my permission you won't tell anybody anything for any reason."

She leaned back again, giving Trotter another look at her face as she thought it over. It tasted bad, but she swallowed it.

"All right," she said.

"Good. And you'll have to promise to do what we ask you. If we do."

"What happens if I say no?"

"It wasn't a threat, Miss Hudson, just a precaution. If at any

**30**

point you feel you can't go along with something we think needs to be done, we call the whole thing off with no hard feelings. You'll still be bound by your promise, of course."

Trotter said, "You're a sadist, Rines, wringing that kind of promise out of a journalist."

"I wanted to see how much she meant it. She went along."

And on the TV screen, that was exactly what she was doing. While she was still nodding assent Rines said, "How long are you going to be in Washington?"

"Three or four days yet. I'm on a story. I'm the editor of the hometown paper, you know."

Rines nodded.

"Well, the Congressman from our district, Farosky, is on that congressional advisory committee."

"There are dozens of them, Miss Hudson."

She smiled for the first time. Very nice. "Not to Kirkester, Mr. Rines. There's only the one Congressman Farosky is on, the one that's to report to the President on the 'sense of the Nation and the Congress on the proper priorities for the forthcoming summit.'

"So I'm doing a feature on Farosky and the committee as an excuse to come here and see you. I'm staying at the Estmoor."

"I'll get back to you before you leave town, Miss Hudson. Thank you for trusting me with this."

She thanked him very prettily for listening and walked out of camera range.

Rines switched off the tape and brought the lights up. The Congressman looked at Trotter and said, "Well, son, what do you think?"

# PART TWO

## CHAPTER ONE

General Dmitri Ivanov Borzov threw water on the stones and heard it hiss at him. He went back to the wooden bench, smoothed the wrinkles from the doubled-over towel and sat. He checked the temperature—ninety-seven degrees. He wondered, not for the first time, why water that temperature, or a mere three degrees hotter, would boil angrily and scald the skin while water-laden air of the same temperature relaxed him and cleared his mind.

He had asked a scientist about it once, a biologist. A brilliant man, but a dissident. A Jew. Borzov had asked him in the midst of an interrogation. The general had found that the occasional innocuous question could get more out of a suspect than a beating could. It was time for such a question, and Borzov had just gotten the sauna (from a store in Finland—all the luxury items enjoyed by ranking Soviet officials were imported from the West into Finland), which he enjoyed immensely, so he had asked.

And the subject had explained, eagerly, grateful at last to be able to talk about something scientific, suspecting, perhaps, that he might never again get the chance. Once his mouth was open, he continued to talk, with only the mildest encouragement, and the friends who had been smuggling his anti-State lies to the West had been caught.

Unfortunately, Borzov had forgotten the explanation. He could, he supposed, visit the asylum to which the scientist had been committed and have him explain again. The place was nearby, and follow-up interrogations, months or even years later, were frequently profitable.

Borzov decided to let it go. He was an old man now. He looked down at his body, as well as he could see it without his eyeglasses. The skin that had once been red with health and covered heavy muscles was now white with grayish spots, hanging in folds where it didn't cling like a thin coat of paint to tendons and bones, covering them but failing to hide them.

And the bones moved so slowly now. It took the heat of the sauna to free them, melt them enough to get him through another day. He had thought of having another sauna installed in his headquarters, so that he could refresh himself at midday, but he had decided against it, settling for a simple shower stall. He had always set an example of Marxist austerity to his men. And he had never acknowledged a need of any sort, other than the needs of the State. A personal need was a weakness, and a man in Borzov's position dared show no weakness. What power Borzov had, and he had a considerable amount, had been bought with fear. But power is just one by-product of fear. The other is hatred. Borzov had survived since the days of Stalin by never letting anyone forget the power long enough to give vent to the hatred. Chairmen came and went, cold war chased détente in an endless circle. Borzov stayed. Quiet but strong. Ever ready to serve the State.

A buzzer rasped. It was time to leave the sauna. The general wrapped a towel around his middle and stepped out onto the tile floor. The Finns would now rush out into the snow and roll naked in it while other madmen beat them with boughs. General Borzov found a lukewarm shower cold enough. All he wanted was something to wash the sweat from him. He wanted to keep as much of the warmth in him as he could.

Even in the days of the muscles, Dmitri Borzov's full height hadn't been impressive, but every morning he put on his uniform (and if Borzov was clothed at all, it was his uniform he was wearing), stood before the mirror and drew himself up to it. His spine protested, but yielded to the muscles that were left. The day it didn't would be the day he retired.

The black Chaika limousine was waiting in front of the building. The driver stood at attention near the rear door as exhaust fumes, cloud-white in the chill of Moscow's early autumn, billowed around her legs. She saluted and held the door open.

Borzov shook off a helping hand and got in. Normally, he would lean back and think. Many officials justified the need for a limousine by saying they worked on their papers in transit. Borzov had never asked for a limousine, and he carried no papers home with him. There was altogether too much committed to paper to please him. The Americans, the British, and those who worked for them could read what was written on papers. He worked during his morning ride, but he worked in the one place in the world he was sure the security was all in order—his own mind.

He would repair to the comfort of it in a moment, but first he had to speak to the driver.

"Your name, Comrade Sergeant," he said.

"Maria Malnikova, C-comrade General."

"Are you nervous?" he demanded.

He had noted, not from interest but because he noticed everything, that while the sergeant was not an attractive woman, she had thick, lustrous yellow hair. She was needlessly pushing it down with one hand.

"Keep your hands on the wheel," he told her crossly, "and don't be nervous."

"I-I'm not, Comrade General."

"Nonsense, your voice is trembling. They have told you all about Borzov the ogre, and you are afraid." He didn't give her a chance to deny it. "You shouldn't be. It is not natural for you. Nervous women do not rise to your rank so young. How old are you?"

"Twenty-eight, Comrade General."

"Have you driven for me before?"

"No, Comrade General. I have replaced Sergeant Brumel, who is to become an officer. To keep the rotation even."

"So I have not told you. Do you remember the War, Comrade Sergeant? No, of course, you couldn't. It was over a decade before you were born. I formed many habits during the War. One was a respect for fuel. I learned to spill my lifeblood itself rather than waste gasoline, and a commitment that strong is not easily changed, even when the times do.

"So, Comrade Sergeant, when the rotation selects you to drive for me again, turn the motor off while you wait for me. It pains me to see a car burning fuel without accomplishing anything."

"I will, Comrade General. I am sorry."

"You could not know; I had yet to tell you. No blame attaches."

"Thank you, Comrade General."

"Just remember what I have said. You drive very well."

Borzov could see her ears redden. He allowed himself a flash of amusement, then leaned back against the cushions and began to think.

# CHAPTER TWO

His thoughts were devoted to one project for the entire trip, but they did him little good. He was glad to feel the car stop (the sergeant switched off the engine when it did), letting him know he had arrived at Dzerzhinski Square. Borzov entered and went downstairs to his office.

The office was another habit Borzov had formed during the War, working in a small, dark room many levels below the street. It had been a precaution against air raids. But he had come to like it. The basements of Lubyanka had been where the most strenuous interrogations had taken place, and when Borzov had something to do with them, it was convenient to have his office nearby, where he could go in peace to digest the results. He had steadfastly refused to move upstairs, and when the KGB built the branch headquarters, a modern monstrosity on a ring road skirting the capital, Borzov had nearly resigned.

He needn't have worried. Plenty of work was still done here. It was convenient to so many other organizations. And even with the advent of new techniques and new drugs, making interrogation just as profitable but with less physical labor, the basement rooms had not been entirely decommissioned.

He went to his desk and called Communications for progress on the American newspaper operation. Only with his request would the reports be printed. An armed courier rushed them to the general's office where he read, then destroyed, them. The whole procedure had taken less than three minutes, and the papers themselves had been in existence less than that. Borzov was pleased, as he always was when things went smoothly.

Things were not going smoothly in America. The woman was being stubborn. She had been given warnings, and she had ignored them. There was no doubt the warnings had been received. The American madman—Azreal in coded dispatches, by his own choice—was perfection, as always. No one suspected that the children had been eliminated by anything but blind chance. Except that woman. *She* knew. And still she defied him.

It made Borzov angry in the most fundamental way. It bothered him even more than the mysterious setbacks of recent years, the foiling of the Liz Fane kidnapping or the defection of Bulanin, Borzov's top man in England. The Americans had been responsible for those in some way Borzov had yet to fully understand.

He could, however, accept it. Even the greatest of chess masters lost from time to time.

But this was different. This was as if he had spent hours developing a strategy, and just as he was about to put his opponent in check, his queen had tried to sneak off the board.

Ordinarily, of course, someone who tried to ignore his assignment without at least having brains enough actually to defect would be doused, painfully, before becoming anything more than a minor annoyance.

The times were not ordinary. Soviet-American relations were on the brink of entering a new phase, and that phase must be carefully shaped. American and Soviet officials had started a round of talks that would proceed, on and off, with cancellations for minor upsets or "spectacular" breakthroughs when the politics of one or the other of the countries demanded, for the next several years. But the talks themselves meant less than nothing. The real decisions would be made by the American people.

Borzov sometimes wondered if the American people believed as much in the efficacy of American Democracy as he did. Because Borzov had known since the War that especially in matters of foreign policy, once most of the people were convinced on an issue, the government had no choice but to go along.

The key to the mind of America was the press. The press controlled access to the people in America, the way the government did here. The press had gotten America into war with Spain; it had driven them from the war in Vietnam. It had toppled a president with scandal and undercut his successors with ridicule.

Most of all, it hid the secret.

The American media were full of Armageddon, Nuclear Holocaust, The End of the World. It had made offending the Soviet Union seem the act of a madman, as witness the editorials every time a president risked it.

"We will bury you," Khrushchev had said, and that slogan was imprinted daily, implicitly and explicitly, on the brain of every American who could read or turn a knob. And, it seemed, that imprinting took up so much of the American brain that the few who could see past it to the secret were scorned as warmongers and fools. Sometimes Borzov found himself wishing a God existed, so he might thank him.

Borzov told himself the secret again, with a sense of wonder at the truth of it, and pride in the wisdom that had let him see it in time to hide it, and to build his nation's policy around it.

*We do not dare bury them.*

We do not dare. Thirty-five percent of our population works to grow food, and it is not enough. The people rose against the Czar because they were hungry, but the Soviet people are not hungry. The Americans grew more food than they could eat (and the press afflicted their conscience with stories of the handful of "hungry"). Much of America's surplus food found its way to the Soviet Union. If the Americans wouldn't sell it to them directly, some ally of theirs would be delighted to serve as middleman.

And the Army had a stranglehold on the economy, on research and development. They were ten years behind the Americans in computer technology, and what they had was the result of the work of Borzov's field agents, or of Americans placing private enterprise ahead of patriotism.

Where would the food come from if they "buried" the Americans? Where would the technology come from, belated as it was, if they ground the West under their heel?

They *needed* the West. Borzov's job was not to destroy America and her allies, but to *control* them. He wanted them to be healthy, but uneasy of mind. They must have the vigor to produce, but lack sufficient will to become a threat to the Soviet system.

There were key events that pushed the balance one way or another. Years ago, Borzov and the late Chairman had devised a system that would give them the edge when some of those events came to be. Now was the time, and the woman was in place. But she refused to do her duty.

It was time for a warning to land closer to home.

The woman known as Petra Hudson was a Soviet spy, and it was time she realized she was expected to follow orders.

# CHAPTER THREE

"You don't ask enough questions to pass as a reporter," Regina Hudson said.

"Where did you get that idea?" Trotter said.

Regina smiled in spite of herself. She didn't know what else this Trotter was good at, but he had a definite flair for snappy comebacks. The first thing he'd ever said to her was, "Don't worry, I plan to carry out the assignment in my Undercover Man uniform, the green one with the epaulets."

And she had to admit she deserved it. But it had been a surprise. When Rines had gotten back in touch with her, he had gone on and on about how this Trotter was their top man, none better, tons of experience, she should have full confidence in him, how lucky he was available, just don't forget about the strict secrecy.

After all that, she'd been expecting—she wasn't sure *what* she'd been expecting. She knew that most real-life undercover men looked like the people they were mixing with, i.e. criminals or middle-level bureaucrats or whatever. On the other hand, Rines had made her expect some kind of cross between Sean Connery and Arnold Schwarzeneggar.

The circumstances surrounding the meeting had added to the impression. No, she wouldn't meet the man in Washington, too many people who were too savvy to shrug things off. It wouldn't do for her to be spotted. They didn't want their man linked with Washington. She tried to tell him it was ridiculous, but Rines had countered with two things—one, she had promised to do what they asked or call the whole thing off; and two, a year and a half ago she had lunch at a diner in Arlington, Virginia, with Congressman Peter Vitkins (D—Mo.), and it had appeared in *Time, Newsweek, Worldwatch*, and six hundred newspapers, many of them owned by the Hudson Group. None of which she could deny.

"Where should we meet, then?" she asked.

"New York," Rines said.

Regina had pointed out that there were numerous savvy people in New York, too. Rines had explained that they didn't care if their man was linked with New York, and the reason became apparent when he explained the cover they were preparing. Their man would be a feature writer, and she would interview him over lunch and hire him to work on the Kirkester *Chronicle*. "Pay him the right amount to make it look good," Rines advised.

So the rendezvous had been set, not at a diner but not in the lobby of the Plaza, either. She met him at a place called Dosanko on Forty-fifth Street between Lexington and Third Avenues, one of a chain of Japanese-style noodle houses. Fortunately, they let her use a fork. The second thing Trotter had said to her was, "Someday I'll teach you how to use chopsticks. If three billion Asians can learn how to do it, so can you. I'm talking because you don't seem to be in the mood."

It wasn't that so much as Regina's not knowing what to say. After all the cloak-and-dagger, this mysterious Trotter had turned out to be a tall young man, bordering on the attractive, with dark hair and eyes. And he wore glasses. Real ones, too. Regina had made it a point to get a step behind him, stand on tiptoe, and look through the lenses. He needed them, all right. So much for fantasyland.

They met as arranged, and the editor-in-chief of the Kirkester *Chronicle* had put out a hand and said, "You don't look anything like I expected you to," at which point he passed her the first snappy remark.

She couldn't hold it against him, though. All the lines were delivered with a smile that drained any possible venom from them. It was a very nice smile.

If she hadn't been told that Trotter was experienced and highly skilled, and all the other euphemisms people like Fenton Rines liked to use for *dangerous*, the thought would never have crossed her mind. Since the notion had been planted, though, she could see how this boyish charm and easy manner could be the most dangerous thing about him.

Since she was supposed to be interviewing him, she decided to make it look good (something else Rines had urged her to do) and ask him a few questions, most of which he refused to answer. For instance, he wouldn't tell her anything about his past, but he would tell her why.

"You just take the background in the résumé for the truth. If that's all you know, you can't get details confused and let something slip."

"But I *know* you never worked for the Baltimore *Sun*."

"It'll check out," he told her. "If anybody checks."

"Why a feature writer?"

"If you made me city editor, I'd be tied to a desk. If I were a regular reporter, I'd have to be turning in copy or the editor would get suspicious. As a features man, by the time anybody realizes I'm not doing any work, my real job could be done."

"Do you think it could be over that soon?"

That was another question he wouldn't answer.

That had been Tuesday. She'd gone right from lunch to the airport and got home early that evening. She spent Wednesday kicking herself. What she had done was more or less to hire the FBI (or somebody the FBI could call on, which amounted to the same thing) the way she would a private detective agency. It hit her like a faceful of ice water. Concern for her mother, respect for Rines's reputation, and (she had to face it) a certain amount of My-Family-Has-a-Fortune arrogance had led her into the folly of approaching them with something this tenuous in the first place. She had nothing but the bizarre phone call and her mother's reaction, something no outsider could be blamed for chalking up to vapors or menopause.

But if Regina had been a fool to ask, why had they gone along? If the FBI was seriously into this kind of thing, she had strolled into a great story, then immediately promised to wipe the whole thing off the record, no matter where it went. She tried to think of some way around it, some alternate path to the same facts, somebody she could quote, so that she could keep her word and still print the story.

It would be completely ethical, she felt obligated to remind herself. Nothing Deep Throat had told Bob Woodward about Watergate had been on the record, for instance. Maybe the thing to do was to become a Deep Throat herself, for some other reporter, just tell him something was going on that ought to be looked into. . . .

No. It wasn't going to work. She'd let her instincts as a daughter override the ones she was supposed to have developed as a journalist. Her mother might be peeved if she found out Regina had gone behind her back about this Cronus business, but she would hit the ceiling if she found out her daughter had given a government man clear sailing to meddle in family business without even the *possibility* of exposure to keep him honest.

The worst thing about it was that she didn't think she could have done anything else under the circumstances. Her mother had never been afraid of anything before—at least that she'd let her children see—but this had her terrified.

She had even (and this was what had Regina terrified) begun to neglect the business. She had missed a *Worldwatch* editorial meeting. Fred Smith, the managing editor, had called Regina in a panic, demanding to know where Petra was. Of course, Fred had been more or less a trial since his son had died, but Regina could understand that. It was the power of one word to change her mother's lifelong habits that got to her.

It had been that phone call that had decided her to get help somewhere. Regina knew herself to be particularly susceptible to emotional states of the people around her, and she was around no one more than her mother. If Petra's behavior was going to drive everybody at the Hudson Group nuts, Regina would be doomed. It would happen all the sooner if her mother kept disappearing.

It turned out that there had been no cause for alarm the day of the missed meeting. Petra Hudson had decided to drop in on Tina Bloyd. The visit, Wes Charles told Regina later, hadn't done Petra much good and had agitated the hell out of the bereaved mother. Besides which, Mother had lied. She'd said she had become so involved in the visit, she completely forgot about the editorial meeting. According to Charles, she had specifically refused to call and say she wasn't going to make it and had forbidden him to do so.

That had really torn it. Regina made an excuse to leave town, and by Saturday she was in Washington. Tuesday was the lunch in New York, and Wednesday was for self-recrimination.

And now it was Thursday, and here was Allan Trotter, for now, at least, the FBI's gift to journalism. He'd shown up in perfect feature-writer camouflage, dressed somewhere between the popular conception of a best-selling novelist, which feature writers wanted to be, and that of an associate professor of English Lit, which is what a lot of them were attempting to escape from. There were, in the two hundred some odd cities where the Hudson Group had papers, probably a hundred thirty colleges, the English faculties of which were going nowhere. At least a feature writer got his name in the paper.

Trotter had come into her office, smiled at her, and said he was happy to be aboard. He'd already said that until they *knew* what was going on, she was to act as if he was exactly what he was pretending to be, in public and in private. Regina was not happy with the implication of the possibility of hostile surveillance, but then she hadn't liked much of anything since her mother came home from that funeral.

All right, she'd told herself as she avoided Trotter's deceptively friendly brown eyes. This was the time to call it off; she hesitated, and was lost.

"Nice to have you," she said, trying to sound as if she meant it. There was a lengthy silence that would give the theoretical listeners-in something to think about but was just Regina's inability to think of anything to say next.

Trotter came to the rescue. "I'd like to see the place, if there's someone to show me around."

Of course, Regina thought. Only polite to show the new employee around. And because she didn't want to hang around a possibly bugged office, she announced she'd do the job herself. Trotter acted as if he'd expected that all along.

She showed him around, not only the *Chronicle*'s little operation in the basement but the whole building. From the *Worldwatch* offices to Group Advertising Sales to the cafeteria, she showed him around. They walked until Regina wished she'd worn sneakers, the way she usually did, instead of dressing up a little to greet the new employee.

It wouldn't have been so bad if Trotter had said anything besides "mm-hmm."

She saved the printing plant for last, arriving, as she'd planned, at one of the few hours of the day the place wouldn't be shaking with the roar and clatter of thirty-foot-high, high-speed presses.

She gave all the statistics, as related to her by the German company that made the machines. How many tons they weighed, how many gallons of ink per second they used. How, since they did not only the magazine and the local newspaper here, but special inserts for the entire Hudson Group, as well as hiring out to other magazines and advertisers, that this was one of the world's busiest pressrooms. She told him that this was all offset, and that the paper went through the machines at nearly two hundred miles an hour.

She pointed at a catwalk that ran down the middle of the room at the level a little above that of the tops of the presses. "You can see it better from up there," she said. "That's where the men go to paste the new rolls onto the web. See, they lower them into position, then glue them to the ones already there. While the press is going. It's a very dangerous job, since the paper going that speed is like a saw and could cut your arm off before you'd even feel it. We have an excellent safety record, though."

Trotter said, "Mm-hmm," and Regina, tired of it, had told him he didn't ask enough questions to pass as a journalist, and gotten the snappy comeback.

Trotter waited a few seconds, then told her, just above a whisper, "Don't apologize or react to this, but you could have just arranged for me to die."

Right, don't react. Regina felt a look of total stupidity spread itself across her face. Trotter pointed discreetly to a man in white coveralls walking briskly along the catwalk to a glassed-in control booth at one end.

"I don't think he heard you," Trotter continued in the same barely audible tone, "but he might have. Let's not take chances."

Then a loud bell went off, and the presses started to roar. She signaled for him to follow her out. The German company had stressed the danger of being in here too long without ear protection.

Trotter smiled and shook his head. He put his mouth close to Regina's ear. "I've been waiting for this," he screamed. She could just about hear him. "Let's talk for a few seconds."

# CHAPTER FOUR

"Don't be silly," the Reverend Mr. Nelson said. "Come as often as you like. I'm here to talk to people, you know. To help them. Or rather, to show them how to ask the Lord to help them. He doesn't care how long it takes, you know." He smiled in that way preachers have, to let you know one of their favorite jokes was coming up. "He hasn't worked to a schedule since the Creation."

Tina Bloyd laughed and thanked him again. Mr. Nelson smiled. He smiled a lot. He had the kind of smile that helped people feel good. Someone at work had told her that, said the new preacher at the Northside Church could help her, and he'd turned out to be right. Tina had thought that after that morning when she'd awakened early to find the sheet damp and her baby dead, she'd never smile again. Damn psychiatrist at the hospital didn't know anything; even Grandma, who'd come upstate on a bus, with her arthritis and everything, wasn't a whole lot of help.

Grandma had urged her to see a preacher, too, but she wanted her to come back home to Mount Vernon and go to *her* church.

No way Tina was going to go back to Mount Vernon. Mount Vernon was a town in Westchester County, New York. A lot of people had heard of the county but only about the houses and the estates and the quaint little villages. They hadn't heard about the downtowns, where the black people lived. Grandma had always said, "BTH, BTH," which meant Better Than Harlem. If that was true, Tina didn't want to know about Harlem. She didn't know much about anything Grandma said, and that had been a mistake.

Tina had been a wild one. She'd been smart in school, when she bothered to go, which was not much. She didn't do drugs, but she did liquor, some, and boys, a lot. It took four years, but the inevitable happened at last. Tina found herself pregnant. She pretended she wouldn't tell who the father was, but the truth was, she didn't know.

Abortion was out. Grandma didn't hold with abortion, and Tina was too scared to lose Grandma, now. She'd always considered Grandma a kind of handkerchief head, running off to the preacher for everything, closing her eyes and rocking back and forth over her Bible, but from behind a bulging belly, Tina could see Grandma in a whole new way. Grandma had raised a baby all by herself, and what had gone wrong had been no fault of Grandma's, just Tina's own damned wildness. She'd have to raise a baby single-handed, now, and the prospect terrified her. She needed that old woman more than anything.

Unless she decided just to walk away from it, put the child up for adoption, and forget it.

Forget it was right. Sure, people were desperate to adopt babies. But they wanted *white* babies. That meant her baby was destined for an orphanage or a series of foster homes.

No way. She wasn't making this baby on purpose, but she wasn't making it so it could be miserable, either.

Tina had gone to the Welfare office to see what she could get. What she got was a surprise. No apartment, and a lot less money than she wanted, but they put her in a training program, learning to set computerized type. She worked hard, found out she liked it and could do it well. She finished her training about two weeks before the baby came, and she went into the hospital in possession of the one thing in the world she never thought she'd have—a job.

Not only a job, but a job with a big company. Turned out they'd more or less sponsored the training program. When she told some of her friends she was going upstate to work for the Hudson Group, they'd told her it was a racist organization. They were in favor of Israel. They were for Welfare cuts. Just read their editorials.

Tina thought about it. She decided at last that she didn't give a damn about Israel, one way or the other, and since when had the Arabs who went around blowing things up been black people, anyway? She also decided that if people had jobs, they wouldn't need Welfare.

So she told the Hudson Group she and her baby would be there as soon as they could. When they arrived in Kirkester, Tina found a clean town, quiet, fresh air. A nice place to live. At the job, she found some people to be friends with. Mostly, they were also graduates of the program, but there were a few local girls, too. White girls. They had a program up here, too, which was so far off the beaten track that even the poor people were white. Tina had seen stories on the TV news about poor white people, but she had never really believed in them.

There was day care for the babies, with a trained nurse there at all times. Since the place was running twenty-four hours a day, what with one publication and another, there was night care, too, and Tina was allowed—encouraged, even—to leave the kid there to go to night school and get her diploma.

She used to go around pinching herself, feeling maybe guilty over doing her best for years to screw up her life, then falling into something like this.

Then the bill came due, and little Clara (that was Grandma's name), a good and beautiful child, had just . . . died.

After Tina had gotten out of the hospital, where they'd sent her for "hysteria"—they'd be hysterical, too, they went in to check on their baby and found the poor little thing dead—she'd headed for the nearest church.

Looking, she thought, for an explanation. If there had been sin involved, it had been Tina's own. Why take an innocent baby?

Mr. Nelson had looked up at her apologetically. He had sandy hair that fell across his forehead, and only some creases around his eyes kept him from looking exactly like a farm boy caught sneaking a fingerful of chocolate icing from the cake.

"I can tell you, but you'll get angry."

"Mr. Nelson—"

"You can call me Will, if you like."

Tina didn't think she could be shocked, but the idea of calling a preacher, a *white* preacher, by his first name came close.

"Mr. Nelson," she said again, "I already am angry."

So he told her. "The world," he said, "is the place where we prepare for the next world. If we do His will, follow His plan for us, when our work is finished, He calls us home."

"You're right," Tina said.

Mr. Nelson looked surprised.

"It *is* making me angry. That kind of talk might be all right if I'd lost somebody who'd lived a *life*. My baby's work wasn't done, for the Lord or anybody else. She didn't even get the chance to *start*."

"Didn't she?" Mr. Nelson had asked.

"Are you crazy?"

"Think of what you've already told me. You were wild, drinking, sleeping around. You talked about sins, you know, those are the worst kind, because they waste God's gift of life. Your own life. But what happened when you found you were going to have the child? You didn't destroy it. You didn't abandon it. You made up your mind to straighten out your life so your child would have every chance. And you did. You've got a new life. You're a respectable person with a future. And you're not going back, are you?"

"But I don't have my *baby*."

"No, you don't. And don't let me or anybody tell you not to grieve. But believe me, Clara's life, short as it was, was not wasted. As I said before, her work was done."

Tina was bitter. "You still didn't tell me what her work was."

"To save you."

She looked at him. "I was crazy to come here."

"I told you it would make you angry. There's just one more thing I want to say."

"Might as well."

"There is a word for souls like Clara's, you know. The ones who come to Earth to help one special person, then return to heaven."

"What word?"

"They call them angels."

*They call them angels.* Tina couldn't get the words out of her mind. For a week, the conversation kept running through her head. It was the same old bull, sure, Speech Number Fifteen, consoling bereft mothers. But he'd sounded so *sincere*. He believed it, even if Tina didn't. The idea that God would waste an angel on her was ridiculous. And she missed her baby, dammit, she wanted her baby! How dare he try to palm her off with—

She'd gone back to give him another piece of her mind, and a few days later she'd gone back again to give him another. Pretty soon she was just asking questions.

Today, she'd gone to him because for the first time, she had found herself thinking of her child without tears welling up in her eyes. Until it came to her that it shouldn't be that way; then the *guilt* made her cry.

And he had made her feel better. Again. "I'm coming to services on Sunday," she told Mr. Nelson on the way out.

"It will be a pleasure to have you."

"It's the least I can do, taking up so much of your time," she'd said, and Mr. Nelson had made his joke about the Creation.

• • •

Special Agent Joe Albright sat behind the wheel of a pickup truck and watched Tina Bloyd walk down the white steps of the church to the walkway that led to Main Street.

**47**

Joe had taken a small garage in the Flats and gone into the junk business—or, as you had to call it in Kirkester, the Salvage/Reclamation business. He had his truck and a pair of khaki overalls with "Joe" scripted in red threads over his pocket. He could go anywhere, at any time, knock on anybody's door, and engage in conversation. He had also made the Government of the United States of America a net profit of $527.68 in the first week and a half. Seems that Albright Salvage/Reclamation was the first black-owned business in the history of Kirkester, and the paper had done an article on him (too bad Trotter didn't write it). The people in town had read the article and had been falling all over themselves to prove that even though everybody they ever voted for, from president to dogcatcher, was a Republican, they were not prejudiced.

That was okay with Joe. That same impulse led people to talk to him a lot longer than they normally would to a junk—a Salvage/Reclamation man. In between "It's good to see a young man starting his own business" and "We don't care what somebody looks like, only what they've got inside," he'd found out a lot about the three deaths. Not much that added up, at least on face value. Joe had a little idea he was developing, though, that *might* make sense of things. The question was, did he, or did he not, tell Trotter?

Another question was, why was he hesitating to approach Tina Bloyd? He'd talked to the other parents without a qualm.

It had damned well better not be, he told himself, because she was black. The day he let race shit get in the way of his job was the day to pack it in. All right. She's been to the preacher so much, she'll be in church on Sunday. I'll put on my best suit, tune up my hymn singing, and meet her there.

# CHAPTER FIVE

"If you think the Russians are crazy enough to blow up the world over a maniac like Qaddafi, you have a lower opinion of them than I do."

Trotter kept himself from smiling—it wouldn't have been appropriate. This was a serious discussion, and he knew Petra Hudson was watching.

It was amusing. The tone and editorial policies of the Hudson Group were very similar to the positions Trotter was taking, so Regina's mother should be on his side. On the other hand, the opposition was James Hudson, Jr., home from college and showing off a previously unsuspected fiancée.

The fiancée's name was Hannah Stein, and Trotter liked her already. She was small, not especially pretty, but with shiny dark eyes that said she wasn't the mouse she seemed to act like. He managed to talk to her long enough to find out she was a sociology major (as Jimmy was) and that her father was the manager of the butcher department of a Food Emporium Supermarket in Queens before Jimmy got wound up on the topic of American intransigence. She looked tenderly at her fiancé, but, Trotter could tell, without illusion. It was the attitude most intelligent women had about men, if they didn't scorn them entirely—"He's really quite wonderful, he just needs a little management."

She was quite good at managing Jimmy already. Every time Trotter made a particularly telling point (the myth of the "Soviet People" for instance), and Jimmy looked likely to lose his temper, Hannah asked him to pass the salt or the butter or something. The tactic drew approving looks from Petra Hudson. Even Regina peered through her week-long haze of irritation at Trotter long enough to nod with thoughtful approval at her prospective sister-in-law.

They were eating in a private room at The Hayloft, Kirkester's finest restaurant, and the only money-losing proposition in the entire Hudson Group. James Hudson, Sr., had opened the place because when the Hudson Group began to take off, there hadn't been a suitable place to take the heavy hitters they were now dealing with to lunch. It was a converted farmhouse with a lot of wood and genuine antiques around. The food was excellent. Trotter had Beef Wellington, and hadn't had to use his knife yet. He'd noted prices when he looked at the menu, and they were quite reasonable.

"Qaddafi isn't really important," Jimmy said.

"He was to the people who got blown up at the Rome airport," Regina put in. Trotter hadn't even been sure she'd been listening. She was still mad at him and promised to be that way for a long time yet. She'd been upset ever since he'd used the covering noise of the presses to tell her he'd have to be her boyfriend, at least as far as the world was concerned.

She hadn't liked the idea. Trotter had told her if he was going to do any good at all, he had to get close enough to Petra Hudson to find out what was bothering her, and being a feature writer for the *Chronicle* just wasn't going to do it.

She still didn't like it.

"Why not?" Trotter had demanded.

By this time, they had been out of the building completely, walking down a tree-lined path around the carefully landscaped grounds of the Hudson Group Headquarters. Regina kicked angrily at dry leaves as they walked. She had her hands in her pockets and her head down.

"Why not?" Trotter said again.

"I have a hard time getting myself taken seriously," she said. "As a boss. As a journalist."

Trotter resisted the impulse to ask if the fact that at this moment she looked and acted as if she were seven years old had anything to do with it. Instead, he said, "So you think people will—"

"I *know* people will," she told him. "They always do. You'll be hearing the whispers about my mother and Charles, if you haven't already.

"So I bring you in to a good job without consulting anybody—even Sally Long, who is now convinced her days as feature editor are numbered, by the way. And you turn out to be my boyfriend. It's going to look sleazy, Mr. Trotter."

"Allan. I'm your boyfriend, you have to call me Allan."

*"You are not my boyfriend!"* It didn't come out as a shout only because she strangled it through clenched teeth.

"Believe me, Allan Trotter will turn in features the like of which this paper has never seen. Pulitzer Prize-quality stuff." That was no lie. One of the Congressman's many captive experts was a former Pulitzer prizewinner who had drunk and gambled himself and his family into serious, not to say terminal, trouble before the old man interceded. Cleaned up and respectable again, he wrote for the Congressman on demand whenever fine nonfiction or pseudo nonfiction was called for.

"Sally Long will come to love me," he told her.

"I won't," Regina said.

"You," Trotter told her, suddenly serious, "don't have to."

"That's good."

He ignored her. "All you have to do," he went on, "is decide what the hell you want. You're the one who was so worried about your mother, you went to Rines about it. Is it worth being the subject of a little gossip to help her or not? Why do I always have to keep bringing up the deal you made? You've got an easy choice—go along or call it off."

"You bastards are never going to let me forget that, arc you?"

"Sure we will. The minute you say it's over." This was a lie; Petra Hudson was a line to Cronus, and no one—not Rines, not the Congressman, and certainly not Trotter—was about to let go of her, daughter or no daughter. But Regina was the best opening they had. It had been part of Trotter's training that if you showed the right amount of hostile indifference, you almost always got what you needed.

It worked again here. She cursed him but went along. She came to his apartment and read books while he played soft music on the stereo. She went with him to the movies and suffered him to hold a cold, unwilling hand. After a week, it was time for him to meet Mother, and she'd arranged that too. Tea at the Hudson home. He had met Wes Charles and told Albright to get a full pedigree on him. He noticed the security system. And he noticed Petra Hudson. The only thing wrong with it, as far as Trotter could tell, was that it placed too much trust in the people who already lived there. It would do a fine job of keeping people out, but if somebody who was in wanted to do some mischief, there wasn't much in the system to stop him.

The woman burned with anger or fear, or both. Trotter couldn't decide. He didn't blame Regina for noticing something wrong. There were definitely things wrong to notice.

For instance, Petra Hudson did not raise a single question about any link between Trotter's recent hiring and his relationship with Regina. Not one. From a woman who should be protecting journalistic integrity and the family fortune with equal vigor, it was astounding. All she did was smile mysteriously and invite Trotter to join the family get-together at The Hayloft.

That had been the last straw for Regina. From that moment, she had been barely civil, forget cooperative. Trotter had been formulating alternate plans, since it seemed that Regina was not going to let the current ploy work.

Until now. Was she forgiving him, or was it that she couldn't stand Qaddafi? Not that it mattered. It had come at the right time, and had been delivered in the right tone of voice, to help the illusion of their intimacy. He just hoped she'd keep it up.

Trotter sized up Regina's brother, hoping he could count on him to keep things going. Trotter had spent half of his still young life flying false colors; like a method actor, he could assume the attitudes and behavior patterns of any type of person, argue their politics better than they could themselves.

He'd been a Nazi and an anarchist and a terrorist. It was one of the ironies of the current situation that it served his purpose to support positions close to what he knew as reality. It was the closest he'd been able to come to being himself (whatever that was) since before puberty.

He'd spent a lot longer time being Jimmy Hudson. Prosperous white liberal, type IIA, the we're-just-as-bad-as-the-Russians type. Trotter wasn't worried. This type could be counted on to be patronizing and smug.

Jimmy turned to his sister. "Bash, Bash, Bash," he said.

"Bash?" Hannah Stein said.

Petra Hudson came back from what Trotter guessed was the vicinity of the planet Neptune and smiled in spite of herself.

"Regina was very shy as a little girl," Mrs. Hudson said. "My husband used to call her Little Bash."

"Mother," Regina said. She was blushing. "For heaven's sake."

Jimmy Hudson smiled, a very different smile from the one a few seconds ago. "Short for *bashful*," he said. "I learned really early how to get Regina's goat by calling her that. I'm sorry, Regina." There was genuine warmth in him now; for the first time, Trotter got a glimpse of what Hannah Stein saw in him.

"I think it's cute," Trotter proclaimed.

Regina looked at him. "You would. The last thing you need is another thing to get my goat."

There was laughter all around. They ordered coffee and dessert and forgot about politics for a while.

# CHAPTER SIX

Jimmy Hudson lay on his back in a darkened room, looking at ceiling shadows of the model P-51 that had dangled there in a perpetual dogfight since a few moments after he'd put it together. He guessed it must have been when he was twelve. He had been heavily into military stuff back then. And, he had to face it, he had no intention of taking the Mustang down. It was still a masterpiece of design. It still intrigued him to study the curves of it, accented now by the glow from the security lights on the grounds.

He held a quick inquiry on the question, Am I a Hypocrite? The answer was no. It wasn't the plane's fault that it had been designed to kill. The speed and maneuverability it used to accomplish its purpose could have been worthy ends in themselves. For an airplane.

What bothered him about the world, and the Hudson Group's (meaning his mother's) attitude toward it, was the decided lack of worthy ends he saw being pursued by anyone. Mother could communicate her feelings to the world through her papers, could hire glib bastards like that Trotter to say and write it for her.

(And what was with this Trotter character and Regina? He used to have hopes for that girl, but if she'd taken up with him, it was all over.)

The *maddening* thing was that Jimmy couldn't even make people see what he meant face-to-face. When he said that the editorial policy of *Worldwatch* and the rest of the Hudson Group was way out of step with the vast majority of important journalism in America, it came out as if he were calling for his mother to adopt some kind of herd mentality, when all he meant was that she might take at least a *look* at what her peers thought. When he tried to say that America should make sure its own hands were clean before sounding off about other countries, he sounded as if he were excusing the Soviet invasion of Afghanistan, or Qaddafi and his terrorists.

He wondered sometimes if this was some sort of curse, or if God was testing him in some way. He didn't talk about that, either. Jimmy was, in a private sort of way, quite religious. He wasn't a staunch Witness for Christ or anything. Up at school, some of the guys made fun of him just for going to the chapel on Sunday. Like a Good Little Boy, they said. He just smiled and said it was what kept him on the dean's list.

He didn't tell anyone he was serious about it. No one except Hannah.

Thank God for Hannah, he thought.

Jimmy loved and respected his mother, despite their disagreements, and he had always felt protective of Bash, despite her being four years older than he was.

But he couldn't *talk* to them. Mother ran the papers, and Regina was being groomed to take over, and if Jimmy ever said their whole business was based on the evil men could do, they'd look at him strangely and ask him if he expected them to change the world.

If he told them he guessed he did, it would be even worse.

Hannah understood. She once said, "To you the world is a lost puppy," but she had (miraculously) not made it seem as if she thought he was a wimp for feeling that way. Instead, she loved him for it. She helped him with ideas making his projects for the

Hudson Foundation sixty-seven percent more efficient. And she kept him from making too big an ass of himself. She'd done it tonight, when Trotter had been taking him over the jumps. Jimmy chuckled softly and rubbed his eyes. He had to be tireder than he thought, to start making puns like that. He should go to sleep.

He didn't want to go to sleep. He wanted to be with Hannah, just to talk to her, talk to the one person who let him be his inadequate, insecure self, instead of guilting him somehow into acting the way they expected a decent-looking boy from a family with some money should act.

He shook his head in the dark. After he'd dated Hannah the first few times, before anyone had told her who the Hudsons were, he became aware of a strange feeling. It had taken him a week to figure out what it was: For the first time in his life he was relaxed. The idea that he would be spending the rest of his days with her was what he needed to make something of himself. Aside from the physical attraction (and Jimmy didn't deny its importance; thank God they both felt it), what he loved about Hannah was the way she made him feel about himself. She made him feel capable of doing some good in the world. She made him feel worthy.

It didn't matter that she was Jewish, at least not to him. It was the fact of the belief that was important, not the form. All that mattered was that she was not so devout that it would keep her from marrying him. What he and Hannah felt for each other wasn't so common that it should be destroyed by *anybody's* traditions.

He was rambling. He wished he could be saying all this to Hannah. It all seemed so much more coherent when she was listening. He wished she hadn't been so tired.

Mother was taking this all surprisingly well, he thought. Not that he'd expected anything dramatic. Petra Hudson had never been one for dramatics. And he knew there'd be no trouble about Hannah's religion. Unlike a lot of people he knew, Jimmy had learned firsthand that being conservative did not automatically mean being a bigot.

But his mother had said *nothing*, except the equivalent of "Bless you, my children." Not a word about springing it on her like this, not a word about letting the family meet the girl before he proposed.

Regina hadn't said anything, either, but that could be because of the way she'd sprung *her* honey on everybody.

But Mother was preoccupied in a way that was almost awe-inspiring, if not downright frightening. It was as if she had things on her mind so huge that simple things like her only son's decision to get married paled to insignificance.

That was something else he'd like to talk to Hannah about. Jimmy wasn't a sexist, but he had to admit that throughout his life he'd never been able to make sense of things he saw girls and women do. Maybe it had to do with his father's dying when Jimmy was so young; maybe fathers were supposed to explain women to their sons, or at least help them deal with the ignorance. Jimmy, growing up among women, had felt the lack. It was another empty part of him Hannah had been able to fill. Not only did she make sense herself, but she was able to explain the actions of other women to him in a way that he could almost grasp.

God, he loved her.

*Well,* he thought, *the sooner I go to sleep, the sooner it will be morning, and I can see her again.* He rolled over and went to sleep with a smile on his face.

•   •   •

Petra Hudson knew it was useless even to try to go to sleep. She shuttled between her bed and the window seat, smoking cigarettes she'd cadged from the humidor in one of the guest rooms. Every puff was like a little inhalation of self-contempt. Petra Hudson had given up cigarettes years ago, and here she was.

She had given up many things years ago. And here she was.

She left the window and threw herself back on the bed. Some ashes spilled from the ashtray and landed on the sheet. All the beds in this house had white sheets. Petra Hudson insisted on them, though they were hard to find these days. She brushed at the linen with her hand, removing the ashes but leaving a gray smudge.

She looked at the smudge, hating it. Then she got off the bed (carefully, this time) and went back to the window. She pressed her face against the glass. It felt cool on her forehead, but it did nothing for the pressroom clamor in her brain.

She was going to lose everything. She was supposed to be one of the most powerful women in America—one of the most powerful Americans, period. It was a power she had striven for, earned, and, she thought, had used responsibly and well. Anything underhanded she had done in the beginning to get to this point had been redeemed dozens of times.

She had told herself that the first time at the side of James's deathbed. That bed over there, the one in which her children had been conceived. A plain, square, king-size bed with a dark oak, unornamented headboard. Too plain for the room, really, but as comfortable as a mother's arms. The bed she had soiled with the wastes of a bad habit she thought she had put behind her.

She was going to lose everything, in spite of her power. Because of it. She was going to lose her children. How comforting *were* a mother's arms? If the woman who had become Petra Hudson was the mother in question.

It had been a simple adventure when it started. Training, then a possibly dangerous assignment overseas in the service of her country. The Motherland.

Cronus had sent her out; Cronus now claimed her. The children who had been killed in this town, the town she dominated, the children of her employees, had been killed as a message to her, with no more concern for them than for a sheep killed to have parchment made of its skin.

Those poor parents. She shared their grief; the guilt was hers alone. With the greatest guilt yet to come.

This was not a society where a mother could order her children into her protected home with her, or force bodyguards on them, or restrict whom they saw. Regina and Jimmy were in horrible danger, and she had put them there. Simply by giving birth to them, she had endangered their lives. She had been an agent of Cronus, and Cronus had been the Titan, the father of the Greek gods of Olympus, who had swallowed his children.

There was no way to protect her children except by persuading them that caution was necessary. There was no way to do that without telling them the truth.

And if she told them the truth, she would lose her children as surely as if Borzov, or his successor if Borzov had finally died, had them shot in the back of the head in the cellars of Lubyanka.

For all she knew, the killers were already in place. Her children might hold hands with their killers before her eyes. They might lie naked next to them. Charles was using all his contacts to check into this Allan Trotter and this Hannah Stein, but she needed to know *now*. Hannah Stein was young, but no younger than the girl who was to become Petra Hudson when she went to work for the Chekists. Hannah Stein was under Petra Hudson's roof at this moment.

Petra looked up for a second, and saw that wasn't true. From her window, she could see Hannah Stein appear through the columns of the front entrance. Her son's fiancée cast a guilty look back at the house, and Petra, with an instinct born of a lifetime of deception, pulled her head back from the window. When she looked again, Hannah was disappearing down the drive, walking off to one side, on silent grass instead of crunching gravel.

Petra had to know where she was going. There was no time to dress, no time even to call Charles. She went barefoot through the house and out after Hannah.

Petra never left by the main door at night—she hadn't known how bright the security lights were. She squinted against them, but she could see no sign of the young woman from Queens.

Petra ran. Too fast, she kept telling herself. Too fast. The idea of this whole performance was to learn something, *something* that would give her the slightest edge, show her some way to hold on to her life and dignity. It wouldn't do her any good to arrive whistling like a teakettle from lack of breath, warning the very person she wanted to surprise.

But, she told herself, it wouldn't do any good to let her get away, either.

Petra felt knives in her at the bottom of both sides of her rib cage; her feet kept thudding into the night-wet grass because she couldn't form her thoughts well enough to make them stop.

Once, she slipped on the wet grass, and on the way down she almost said "Thank God" at the thought of an opportunity to stop, but the cold and wet hit her face and body like a slap, shocking her back into the knowledge of what was at stake. She got up and ran again.

Another two hundred yards, she could see the gate, and the road beyond. Hannah was framed between pillars. She had just grabbed the door handle of a big, dark car that was idling in the road. Petra saw the girl open the door and get inside.

Petra kept running. She'd get the license number, at least. *Something.* She thought she would die before she made it to the road, and then she knew it, but she kept on. She got to the gate just in time to see the car disappear. She couldn't read the license number.

Petra stood there, grabbing the white stone of the pillar, retching, sobbing. Knowing that she was a failure, and that she was going to lose everything.

# CHAPTER SEVEN

"Made it!" Hannah said as she pulled the car door closed. "Did anybody see you?"

Hannah smiled. "I don't think so. Nobody said anything, and I think they would have if they'd seen me."

"Makes sense to me. Just making sure."

The smile widened. "Thank you for doing this," she said. "All of it. Especially for helping me keep it all a secret. I know it's silly, but it's important to me."

"I understand."

"I thought I'd have a heart attack, though, crossing the grounds under those lights. I don't think it gets that bright in the daytime. There's a lot of electronic security stuff—Jimmy's mother just had it put in a little while ago—but it's all designed to keep people from getting in." She laughed, something between a snort and a giggle.

The driver found it charming. She was a lovely girl.

"What are you laughing at?" he asked.

"I was just thinking it's a good thing Mrs. Hudson doesn't go in for Dobermans." She said "Mrs. Hudson" as if she liked the sound of it. "I'm not sure we can keep doing this at night, though. I don't know if this was such a good idea."

"When else?" her companion asked reasonably. "You're with your fiancé all day, aren't you?"

"That's true. He even wants to come shopping with me these days."

"There you go. You just can't *do* something like this, you know. You have to prepare. We need some time to work together."

"I know," she said. "It's just that I think it might have been a mistake to try to do it this way. Not only with Jimmy. My parents would kill me if they knew I was doing this."

"I hope you're not getting cold feet," the driver said. He had never been more sincere.

"No, of course I'm not getting—hey, we're downtown, right? I recognize the statue. The guy on the horse in the middle of the fountain."

"That's General Sherman."

"We ate at a restaurant near here tonight."

"Did you have a good time?"

"The food was all right. Jimmy and my future sister-in-law's boyfriend put on territorial displays. But where are we going? I thought it was in the other direction entirely."

"One brief stop first. I have other people depending on me, too, you know."

"Of course. I'm sorry. I'm just a little jumpy. All this cloak-and-dagger stuff seems so incongruous."

"Please, don't trouble yourself. As I said before, I understand. Besides, it will all be over soon."

Hannah brightened. "That's good news. How soon?"

The car rolled up to the curb and stopped. Roger smiled at her. "Before you know it," he said, and reached for her neck.

# CHAPTER EIGHT

Regina looked at a disk of dim light on the ceiling and said, "I didn't need this."

Trotter kissed her on the belly, sternum, throat. "I did."

"Don't make fun of me," she said. She managed to make it sound like a command instead of a plea, but that didn't change the fear.

"I'm not, Bash," Trotter protested. "I wouldn't."

She kept looking at the ceiling. If she looked at the man whose bed she had climbed into so willingly an hour or so ago, she would have burst into tears.

"You would. You're doing it now."

"No, I'm not." The beginnings of a laugh were in his voice.

"You called me Bash."

Now he did laugh. "I'm sorry," he said. "Really. It's just that since we met in New York I've been trying to figure you out, and it turns out your father had already done it for me."

"Leave my father out of this. You can't use my father against me."

"What are you talking about, 'against'? I'm just saying that he was *perceptive* when it came to his children. You're one of the most visible young women in America, what with your job and your family and your money; you do a highly visible job very well, a job you like. Don't you?"

"You're doing the analysis," she said, "Dr. Trotter."

"You only need a doctor if there's something wrong with you. But I'll go on. You *love* your work. You actually believe in the stuff most journalists only give lip service to. You know what it takes to be a good editor, and you do it, *but you're bashful*. You have maybe twenty percent of the self-confidence you deserve to have."

"That's enough," she said.

"Not quite. Why did you come home with me?"

"You were driving."

"That's not an answer. I know why I brought you here. Why did you get out of the car? Why did you come upstairs? Why are you naked in my arms right now? Hard as a statue at the moment, but naked in my arms all the same. I hope you're not going to claim I raped you."

Why had she come here? Why had she let it all happen?

With herself she could be honest. It was because she had wanted this since she'd first seen him. He was big, and handsome enough, but more important, he was intelligent and confident. And dangerous and mysterious; any woman who denied the attraction of danger and mystery was lying.

And he seemed attracted to her. From the very first. Regina had never thought of herself as the kind of woman who would be attractive to that sort of man. Regina had had two love affairs in her life, a number so low compared with some of the other girls at school, she refused to speak about it at all, even with her closest friends. They probably thought she was a virgin. One was with the son of the president of a lumber company, who saw their relationship like some kind of arranged marriage of the Renaissance, with the son of the King of Pulp Production marrying the daughter of the Queen of Newsprint—a sort of Ferdinand and Isabella of the paper world. The other had been with a poor but honest boy from Buffalo who (and Regina would always love him, at least for this) had asked her out without knowing what Hudsons she belonged to. It was wonderful until he found out. Then he spent two thirds of the time intimidated to the point of impotence at the thought of her wealth and his unworthiness to share it, and one third of the time acting like a hunter who has brought down a record trophy. He seemed almost relieved when Regina had called it off.

She had dated other men, but they had all been variations on a theme, and Regina had made her retreat each time before things got as far as the bedroom.

The worst of it was, she *liked sex,* and she suspected she had a natural flair for it. But self-respect was more important, and if who and what she was meant that she had a choice among being seen as a commodity with an incidental vagina, being held in something like awe, or resorting to cheap anonymous pickups, she could do without.

But it got difficult. She got lonely and she got horny, and whatever there was to say about Trotter, one thing she was sure of was that he couldn't be placed in one of the three categories.

He kept her guessing; he drove her crazy. She wanted nothing to do with him. But she also started taking the pill again. She stayed angry with him for a week, but when he said he wanted her to come to his apartment to talk, she had gone willingly.

They'd talked. He liked her brother, in spite of his naive politics. He liked Hannah Stein.

Regina had said she liked her, too, Jimmy needed someone like her.

Trotter hadn't asked her what she needed, he just gave it to her. He took her in his arms and kissed her gently, then hard. Regina seemed to remember that hers had been the first tongue to cross the frontier. Then she was in the bedroom, naked against him, coming, more than once, almost before she knew what was happening.

A thought—something about loving this man—flashed across her disarranged mind just before sanity set in, and she realized this man was some kind of undercover agent. Deception was his livelihood, his way of life. Convincing a woman he wanted her, and "proving" it, were probably all part of a day's work. She wondered how she could have been stupid enough to hide that from herself all this time. She stared at the circle of light on the ceiling and wished she were dead.

"I'm leaving now," she said, and started to get up.

One strong hand on her shoulder forced her back to the mattress. "Not yet," Trotter said. Regina felt a small tickle of fear.

It must have shown on her face, because Trotter said, "Don't be afraid. You can go in ten seconds. You can go now." He let go of her shoulder. "I'll drive you home, if you trust me. Just answer my question or tell me positively you won't."

She looked at his eyes, close to hers because of his myopia. They were eyes that had seen too much and had given up everything but hope.

No actor could put that much in his eyes, no matter how practiced at deception. Could he?

"If I trust you," she whispered. Part of her brain called the rest fool; if she didn't get up, dress, walk out the door, and call this whole business off this second, she'd have only herself to blame for anything that happened after.

"Don't hurt me, Allan," she said. This time, it *was* a plea, and she didn't care.

"I won't," he told her. "I wouldn't." His hands were gentle.

There was a noise on the stairs. Trotter froze. Regina felt the tension in him and froze, too.

"What's the matter?" she whispered.

"There shouldn't be anyone out there. There's only this apartment over the garage, and the people I rent from are away for a couple of days."

Regina watched, fascinated, as Trotter went into action. He was out of bed and into his pants in seconds. There had been no sound; he hadn't even made the bedsprings creak or the change in his pockets jingle. He went silently to the door, listened at the crack as he eased off the lock and the chain bolt, then threw the door open and plunged into the stairway. She heard his voice yell, "Call the police!" then the slamming of the outside door.

Call the police and tell them what? Regina would have to look at whatever it was in the hall, and quickly, but she was naked and didn't want to be. As she stood up, she pulled the bedspread free and wrapped it around herself. Shaking under the rough cotton, she went to look at the stairs.

Someone was lying there, faceup, head down. It was the body of a woman, but the face was no longer a woman's face. The color was wrong, and the expression on it could not be described as human.

Regina recognized it, anyway. Hannah Stein. My God, Hannah Stein.

Regina found herself sheltering a sudden hope that the figure on the stairs might be alive, a hope that had been let in by her love for her brother. She picked her way down the stairs to see if she could help.

Hannah Stein couldn't be helped. Her head was at a right angle to her body, and there was a smell in the hallway that told Regina that death had not even left her brother's fiancée the dignity of continence.

Regina would have been sick, but there was something taking up too much of her brain to make room for nausea.

Hannah's hair was wet, plastered by water into dark spikes. It didn't make any sense. She'd have to talk to the police about this. Talk to Allan.

Why in the name of God should Hannah's hair be wet?

# CHAPTER NINE

Trotter caught sight of the heel of a black shoe disappearing through the doorway. He stopped just long enough to see that nothing could be done for the girl, then took off after the owner of the heel.

Gravel dug into his feet as he ran up the driveway to the road. Trotter ignored the pain. If there was a chance to grab one of these guys, to sit him in a chair, and squeeze him and make him talk, Trotter had to take it.

According to his father, the Objective was everything; you had to look at the Big Picture. You had to be willing to let A, B, and C die here today in order to save a whole alphabet of lives tomorrow, somewhere else.

Trotter knew that sometimes there was no other way. But he also knew something he had never been able to convince his father of—a picture is the sum of its elements of design. If too many details are ugly, the Big Picture will be a mess.

What was going on here in Kirkester was very ugly. If he could stop it now, he would. Let his father worry about getting the Russians by the balls. Trotter would save a few lives, if he could.

Trotter reached the road in time to see a car driving away, slowly now, but picking up speed. It was a dark car, black in the artificial light of the street lamps, maybe a dark blue or dark gray in daylight, That was all Trotter could make out, because like an idiot, he had run outside without putting on his glasses first. He squinted. He put the tips of the thumb and forefinger of both hands together in front of his left eye and pressed to get a pinhole focus, but it was no good. Trotter watched the fuzzy shape of the car disappear in the distance, cursing himself under his breath.

Failure, he thought. Acknowledge it and forget it. Get on with something constructive.

The first constructive thing to do was to ask himself if the car going by had been coincidence, and that whoever he'd seen leaving the stairway was still around, ready to jump him as he headed back to Regina.

Or had doubled back to Regina already.

Trotter put a lid on the panic that was trying to boil over in him. No. He'd heard footsteps ahead of him on the gravel. Then the crunching sound had changed to the tap of leather on a sidewalk. The footsteps stopped, the car door opened, the car drove away. Regina should be safe enough. Even if she weren't, there was something he had to do. He had to look at his own Big Picture.

Trotter became aware of the cold pavement under his bare feet, and the cold night air on his chest and back. He waved his arms around to speed his circulation. He hoped no one looked out a window and saw him; dealing with the police would be a big enough pain as it was.

Trotter squinted again and made out a rectangle of light that could only be the neighborhood pay phone. He ran to it, went inside, put a quarter in, and dialed a local number.

The phone rang seven times, driving Trotter half crazy with impatience, before a sleepy voice said hello.

"It's a good thing you're there."

"Where the hell else would I be?" Special Agent Joe Albright sounded amused. "I thought you'd forgotten all about me."

"I never forget anything. Listen. There's been another one, but they've stepped it up. The Hudson boy's fiancée. Dumped on my doorstep. Get on a safe line and put Rines to work on it."

"On what?"

"The victim. Name's Hannah Stein, from Queens, New York. I want family, background, the works."

"I thought these people were just supposed to be examples to put the fear of the Sickle into you-know-who."

"Where the hell did you get a stupid idea like that?" Trotter demanded.

"Relax," Albright told him. "Nobody leaked. I do have a brain, you know."

"Brains can be dangerous. What's different is that the last I saw her, she was about to be tucked away safely in a secure mansion. I don't think anyone could have gotten to her without her help."

"I'll get right on it. Anything else?"

Trotter took a second to think. "No," he said at last. "Not now. Just get me up-to-date on anything they've turned up on this. I'll get back to you later."

"Good-bye, sleep," Albright said.

"You want to sleep, become a politician. Meantime, the place is going to have cops all over it in a minute, and I want to be available to welcome them."

Trotter hung up the phone and found himself squinting into a flashlight, the glint of a badge, and, he supposed, a gun.

"Police officer," the police officer told him. "Out of the booth. Hands up."

Trotter complied. "High enough?" he asked.

# PART THREE

## CHAPTER ONE

The Reverend Will Nelson looked out at the congregation with a feeling of satisfaction. He was always aware that he was the custodian of the faith and trust that had been earned by the men he substituted for, and he tried never to mishandle that trust. He even, like a banker entrusted with mere money, endeavored to make it grow while in his care.

It was a nomadic life, but the job he did was an important one. God bless Donna for understanding. More than once, the preacher he filled in for couldn't return for one reason or another, and the congregation had asked him to stay. He knew Donna would love to settle down somewhere, establish a household where *she* could decide what drawer to keep the hot pads in. It was the one sadness of an otherwise perfect marriage that Donna couldn't have children, but wherever they went, she taught Sunday school and came to know and love the children of each new town. It was always a wrench for her to say good-bye.

But Will just couldn't accept it. Everyone had his work to do for the Lord, and his was very special. When it was time for him to stop wandering, the Lord would call him to his One True Home.

Currently, he was minding the store for the Reverend Mr.

Nethercott, who'd led the Kirkester congregation for twenty-seven years. Mr. Nethercott was in New Hampshire, at the bedside of his son, who had been hospitalized since February when he'd received a serious head injury during a skiing accident. Will had spent some time in that part of the world himself. He prayed daily for young Nethercott's recovery.

Will was pleased to note that attendance had held steady during his tenure in Mr. Nethercott's place. Attendance today was even greater than usual, it seemed.

Of course, tragedy would do that, and there had been tragedy here. Tragedy in human terms, at least. It was one of the few unresolved questions of his theology: Why is it that humans, even Christians, who should know better, are incapable of seeing the reunion of a soul with its Maker as the joyous event it should be? Even he, who had counseled many of the bereaved, sometimes felt twinges of doubt, tiny but real. At times like that, he called upon his Faith. It had seen him through war, and it would see him through doubt, however small.

The Hudsons were here today, even young Regina, who hadn't been here in ages. They were back from New York, where they'd attended the poor Stein girl's funeral. Young Jimmy was still shattered by the loss, but he was young, and his Faith was strong; he'd prevail. God willing.

The pressure seemed to be telling on Mrs. Hudson. She looked paler than ever, in her black clothes, and she trembled during the sermon.

He preached on Courage and Humility, Christian virtues he judged were essential at times like these. Humility to submit to the will of God, and Courage to carry out the responsibilities one has assumed.

As always, he took the pulpit with just the barest of notes. He always preached better when he preached from the heart.

And as always, he felt joy as he saw his words have an effect. Tina Bloyd began quietly to weep, and Will knew at last that she had come to be at peace with herself.

It would be a long time before Petra Hudson would be at peace with herself. Her trembling had become an undisguised case of the shakes, and she couldn't make it to her feet unaided. Her son and her chauffeur helped her from the church. Jimmy Hudson looked contritely at the reverend. Will nodded benignly, but kept preaching, so as not to make a bigger spectacle of the woman than was unavoidable.

He was nearly done, anyway. He blessed the congregation and finished up. As always, he went around front to mingle with the people leaving, but this week he hurried, to see if he could do any good with Mrs. Hudson. It was too late—the big black car was leaving.

He did see one thing to lighten his heart, though. That nice Mr. Albright was talking earnestly to Tina Bloyd. She was using his handkerchief to dry her eyes, and smiling shyly at him.

Life does go on, he thought. In spite of everything, it is His will that life go on.

# CHAPTER TWO

While the Hudsons all went to Queens for Hannah Stein's funeral, Trotter went to Washington to talk to his father and Rines. Nobody Trotter knew was being buried in Washington that day, but the weather was gloomy enough for a horror movie. A cold wind whipped sheets of rain across the parking lot of the Agency's new headquarters, a small shopping center in Fairfax, Virginia.

There was more furniture around this time. Trotter was allowed in by his father's own hands, which, he supposed, was an honor. It was ironic, Trotter thought, that if you had an appointment and he was willing to see you, it was much easier to get to the Congressman in his guise as the head of a secret espionage organization than it was for one of his constituents to see him on Capitol Hill.

His father told him to sit down. Trotter settled into an old, leather-covered armchair that faced the old man's desk. It was probably the most comfortable visitor's chair in the D.C. area, and Trotter was half convinced the old man lugged it around from office to office as a point of vanity. The Congressman didn't subscribe to the theory of management that prescribed uncomfortable chairs for office visitors. The idea was to shorten appointments, and by keeping the visitor from relaxing, give the owner of the office an edge. In this theory, an uncomfortable man (or woman) was already halfway toward being intimidated.

The Congressman didn't need *furniture* to intimidate anybody. He did it with his eyes. And his voice. Sometimes, Trotter was convinced, he did it just for practice.

Like now, for instance. When Trotter had called the Agency's special eight-hundred number (never knew when an agent might have a tip-off on the start of World War III to pass on, but no change in his pocket) to set up this little visit, the Congressman instructed his secretary (who, along with the technicians who ran the Agency's communications network, worked in another building entirely) to set it up without a word of protest.

Now, if you could believe the expression on his face, he was disgusted with the whole idea.

He looked sternly at his son. There was a time Trotter would have squirmed under those eyes, at least internally, but that time was long over. It ended the day he'd first run off from the old man and the Agency.

The Congressman saw he wasn't getting anywhere with a glare. He switched to a cold scowl. "Well?" he said.

"Where's Rines?" Trotter asked.

"He's in New York, lookin' after your girlfriend and her family at that funeral. Usin' some of his own boys. Don't know how he's justifying that to the Bureau, but it's nice for me. All my New York people are keepin' an eye on Libyans."

One thing about his father Trotter would never understand was the old man's inability to stop playing word games. His son, of all the people in the world, *knew* that the Agency never "kept an eye" on anybody. What the Agency men in New York were undoubtedly doing was setting Libyans up to be: a) arrested by U.S. authorities; or b) killed by fellow Arabs in the most embarrassing way possible for the enemies of the nation.

Suddenly, Trotter started to laugh.

"What's so funny, dammit?" the old man demanded. "Sometimes I worry about you, son."

"That's really touching," his son said, "but don't trouble yourself this time. I just got a flash of Rines and a bunch of his men wearing yarmulkes, trying to look inconspicuous in a Jewish cemetery."

"Doesn't have to be yarmulkes, you know. I went to a service for Javits, found out it can be any kind of hat."

"I know that," his son said.

"Then what's so funny?"

Trotter sighed. "Never mind." The vagaries of his father's sense of humor were something else he'd never understand. "I assume you've run those checks I asked for. Or Rines has, since he seems to be doing all the work around here these days."

That the old man smiled at. "The reports have been done," he said.

"Anything interesting?"

"Well, the bodyguard is clean. Wesley Charles. Ex-Special

Forces, did a lot of fancy anti-kidnapping driving in Italy during the worst of the Red Brigades stuff. Divorced. Ex-wife is an interior decorator out in California. Makes good money. One child, daughter. Goes by mother's name; in school out there. Charles puts money away for her."

"And he's clean."

"Absolutely. Unless he's just gone over. It does happen, but I can't see it here."

"All right. Just a thought."

"Thoughts should be shared, son."

"In a minute. Tell me about the girl."

"Why did you want to know about the girl?"

Trotter had promised himself years ago he wouldn't let his father goad him into losing his temper. He now broke that promise for the three hundredth time. "Why do you keep *testing* me? From my first breath, you trained me for this goddam job. No matter how hard I try to run away from it, whenever something nasty turns up, you haul me back again to handle it. So why don't you just have a little faith in your creation, and believe when I ask you a question, there's a reason for wanting to know the goddam answer?"

The Congressman's voice took on a tone of sublime patience that made Trotter want to kill him. "I *know* you have a reason, son. I just wanted to know what it is."

"Is there anything on Hannah Stein?"

"On her? Not to say *on* her. She signed a few petitions against nuclear power. She's a Democrat."

"So are you."

"That's only for elections. I," the old man pronounced, "am above politics."

"Yeah," Trotter said. "Or below them. Was Hannah Stein involved in something beyond the stuff any ordinary citizen has a right to be involved in?"

"No. I could have told you that twenty minutes after she died, but we listened to what you told Albright, and did the business up, got reports on her womb to tomb, and a more normal little girl I never hope to see. Did my heart good, checkin' up on somebody who stood up to it so well. I thought, this is the kind of person we're fightin' to save the country for. Then I remembered she was dead."

"Because she got too close to Cronus."

"It's your theory, boy."

"Do you have a different one?"

"No. We're together on that one, all right. But you're actin' like there's still some kind of mystery about it."

"Not about why these young people are getting killed—they're putting pressure on Petra Hudson. First children of her employees, now her son's fiancée. Closer to her own children all the time."

"This could be a good time to talk to her," the Congressman suggested.

"Not yet."

"Why not?" The Congressman lit one of his thin black cigars. "I'm not testin' you, by the way. If you're goin' sensitive on me. I just want to know."

"Okay. If we're right about this at all, Petra Hudson is—or at least was—a deep-cover Cronus operator."

The Congressman nodded. It was one of those things too obvious to say for any reason except to establish it as a basis for further discussion. Of *course* the Hudson woman had to be a Cronus operative. The fake telegram her daughter had heard by mistake had threatened her with Cronus, and no one but a Cronus operative would know what it even meant.

"All right, then. That means she got the best training that Russians could offer. Could threats to her personally have any effect? Could torture?"

The Congressman remembered his son's reluctant mother. She'd been a Cronus operative, too.

"No, son, it wouldn't." He finished his son's argument. "And if she's defying Moscow, which she apparently is, though I'm damned if I can even guess why—you got any ideas on that?"

"No. Although it would be nice to know, wouldn't it?"

"Yeah," the old man said. "It would be nice to know what the Russians are planning that's so disgusting a woman who signed on as an agent for the Cronus project wouldn't do it."

"Something worse than Cronus," Trotter said. "It boggles the mind."

"Yeah," the Congressman said. "It might be a good idea to find out what it is."

"Sure," his son said. "But the time is not yet."

"I caught up with you a while back, son. Seems like the only leverage to use on the woman is threats to her children, and leaving aside the fact that it isn't my favorite way to operate . . ."

Which means, Trotter thought, that it's the kind of thing he'll do only if he can't think of anything else.

". . . we *can't* do it because the Russians are doin' it already."

"Right."

"So what are you going to do?"

"Well, three things can happen. The Russians might offer Petra

Hudson another chance to cooperate, now that they've shown they can reach into the woman's own house for a victim."

The Congressman held up a palm. "Wait a second, son. That one of the mysteries you were talkin' about a little while ago?"

"Yeah. That's the big one. The cops in Kirkester aren't even looking at it."

"Why the hell not?"

"They're convinced she was sneaking out to see me. The body was found in my hallway, after all. They've been round and round with me on that one. 'What was she doing *there*, Trotter?' Why is it that the dumber a cop is, the more sure of himself he is?"

"It's not just cops you have to complain about, son. Just hope you never get elected to Congress. What did you tell them?"

"Testing me again? I told them I had no idea, that I could conceive of no reason why she'd be coming to see me and would fall and break her neck on my stairs."

"They're still sold that these have all been accidents."

"They'd love to call it murder, with me in the starring role, but considering that I was making love to one of the town's most prominent citizens at the moment, they're inclined to accept my alibi. I was hardly going to teach the cops better. What was I going to say? A hit man working for the Russians killed the fiancée of one of Petra Hudson's kids and dumped the body on the stairway of the other's boyfriend to show the town's leading citizen they could get to anybody?"

Trotter shrugged. "So, as far as they suspect anybody, I'm the suspect. Back to the mystery. Hannah Stein was tucked up in bed, safe and sound. If the Russians got her out of that house, how did they do it? I don't think *I* would be able to get past all the electronic stuff they have there. Hannah must have sneaked out of there, but *why?*"

"You were lookin' for some kind of guilty secret she'd sneak away for. Or maybe she was an agent planted on this Jimmy Hudson strictly in order to be sacrificed."

"I was looking for something," his son said.

Trotter took a breath. "Anyway, that's the big mystery. And believe me, whoever is running this is going to play it to the—"

"What's the little one?"

"Huh?"

"You said, that's the big mystery. What's the little one?"

"Oh. Her hair was wet. No other part of her body. Just her forehead and hair. There was no rain."

"You go swimming, hair is the last thing to dry."

"Tap water, according to the State police lab. I thought of a lake, or a river, or a swimming pool, or even that she'd stopped somewhere and took a shower. But it was just plain water, with traces of chlorine and stannous fluoride. No soap. No pond or river life."

"Tap water," the old man said.

"Or fountain water. There's a Civil War memorial in the middle of town, and she'd have to pass it to get to my place, but why the hell should she go dunking her head?"

"Or why did the killer dunk it for her?" the old man said. "Son, I don't like this."

"Whereas I, on the other hand, love it."

The Congressman looked at his son and wondered if the boy knew how right his supposed sarcasm was. He should see himself now, the old man thought. Eyes bright behind the glasses, his whole mind and body alert and clicking away. Of *course* he loved it. He *had* to love it. Loving it was in the chromosomes the Congressman had given him, and just as much (maybe more) in his inheritance from his Russian mother. It was a job that had to be done, and some people were suited to do it. The young man who currently called himself Allan Trotter would be a lot happier, his father knew, if he could just admit to himself that this job was his destiny.

He'd said as much to his son, on occasion, and had been rewarded with scorn and rebellion. Now, he just said, "They've shown how close to home they can strike, they might give the Hudson woman another chance to come across. That was one possibility of three."

"Possibility two: They might come after me."

"That would give you the hit man. Think he knows enough to make it worthwhile catching him?"

Trotter grinned. "Thank you for the compliment. *If* he failed to catch me, and I got him instead. If he even tried. I don't think it's too likely. Since I took up with her daughter, and especially since she found out Regina and I have been sleeping together, Petra Hudson would smile while she watched me being flogged, then give me a sodium chloride rubdown.

"The third possibility, of course, is that they'll try to decide which of her children she cares about the most, then kill the other one."

"That one doesn't sound too likely to me, either," the Congressman said.

"No," his son agreed. "If she's tough enough to stand still and let other people's kids be slaughtered, she's tough enough to really go nuts if anybody actually hurts her own kids. She'd have nothing left to lose."

"So we look for an approach to Petra Hudson."

"We draw a circle around Petra Hudson. And when the Russians make their move, I make mine."

# Chapter Three

Trotter paid two more calls while he was in Washington. The first was to a dead woman.

Her name, since the Russians had sent her to America to institute phase one of the Cronus project, was Sheila. As soon as it succeeded, she was Sheila Fane. No one but she and possibly Borzov knew what the name she'd been given at birth was, and the Congressman and those who worked for him had stopped trying to find out. The woman called Sheila Fane had been induced, over the last several years, to part with many secrets, but she would not tell her name.

Trotter had heard about the name business from his father just before coming here to see her.

"She'll talk about anything, now," the old man had said, "but she hangs on to the secret of what they called her at birth as if we really gave a shit what it is."

Trotter figured it for a face-saving gesture. "Sheila Fane" had been defeated and disgraced and ultimately wiped out of existence. None of this had happened to the young Russian girl who'd loved her country so much she volunteered to go to a strange land, bear an enemy's children, and ultimately sacrifice them for the good of the Motherland.

Because that was what the Cronus Project had been all about. Borzov had targeted one hundred American men, all those years ago, men who seemed certain to become important to their country—in science, industry, politics or whatever. The men were watched and studied. Analyzed. Soon Borzov knew more about each man, about what he wanted, than the man did himself.

Then he recruited one hundred young women, the smartest and most dedicated he could find. Each was assigned one of the men, told to study him, learn what he wanted in a woman, *and then to become that woman*. Then, a few at a time, with the best cover stories and documentation the experts at the KGB could provide, the women infiltrated the United States. Their job was to meet the man, marry him, and bear his children.

Children who, when the time came, when one key man's actions could affect that constantly shifting abstraction called the balance of power, could be taken, or killed, or hurt, or whatever seemed necessary. It would be easy, because the essential inside help would be provided by the child's own mother. It would be safe, because the Americans would never suspect someone's *mother*, now, would they?

In a fit of poetic fancy, Borzov had named it the Cronus Project, after the father of the gods, who had swallowed his own children as they were born.

One hundred women, according to Sheila Fane, constituted the Cronus invasion force. One, because of the press of urgency during the Korean Conflict, had been diverted to other duties. She had been captured, and she managed to kill herself without passing on any information. She had not, however, succeeded in destroying the baby she carried. The Congressman's baby.

Trotter sometimes pondered how close he'd come to never having been born, then tried to decide whether he was glad or angry that he had been. On the one hand, his was not exactly a happy life. On the other hand, he was here to do something for the other children of Cronus. Like Trotter himself, they were monsters—children not even of hate but merely of *tactics*. He was born to be a tool; they were born to be victims. He'd fight that with whatever strength and skill and ruthlessness his father had managed to instill in him.

So. His mother had been one. Sheila Fane, who had sent her daughter to be defiled in body and mind by a gang of psychopathic terrorists, was two. Petra Hudson was almost certainly a third.

How many more? There could be ninety-seven more Cronus women out there, hundreds of children and young adults with an invisible knife held to their throats by a loved hand. Trotter didn't think that was the case; *no* intelligence operation of that magnitude achieves a hundred-percent success.

But there had to be some. Thirty successful women wasn't beyond the realm of possibility, or even forty. One was too goddam many.

They kept Sheila Fane's body in a private hospital. Her body was alive; only her past and future were dead. Her past had died in the flames of a staged car wreck, with a borrowed corpse standing in for Sheila Fane. The same fire had also burned one of Trotter's previous identities, but he was more used to changing them.

Her future was dead because she had no future, aside from the pale green corridors of the small private hospital she was confined to. Just how private this hospital was could be seen in the fact that it was listed in no telephone book anywhere. That it took no patients, except those referred by certain doctors with whom it had long-term working arrangements.

The doctors also had long-term working arrangements with the Congressman.

For the record, the woman who had been Sheila Fane was now known as Jane Peterson, a paranoid schizophrenic. This was to cover the (extremely) remote possibility that she might somehow wind up speaking to someone who had not been approved by the Congressman.

Trotter showed a guard, a nurse, an orderly, and a doctor a sheet of letterhead from a psychiatrist's office. Between the address and the signature were a few innocuous words constituting a coded message, instructing the staff to let him see the patient.

They led him into a small white room. He sat on one of two wooden chairs and admired the white-painted metal filigree grating over the window. So much more attractive than bars, and every bit as effective.

A few seconds later they brought Jane Peterson to him.

She was very different from the fashionable suburban matron she'd been before. Now she was gray. Hair, face, everything. She was dressed in a gray sweatsuit and sneakers. She looked washed out, like a bad photocopy of herself.

Until she saw Trotter. Then her eyes flashed and her spine straightened. If she had claws, she would have unsheathed them.

"You," she said.

Trotter told her to sit down, then dismissed the attendant, who looked disappointed. Trotter made a mental note to tell his father—curiosity was not a trait to be encouraged in that kind of job.

Trotter looked at the woman. She hadn't taken her eyes off him. "I'll call you Mrs. Fane," he said. "I'm used to it."

"This is it, then," she said.

"This is what?"

"I'm glad it's finally here."

"Glad what's finally here?"

"The end. You've come to kill me, haven't you? You've taken everything else."

"No," Trotter said. "We're not going to kill you. Not yet, anyway. You've been very valuable. Very cooperative."

"Do you know what they've done to me here? The drugs, the indignities?"

"I could guess. Anyway, after what you did, you have no claim to any kind of dignity."

She flinched as though she'd been struck. Trotter, to his own surprise, felt a twinge of sympathy. He suppressed it. It wasn't hard. All he had to do was call up the image of this woman's daughter after she'd been raped, tortured, drugged, brainwashed, and left to die, all with her mother's connivance.

"Hypocrite! You are as bad as I am. You have no claim to human dignity, either!"

Trotter smiled. "And I make none. But you're wasting my time. I have some questions. Are you going to cooperate?"

"You know I will. I have no choice. If I refuse, they'll take my mind away from me again. Anyway, I don't believe you."

"You don't have to believe me."

"Why is it you? Many people have asked me questions, but never you. Why are you here now, if not to kill me?"

"I haven't needed you."

"*You owe it to me!* I gave up everything—my homeland, my language, my name. I had a family I dared not love. All I had was my mission, and you took it away from me. You took the purpose of my life, and you even took the lie that surrounded it. You owe it to me to kill me now."

Trotter took an envelope from his inside pocket. "I have some photographs here. They're all of the same woman. I want you to tell me if you recognize her."

He held out the pictures. The woman he had known as Sheila Fane took them from him without a word. Tears ran down her face, but she refused to acknowledge them, even to wipe them away.

Trotter waited. Finally, she began shuffling the photos. After one or two, she said, "This is Petra Hudson, the publisher."

"Keep looking," Trotter said.

There were a lot of photos; the media tend to cover themselves fairly thoroughly, and Trotter had been able to find at least two photos of Petra Hudson a year in the morgue of the Kirkester *Chronicle*, going back to her wedding picture. There were no childhood pictures—at least, Regina had never seen any. It made sense, of course—if the theory held up, all the childhood photographs of Petra Hudson would be in the hands of the KGB, or more likely, a pile of ashes long since scattered to the winds.

Trotter had stacked the pictures most recent to oldest, with the wedding picture last. One of his father's experts had cropped James Hudson, Sr., from the picture, leaving only a young Petra, looking pretty and virginal in her white veil.

Sheila Fane held up the bottom picture. "We called her Nina," she said.

**76**

"Where did you call her Nina?"

"At the village. Centerville."

"The American village. In Soviet Georgia. Where you trained for Cronus."

"Why do you ask about the obvious?"

"Just making sure," Trotter told her. "Tell me about Nina."

"I've told you. We trained together. I didn't *know* her. We weren't encouraged to become friends."

"Tell me what you know about her."

"She was brilliant. The best at everything, the quickest to catch on. Borzov himself came one day and spoke to us. He singled her out; he said a commendation would be placed in her record, since the nature of the mission ruled out any direct presentation.

"He said—he said he was proud of all of us, but if there was to be only one of us who would succeed, it would be Nina."

She looked at him. The tears had dried to salty streaks on her face.

"Have you been helped?" she asked.

"Maybe."

"I curse you," she said tonelessly. "May you live a life of total emptiness, as I do. And may it be a long one."

Trotter smiled at her and rang for the attendant.

# CHAPTER FOUR

The next day, Trotter went to visit Grigori Illyich Bulanin, formerly of the KGB. Bulanin had defected to Trotter in person, in a Chamber of Horrors in London. He was one of the loose ends that had had to be tied up in the aftermath of the Russians' first attempt at a Cronus operation.

Bulanin's defection had been one of practicality, not of conviction. In a move to gather enough glory to propel him to the Politburo, he had gone far beyond his authority as "agricultural attaché," and had mixed himself up in the kidnapping of a former top British Intelligence man. When it all fell apart on him, Bulanin had been wise enough to know that ambition should come a distant second to survival. He'd cast his lot with the Congressman and the Agency.

It was possible (though unlikely) that once out of his immediate peril, Bulanin might devote his time to gathering enough information to make himself valuable to Borzov once again.

To guard against this possibility, Bulanin was kept in a safe house. The Congressman chose safe houses for this kind of thing on two criteria: one, the safest house is the most inaccessible; two, the safest house was the one that could summon the most armed men to guard it.

Therefore, Trotter had not been surprised to learn that Bulanin was being kept in a cabin in the Maryland mountains, not far from Camp David. His father had offered to have him helicoptered out to it, but Trotter said he preferred to drive. He checked out a four-wheel-drive car, because it rained a lot in that part of the country at that time of year.

It was a small compound, and the guards were unobtrusive but definitely present. They were armed to the teeth under their plaid hunters' coats. Trotter could see the lumps and bulges under the wool. They pulled Trotter over and took him into a small log cabin that turned out to be lined with tile and fluorescent lighting and contained communications and security equipment. They patted him down, found nothing, walked him through an X-ray machine, and finally pulled a set of fingerprints, which a computer compared and said were okay.

Trotter was glad to see a human being cross-check the results before they let him through—the computer was the weak link in the security. Someone who knew what he was doing could probably reprogram that thing to let in Pol Pot.

Then they took him in to see Bulanin, who was watching a tape of *E.T.* on a big-screen TV.

One of the men in the plaid jackets said, "Mr. Trotter to see you. Top clearance." He and his companion withdrew, but not out of sight. Probably not out of earshot, either, but it didn't make that much difference. Trotter had once worked with one of these guys during an assassination attempt, ex-Israeli army captain who had no curiosity whatever—he lived solely to contemplate the beauty of proper security procedure, and to go into action when someone tried to penetrate it. He told Trotter, "Shooting is my food," and he was fairly typical of the breed.

Bulanin looked up at Trotter. A warm smile lit up the Russian's movie-star-handsome face. "Welcome, welcome," he said. "So you are Trotter now."

"Names come and go," Trotter told him.

"As do the men who bear them, no?"

"We're still here," Trotter said.

Bulanin laughed. Trotter had never seen him laugh before. He reached out and switched off the television and the tape player. "I've seen the film before," he said. "A wonderful fantasy. Let us hope it never comes true."

"Why is that?"

"Because if a visitor ever did come from another world and landed in one of our countries, the other would learn of it and immediately launch the missiles before the visitor could give the first secrets that would shift the balance of power. They would have to. Don't you agree?"

It was too obvious even to acknowledge. If the kind of work Trotter did, and Bulanin had done, could be reduced to one commandment, it would be Think the Worst.

Trotter asked his question instead. "Who kills for Borzov?"

Bulanin looked at him in surprise, then laughed again. "Dozens. Hundreds. Russians. Bulgarians. Poles. East Germans. Arabs. Irish. Italians . . . How many nations are there in the world? You may recall a certain countryman of yours named Leo Calvin."

"This is different. This is an American, or someone who can pass for an American for a long time. He's done four so far, maybe, with at least a month between each."

"Maybe?"

"He makes them look like accidents," Trotter said. "He's very good."

"So some of the deaths you're wondering about might have indeed been accidents."

"It's possible."

"He must be very good indeed if he has you, of all people, as worried as this."

"I'll admit I'm worried," Trotter admitted. "He's someone we never heard of."

Bulanin nodded sagely. "Or you have heard of him, and you are asking me in order to check your information. Or this is just a fishing expedition, because it is always good to know if the enemy has come up with a new approach before you have thought of it."

Trotter smiled. "Grigori Illyich, please don't teach me interrogation techniques. It so happens that now I'm telling the truth."

"What harm can there be? My life is a restricted one, if pleasant, and the only people I ever talk to are these robot guards or visitors handpicked by your father. He's offered me a woman."

"Big of him," Trotter said. "You're stalling, my friend. It makes me think you have something to tell me."

Bulanin sighed. "You know, the only man I ever killed was Leo Calvin, whom I shot to keep him from shooting you."

"And to keep yourself from being sent back to Moscow so Borzov could have a go at you."

"There was that," Bulanin conceded.

"Anyway," Trotter went on, "how many deaths did you order? You lose points for ordering them, too, you know."

"Then I *am* in trouble," Bulanin said with a smile. "Not only did I order many, but most of them were carried out. Not all, though. I ordered your death three times in the space of two weeks, and look where it got me."

"I am not the person to come to for sympathy," Trotter told him. "Are we through wasting time?"

"I have no facts to give you," Bulanin warned. "I can't even dignify it as rumor. I spent most of my career in the West; Bonn, Washington, London. Perhaps if my work had kept me more in Moscow, I might know better—"

"You're doing it again. If it's not fact, and not rumor, what is it?"

"Legend."

Trotter looked at him. To a spy, a legend was the network of false documentation that supported him (or her) on a clandestine mission.

Bulanin saw the question on Trotter's face. "I don't mean the word in the professional sense," he said. "I mean a legend, like the Flying Dutchman. I don't suppose anyone knows the truth of it but Borzov, but word filtered out."

"Word filtered out," Trotter echoed.

"It always does. You know as well as I that the largest risk in a security agency is not that your people will tell outsiders, but, like workers at a tire factory, will gather and talk shop. So word inevitably filters out."

"I understand that. What I want you to tell me is, what did the word *say*?"

"Azrael," Bulanin said.

"Azrael." It irritated Trotter to be repeating the other man so often. "Sounds like a Borzov special."

Bulanin looked surprised. "You are aware of the man's idiosyncrasy, then?"

For the first time, Trotter really believed Bulanin would be content to spend the rest of his life in this cabin, or in similar lodgings arranged by the Congressman.

Because it was true. Borzov's one weakness was his poetic streak. The man found it literally impossible to resist giving an operation an appropriate mythological name. Intercepted Russian communications with mythic connotations had already helped lead to an understanding of the workings of two operations. Vulcan, which was a plan to destroy a nuclear plant in France, and the fateful Cronus.

In five words, Trotter had made two unforgivable mistakes. He had revealed that the Agency had the means of learning the code names of Russian operations, and that they were aware of their significance.

And Bulanin had made his own mistake by showing he had spotted Trotter's. If he ever left the Congressman's custody now, it could only be by death. He couldn't be allowed to have even a *chance* of taking or sending that information back to the Kremlin. Trotter would make sure everyone knew that, despite the fact that it would show him up to be the idiot he was. If he didn't, the men who watched the wiretaps in this room would.

"Tell me about Azrael," Trotter said.

"The legend, you mean."

"Tell me the legend."

"It's the legend of the perfect assassin. Skilled, secret, fearless."

"An American?"

"Apparently. A free-lance. He'd work for us, the Mafia, big business, anyone. No ideology at all."

"And Borzov called him Azrael."

"So says the legend," Bulanin said quietly. "It might have been his own idea. That would explain why Borzov is so high on him. Like minds, you know."

"Azrael was an angel, wasn't he?"

"The Angel of Death," Bulanin said. "I got curious once—a dangerous trait, but from time to time I succumb to it—and I looked it up."

"The Angel of Death," Trotter said, not realizing he was again parroting the Russian. He was remembering Hannah Stein, with her broken neck, lying in his hallway. With her hair wet. And he thought of the other deaths, the ones that had already happened and the ones to come.

Borzov, once again, had been on the money. Trotter was going to make it his business, though, to find out just how appropriate that name was.

# CHAPTER FIVE

There was a party at the home of the department chairman this evening. Dr. Smolinski was there; he was always there. One had to be polite. One had to be grateful. Smolinski was a refugee, after all, an exile of conscience, having left Poland in protest of the crackdown on the workers in the wake of the Solidarity movement. He was a noted scholar; in that instant of the evanescent American consciousness, he was a hero, though he was sure he had been completely forgotten by now. *The New York Times* had done an article on him, and before the week was out, Sparta University, an institution suffering the martyrdom of being more famous for television sports announcers and petroleum engineers than first-rate scholarship, had invited him to be a guest lecturer.

The invitation specified no time limit, and Smolinski was still here. His tasks were not onerous. Twice a week, he met with two sets of graduate students, and discussed the modern history of Eastern Europe. Occasionally, he repaid the *Times* by favoring its readers with a piece for something called the op-ed page. He worked on his book, but aside from admitting the project was in motion, he said little if anything about it and refused to project a time when an eager academic world might be allowed to see it.

He had, several times, subtly reassured the Dean of the School of Arts and Sciences, in response to questions subtly asked, that when the time came, the hospitality and encouragement of the administration and faculty of Sparta University would be fully acknowledged.

And he attended parties, though he had little interest in the main activities his colleagues engaged in for amusement. Since he did not seek advancement, he had no need to perform character assassinations on potential rivals or to lick the boots of those with power. Since he was not married, he had no need to arrange adulteries. Smolinski was well content to restrict his liaisons to a coterie of attractive, but undemanding, single women. He was a guest here, after all.

And being a Pole, he did not need to find some hypocritical excuse to drink liquor. If you wanted to drink, then *drink*. If you wished to be drunk, you should get *magnificently* drunk, in the company of like-minded companions. And stay off the road.

What one should not do is to get drunk when others are sober, or get drunk and pretend you haven't.

Here was the Department chairman, now. His tie was askew, and his eyes were abnormally bright. He would have another Polish joke. The Department chairman would rather be flogged than tell an ethnic joke while sober, but when sufficiently drunk, he told Smolinski incessant, vulgar, stupid jokes that bore no relationship to the reality of the Polish people.

"Stan," the Department chairman said earnestly, "I've got another one for you." He was always "Dr. Smolinski" when the man was sober.

"I somehow suspected you did."

"Who's the most important Pole in the United States?" Even drunk, the Department chairman would not say "Polack." As much as he loathed them, Smolinski knew that none of these things could be funny, even to the fools who laughed at them without the word "Polack" in them somewhere.

"I don't know," Smolinski said. He wondered if the Department chairman remembered these little incidents when the alcohol had been metabolized, and what he thought of himself if he did. "Who is it?"

"Stashu Liberty."

Smolinski laughed politely. He always laughed politely. It was part of his conception of the obligations of a guest. At that, the Department chairman was improving—this joke was merely moronic.

"Thank you, sir," Smolinski told him. "A smile to send me home."

"Oh, don't go. The evening is young."

"Young enough to be pressed into some productive work, I hope. My book, you know."

The Department chairman tried to change his mind, then turned the task over to his wife, who ignored her assignment, and instead offered, for the hundredth time, to "show him around town." This was accompanied by a repertoire of lascivious gestures that stopped just short of baring her bosom, but Smolinski was heroically obtuse. He escaped from the house about forty-five minutes after announcing his desire to leave, which was better than the average.

Smolinski rented a three-room cottage a short walk from campus. It was comfortable. He could work there, and he was eager to arrive, because he had much work to do tonight.

It was a cool night, but Smolinski enjoyed it. The weather here was much like the weather in Poland. He liked to ski and had tried it last winter, but too many people crowded the slopes for him to enjoy himself.

Smolinski entered his house. He locked the door behind him and made sure the shades on all the windows were drawn. He always did. No one noticed. If anyone did, it still would not concern him. He was a refugee, after all. He is bound to want his privacy, they would say. It is natural that he is cautious.

It was more than natural that Smolinski should be cautious. It was imperative. Dr. Stanislaus Smolinski was the KGB's regional director for Upstate New York. He'd been preparing to play this role for years, since first he showed intellectual promise at school. Smolinski had always been intelligent enough to know where the power was, and the power in Eastern Europe was in Moscow. There was no more to be said. As one dedicated to Lenin's principles of revolution, he had always been drawn to Russia.

The irony was, he had never been there. Once he had been groomed to be a "dissident," it would have been a grave mistake to bring him East, across the border.

One day he would go. He would see the body of Lenin with his own eyes, and he'd offer the long, uncomfortable ordeal he had endured in his native land and in the West as a tribute to the great man.

In the meantime, he served the KGB, in the tradition of Felix Dzerzhinski, the Pole who began the organization that would become the Komitet Gosudarstvennoi Bezopastnosti, and Beria, the Pole who succeeded him.

Borzov was not a Pole, but Smolinski looked upon him as a patriarch. It had been Borzov who realized that secret was not always best; that a man set up in the easily dazzled eye of the American media as an underdog hero against an "oppressive Communist regime" (in the phrase Smolinski had trained himself to say almost by reflex) would be able to pick among a dozen fine opportunities for spying.

And this was the one he had been instructed to choose.

Smolinski had been surprised, at first. He had been offered a lecture tour; he had been offered a post at a Washington think tank. No. Visiting Professor at Sparta University in upstate New York was what Borzov had said.

Smolinski had had sufficient presence of mind to hide his surprise from the man at the other end of the scrambled radio signal. It was a good thing, too, because later, when he thought the situation over, Borzov's wisdom had revealed itself to him.

Because Stanislaus Smolinski had not been chosen simply to be a "mole," as the British writer had put it, he was to do in the

West what he had done in Poland—act as a sort of litmus paper. By their reactions to him, as a public opponent of the world he had left behind, he could judge who might and might not prove to be useful.

In addition, he was to gather whatever intelligence he could, and to supervise special operations as they arose. He could hardly do that while on a lecture tour.

And Washington was too close to the center of things. A refugee from a so-called Iron Curtain country would be screened much more closely if he chose to join a Washington think tank than if he went to a second-rate college in New York State.

Yet there was much for Smolinski to do in northern New York State. There were missile bases and Air Force bases. It was major supplier of water power for the Northeast Power Grid. There was all sorts of government and defense-related research going on at the many colleges and universities in the region. There were several hundred miles of unguarded land-and-water border with Canada. An agent could travel much more easily to Canada than to the United States from the Soviet Union, sometimes by way of Cuba, sometimes not. It was then a simple matter to sneak them into the United States. Until recently, these agents would disperse thoughout the country to their various assignments. In recent months, though, they had been placing themselves under Smolinski's command. He now had close to a dozen men working for him. He had met few of them face-to-face, but through coded phone conversations and letters, he kept in constant touch.

It all had to do with the operation going on in Kirkester, some hundred miles east of Sparta. There was an agent working there, answering directly to Borzov. Smolinski had no idea what he was up to, but it involved the Hudson woman. Smolinski was responsible for support services for the mission—he had given the order for the faked telegram to be read to the Hudson woman over the phone. It was his men who passed frequently through Kirkester (Smolinski had been ordered to keep any of them from trying to set up operations in the town itself) and photographed newcomers to the town.

And it would be Smolinski himself who, in a very few days' time, would relay Moscow's demands to the Hudson woman. He had received the orders, along with assurances that he need not fear his cover being blown, earlier today. He was excited, and proud.

But he would not meet with the woman until a certain other matter had been attended to. One of the photographs had been recognized in Moscow. They knew him as Jeffrey Bellman, and it was he who had gone to England and induced the defection of the traitor Bulanin. He called himself Trotter now, apparently, and he looked different—spectacles, different eye color, loss of weight, etc.—but not so different that the experts in Moscow could not recognize him. He was too dangerous to be left around when the plan (whatever it was) went into high gear.

Mr. Trotter would be attended to. Tonight.

And if he turned out to be the wrong man, what did it matter? There had been so many mysterious deaths in the town of Kirkester already.

# CHAPTER SIX

Joe Albright went upstairs and began straightening out the apartment above the shop. He'd furnished it entirely with junk—with salvaged/reclaimed items—and it didn't look bad at all. All he'd needed to buy new was a TV set and cushions for the sofas and chairs. He knew this was something big and a little off-center, and he found himself nervous about making a good impression.

He knew it was stupid. The FBI hadn't hired him because of his domestic skills. Still, he was glad he wouldn't have to receive a heavy hitter like Trotter (and who *did* he work for, anyway?) in a messed-up, uncomfortable place.

The only hard part of setting up the meeting was arranging things so that Trotter could come visit him without anybody knowing. It couldn't be during business hours, because in the mornings Joe was out in his truck, collecting merchandise and information, and in the afternoon he was in the shop, selling stuff and writing coded reports for Rines in his spare moments, which he didn't have a whole lot of. Lot of traffic through that door.

It was still the fallout from that article. Joe had never been in a situation like this before. It occurred to him that if there were only, say, five or six black families in America, there would be no prejudice whatsoever. There would also be no basketball worth a damn, but that was another problem. But he could see it in this town—there weren't enough black people around to scare the whites. His store was booming because people were coming to see the Amazing Colored Man, not because of a sudden passion for secondhand furniture.

Trotter rapped out the code they'd agreed on, and Joe went down to let him in. He waved Trotter up the stairs first, figuring good security was good security.

"Where'd you park?"

"Around on Asket Street. I didn't want the folks at the body shop to see me."

"That's the owner. Greek guy. Greek name, anyway. He never goes home. I got back from church Sunday, there he was."

"Learn anything from Tina Bloyd?"

"I learned she's a real brave lady who's had a tough time."

"I know."

"I don't like messing her around."

"What, messing her around? Did I ask you to rape her? Seduce her? Kiss her hard? I just want you to make friends and find out if there's anything about the baby's death that didn't turn up in the reports."

"Like what?"

Trotter looked at him. Joe realized his good impression was slipping, but he cared less than he thought he would.

"Like if the killer dropped a mongrammed cigarette case in the crib," Trotter said. "Look, Joe, if I knew like what, I would just go and ask her yes or no. What's the matter with you? You fall in love or something?"

"That's ridiculous. What's today, Tuesday? I didn't even talk to her until Sunday."

"Since then?"

"Once a day or so on the phone."

"You gonna answer my question?"

"I already said it's ridiculous."

"Love is ridiculous."

"If I said yes, you'd pull me off the case."

"Well, hell," Trotter said. "We can't have that. Never mind, don't answer."

"You get the stuff from Rines?"

Albright unlocked an old rolltop desk made, as far as he could tell, of solid oak. He twisted a flower, and part of the inside facing popped open. Albright reached inside, pulled out a manila folder and handed it to Trotter.

"How very E. Phillips Oppenheim," Trotter said.

"Who?"

"Never mind." Trotter untied the tape and opened the folder. "Did you look at this?"

"No. I had no instructions."

"Okay, instructions. Anything that comes through Rines, you

should read. If I trust you with the questions, Rines can damn well trust you with the answers. Anything that's too delicate for you to hear will come to me by a different route."

"If that's the way you want it."

"That's not only the way I want it, it's the way we've got to do it. I could wind up disagreeing with something that eats me in this thing, and you'll have to brief whoever comes next."

Trotter had been reading all the time he'd been talking, a skill Albright would like to develop. Trotter handed him the first page; Albright took it and read.

It was a report on suspected Russian and Eastern Bloc infiltrations of the area within a two-hundred-mile radius of Kirkester.

"Five of them," Albright said.

"That's just the number they suspect," Trotter told him. "Figure seven or ten."

"How the hell do you know this?"

Trotter smiled. "This your first counterespionage assignment?"

"Until you opened your mouth just now, I wasn't even sure *this* was a counterespionage assignment. But yes, I'm usually working drug-related stuff. The West Coast is lousy with Mexican drugs, lately."

"You use informants, don't you?" Albright nodded. "Us too," Trotter said.

"I have been trained, you know. I *know* you get told by somebody. I was wondering what *kind* of somebody."

"Lovers of freedom." Albright wanted to laugh, but Trotter cut him off. "I'm not joking. These people sit in the middle of it and smuggle these things out at the risk of death, 'mental care,' or life imprisonment. What happens when the Bureau catches a spy? He gets a couple of years in jail, then the Russians trade him for some poor innocent schmuck they pull off the street."

"And that's why you don't tell us about these foreign guys sneaking in."

"That, and for what we can learn from them."

This, Albright reflected, was one weird conversation. The words were about stuff so basic, it was almost embarrassing. Yet once he'd started the conversation off, he got the feeling that Trotter really wanted to go on with it. Not so much for content or anything, but to sublimate some kind of strong emotion he was embarrassed to say out loud.

Trotter went on talking. "If you pull them in, we don't learn anything."

"Whoever *we* are."

"Albright, you don't want to know."

"No, I certainly do not. Even now, I get an occasional twinge I'm finding out too much. Still, you do seem to have a flexibility about what you want to do to get things done. The rules fit a little tight around the collar sometimes."

"Don't complain about the rules. One of the miracles of this country is that we can have things as good as they are with ninety-nine point nine percent of the government sticking to the rules."

"That much?"

"Make it seventy-five percent, and we're still doing better than anyplace else I can think of."

Trotter finished looking at the report. "Four Russians, one Czech," he said.

"So?"

"No Bulgarians. Bulgarians are the Russians' favorite killers. They specialize in it. They like it."

"You say there's two to five guys they didn't hear about."

"True. But I doubt there's any Bulgarians there, either. They don't need any journeyman killers on this trip. They've got an ace."

"I'll say. And what are we gonna do with him when we catch him? There's not a damn bit of evidence that these even were murders."

Trotter smiled at him, something halfway between sad and cynical. "Keep playing by the rules, Joe," he said.

Trotter thanked him for the hospitality, asked him to try to hurry Rines up on those background reports he was supposed to be getting.

Albright was tempted to ask him if there were any in particular he was interested in, but he fought it down. He already felt childish and unsophisticated. He didn't want to see that damn smile again.

They shook hands; Trotter left. Albright sat and thought about what he could do for his country. The only thing he could come up with was to get closer to Tina Bloyd, a pleasant assignment if there ever was one.

He was working on ways and means when he heard the shots.

# CHAPTER SEVEN

If it had been August instead of October, Trotter would already be dead. In the summer, people stay out later, television sets blare through open windows. Insects and the birds that eat them fill the air with their cries. The soft click of the hammer of a .38 being cocked would get lost against all the other sound.

In the chilly nights of autumn, people stay indoors with their windows closed. The bugs are dead or sleeping, and the birds have migrated to warmer places. A man who's heard the gun noise before will hear it now and recognize it. He'll drop to the macadam of the road and let the bullet spiderweb the window of the door he'd been about to open.

Times like this sometimes made Trotter want to reconsider his policy about carrying a weapon. Generally, when he carried a gun, he found himself constantly *thinking* about it, as if it were a boil that had come to a head, and that he was tempted to squeeze for the explosion. He would catch himself not listening to people because he was thinking about the gun. He had decided long ago that he would only arm himself when he thought there was a definite possibility he'd have to kill someone before he got back home.

It was a decision he'd been happy with, but it had the flaw of making no allowance for times when bullets came at you out of the dark.

Trotter was off the ground again in a second, scrambling around the front of the car. He wanted to get the mass of it between him and whoever that was behind the tree across the street. He couldn't really see anything—it was a big tree, and the street lighting in this part of town was nonexistent.

Trotter didn't mind the dark. It was the one thing he had working for him. He crouched behind the left front tire and took big, silent breaths while he sized things up.

He heard no footsteps, which made sense. His playmate across the road had no way of knowing Trotter was unarmed. It would, unfortunately, occur to him eventually, and he would gather his courage and come look, and shoot Trotter dead.

It would do no good to try to get into the car from the passenger side. No matter how quickly he got in and started the motor, he couldn't keep the dome light from giving him away, and he couldn't drive off in less time than it would take a man to get close and kill him.

So he had to run. The idea was to do it in the way that gave him the best chance for survival. The destination was easy—back toward Albright Salvage/Reclamation. Better to be running toward help than away from it. The whole neighborhood would have heard the shot, but, Trotter knew, they'd chalk it up to a car's backfire or something. To most Americans a gunshot was that dynamite-bomb-in-an-echo-chamber effect they dubbed in for movies or television shows. Joe Albright, though, would recognize the sound for what it was, and he'd come to investigate.

Trotter had about eight yards to go before he could reach the corner of Wilvoys Road, and for the whole distance he'd be naked to gunfire. There wasn't much he could do to hide, either. The light was bad, but it wasn't *that* bad.

In front of him was the car, and in front of that was a man with a gun. To either side was bare sidewalk. He might dive for it and scramble behind the next tree, but behind the tree, he'd have all the same problems he had now.

Behind him was a privet hedge. It was a tall privet hedge, as tall as Trotter himself. He could get over it, but he couldn't do it without letting the man with the gun know what he was up to. It *might* not matter. Even if it did, it was the only chance he had.

Still in his crouch, Trotter turned quietly until he had his back to the car. He planted his left foot against the tire and brought his right knee up to his chest in a classic sprinter's stance. He was sizing up distances and guessing the effort required when he heard footsteps crossing the road. That was enough; no starting gun was needed. Trotter exploded toward the hedge. About five feet away from it, he launched himself into the air at a forty-five-degree angle, exactly as if he thought he was Superman and could simply fly away from his troubles.

He was in the air before he thought of Cyclone fences. People often grew privet hedges around Cyclone fences—the fence for security, the hedge for looks. There hadn't been enough light to inspect this particular hedge, but if there was a metal fence in the middle of it, Trotter was in big trouble.

Because to get to the other side of a privet hedge, it is not necessary to jump clean *over* it. All you've got to do is jump high enough to hit it with your body below your rib cage, let your weight and momentum bend the hedge under you, and lower you softly to the ground on the other side.

If there is a Cyclone fence, or anything unyielding in the middle, you will rupture your liver.

Trotter was in luck. Not only did he encounter nothing unyielding, he also missed the ancient Sears Roebuck J. C. Higgins Flightliner bicycle someone had left to rust away in the front yard of the boarded-up house the hedge had been guarding the privacy of.

It would probably take a few seconds before the man with the gun decided to follow him. Trotter decided to invest a little of the time moving the bicycle so that it rested right on the place the hedge had left him. Trotter took off around the house. The grass was tall and made for slow running, but at least it was quiet. Once he had the corner of the building between him and his pursuer, he'd be hard to catch.

As he reached the shelter of the side of the house, Trotter smiled as he heard the jangle of metal, and curses mingled with grunts of pain. That would teach the bastard to take the easy way over a hedge—from now on, let him bend his own bushes.

The hedge ran around the entire lot, so Trotter had to do his trick again. This time, though, he deposited himself neatly on top of a metal trash barrel filled with empty oil cans. Albright's neighbor, the garage. He'd forgotten.

The noise was astounding.

And that will teach *me*, Trotter thought, not to be overconfident. He could hear his father's voice—"Keep alert, son. It might take the other fellow a while to realize you've turned the tables on him."

Trotter had smashed his foot against the rim of the barrel. He wasn't doing much more running, at least on that foot. He'd have to stand and fight. Or crouch and fight, or crawl and fight. "Fight" was the operative word.

By now, the pursuer would know Trotter had no gun. He would also remember the bicycle trick. *All right*, Trotter told himself, *enough about your disadvantages. What have you got going for you?*

Well, for one thing, he wouldn't know about the sore foot. And he might not know about Joe Albright, who would be coming to the rescue any minute now.

Trotter hoped.

Another possible advantage Trotter could see was that while the man with the gun would know that among pieces of cars and scrap metal there'd be something Trotter could use as a weapon, he wouldn't think there would be anything that could be effective long-distance.

Trotter knew better. He limped around to a few cars and armed himself. He was glad the owner of the garage did not keep a dog.

Trotter heard the rustling of the hedge before he was ready. He'd meant to get a lot more stuff, but he'd have to be content with two hubcaps and a car antenna. He dragged his foot to cover as quickly as he could.

And here I am again, he thought, crouched down behind an automobile, waiting for a man with a gun.

Who had, as Trotter guessed, wised up since last time. He was going through the hedge the hard way, walking his way through by main strength. Trotter had hoped that might be what he'd try.

The hedge stopped rustling; there was a dull clang as a piece of metal got kicked into the garbage can, then silence.

Trotter pulled the radio aerial out to about half its length, and held it in his left hand. With his right, he grabbed one of the hubcaps by the rim, concave side toward his body. He was all set, assuming his pursuer passed Trotter's hiding place to the right.

It was a fifty-fifty chance, but Trotter had learned that the way to stay alive in this business was to figure out a way to adjust the odds. It frequently didn't take much. In this case, it took a pebble. Trotter put the aerial down for a second, picked up a pebble, and threw it across his body, where it pinged against the door panel of another car.

Trotter backed a few feet away from his hiding place, to give himself room to move. The man with the gun smelled the kill, now. He let his footsteps crunch the gravel. He might as well have been yelling out coordinates.

The gun appeared first, followed by a black sleeve. If Trotter'd known that was how it was going to happen, he would have forgotten the hubcaps completely and held the antenna in his favored hand. Still, he'd made his plan, and was stuck with it.

But the pursuer wasn't cooperating. He just stood there, gun and disembodied arm. The temptation to switch hands and lash at the wrist was enormous, but Trotter resisted it. He didn't dare breathe, he didn't dare *move* until he made *the* move, the one that would decide whether he was going to live or merely go down fighting.

The waiting went on forever—about twenty seconds of objective time. Trotter couldn't take much more of it. Forget mental pressure. He was crouching on a painfully twisted ankle, and he was going to have to stand up soon or collapse altogether.

To hell with it, Trotter thought. He screamed, very loud.

The pursuer became a victim of his own professionalism. Since he knew Trotter had no gun, he wanted to make sure of a clear shot. He stepped around the front of the car, put both hands on the gun, bent his knees and fired. But by the time he pulled the trigger, Trotter had already Frisbeed the hubcap into his stomach, and the bullet plowed harmlessly into the gravel.

It probably caused more surprise than damage, but it would

do. Trotter whipped him across the neck with the aerial before he could recover enough to get off another shot, then dropped the antenna and launched himself on the man in a low, one-legged dive.

Trotter grabbed the wrist of the gun hand and began beating it against the gravel. Once the gun came free, it was all over. Trotter suspected it might. A lot of gunmen identified so thoroughly with a hunk of metal that depriving them of it was like shaving Samson's head.

A voice said, "Nice job."

Trotter looked behind him. Joe Albright. "Nice you could make it," he said.

"It's a goddam maze back here."

"You got a gun?"

"Get real, will you? Of course I've got a gun."

"Good. Keep this clown covered while I talk to him. He has a great respect for guns."

Albright nodded and pointed the weapon at the man's head.

Trotter said, "What's your name?" and got no answer. He tried Russian and got more silence, but there was a flicker of fear on the man's face.

"Was that Russian?" Albright said.

"Pig Latin. Shut up, okay?"

Trotter turned to the prisoner and spoke more Russian. "Who sent you?"

This time he got an answer. "I had orders to shoot you."

"Yes. I didn't think it was your own idea. Where did you get the orders?"

"They came. Over the telephone."

"The number?"

"I receive calls only."

In English, Trotter said, "The saddest thing about you is that you think I care whether you're telling the truth."

The man's eyes widened a little at that one. So he spoke English. Big deal. The Russians would hardly send in a man who didn't.

The big question was, what was he going to do with this guy? Chances were he *was* telling the truth, and didn't know much. It was damn certain this wasn't the man Bulanin had told him about, the one Borzov called Azrael. This was one minor wet-job specialist, willing to kill, but not especially able. He'd been sufficiently trained to take out an unsuspecting businessman, or untrained women and children, but sending him after a professional like Trotter was like chopping off his head.

Which meant whoever had sent him either didn't know Trotter

94

was an agent (which seemed unlikely, after that visit to the Soviet embassy in London), or they were ready to sacrifice this guy to some purpose. Something connected to Petra Hudson? Or something totally different?

"You," Trotter said in Russian, "are a complication." The guy probably knew nothing. Even if he did know something, it would take hours and expert persuasion to get it out of him. Trotter had the expertise but not the time. He also lacked a place to keep this guy until his father could send other experts. He sure as hell couldn't take him to the police.

"Joe," Trotter said, "go home."

"What are we going to do with this guy?"

"Just go home, I'll handle it."

"But—"

"Somebody may report these gunshots. You want to be home if the cops canvass the neighborhood."

"Trotter, I can't—"

Trotter turned to look at him. "All you have to do is go home. Go."

Albright stood there for a few seconds. Then he shrugged and left.

Trotter turned back to his prisoner to see the man scrabbling urgently in his pocket. Trotter grabbed the man by the wrist and squeezed until the fingers came open. Trotter turned the man around and slammed him against the car, then went through his pockets himself.

He found no weapon, just some loose change and something the size and shape of a vitamin capsule. It was made of glass and had a brownish fluid inside.

"Oh, for Christ's sake. I should have let you."

He turned the man back around. He forced himself to look into the gunman's eyes. He wouldn't let himself forget that this was a human being. Not much of one, maybe, but a human being all the same.

In an hour, he would be part of a landfill on the west side of town.

Trotter pulled back his arm, then struck once, knuckles on throat.

# CHAPTER EIGHT

Regina turned her face to Allan's chest and bit him. She'd never bitten a man before; she only did it now to avoid screaming, in pleasure or frustration, she couldn't tell which.

Trotter kissed her gently on the forehead, held her more tightly with the left arm that cradled her. His right hand played in the wetness of her, finger gliding without friction, teasing, teasing, bringing her closer and closer but not quite there. It had been going on for some time now. Regina was afraid she'd lose her mind if it didn't stop, but she didn't want it to end.

She didn't think he'd said a word to her yet. She'd heard the door bell ring in the code he'd arranged. She opened the door, he stepped inside.

There was something in his eyes she hadn't seen before, something sad and vulnerable. It unsettled her. He was the man with the quick answers, confidence itself, the source of any hope she had that whatever was stalking her mother and those close to her (including Regina herself) could be thwarted. Now he looked like a little boy.

"I—I tried to phone you," Regina had said. "I was worried about you."

Then he caught her in his arms and kissed her, hard. He took her to the bedroom and threw her on the bed and began making love to her.

They were naked now, but still on top of the bed, on the quilt she used for a bedspread.

Allan moved now, taking his hand away. Regina gasped, disappointment mingling with relief. Allan kissed her, mouth, throat, breasts. He stroked her and squeezed her, and soon she was gasping again.

She reached for him, feeling him warm and hard and ready. She said, "Now. Now, darling."

Now it was. He moved over her, and inside. He kissed her, and his tongue mimicked the thrusts of his hips. Regina exploded almost immediately, but it went on. Again and again she felt herself tighten around him, felt the shudders go through her, heard her helpless, animal moans. Then one last time, when he moaned, too, then kissed her fiercely, and rolled off.

She put her head on his chest. He stroked her hair. He murmured something; she heard it as a rumble in his chest.

"What did you say?" she asked.

"I said it's good to be alive."

•   •   •

They made love again in the morning. Regina's idea. I'm becoming positively wanton, she thought.

When it was done, she volunteered to fix breakfast.

"Okay," he said. He was smiling. Together, they'd exorcised whatever had been troubling him. "But let's be liberated about this. Next time, I'll get the breakfast."

Next time, she thought, and caught herself starting to hum. Like Scarlett O'Hara. No. That turned out badly, didn't it? Not that she kidded herself that the prospects here were any better. Today, she just didn't want to think of it.

Then Allan went off to the bathroom and started singing in the shower, and she had to fight down a whole new series of crazy hopes.

"French toast," he said as he sat down at the table. "I'm impressed."

"Frozen," she said. "From the toaster. I did the bacon myself."

"It's delicious," he told her. "A tribute both to you and to American technology."

"This is wonderful. I can be sexed-out and patriotic at the same time."

"You called me darling last night," he said.

For a split second, Regina paused with the fork halfway to her mouth. Then she finished the maneuver, chewed and swallowed before she said, "Did I?"

"You did. And I want you to know, I liked it."

"I thought you were going to tell me it was a mistake."

"It might have been. But I liked it. More, I needed it."

"You're welcome." She looked down at her plate. "I didn't expect any of this."

"I did. Your part of it, I mean. I can make women . . . care about me. It's part of the training."

Regina looked at him. She wanted to be dead. In a few seconds, the growing sense of humiliation she felt would kill her.

He was still talking. ". . . but this is new. In a way, I don't like it. It could be dangerous for me, and for you. And we don't have much of a future, because *I* don't have much of a future."

"What are you trying to say?"

"Look. I came here to do a job, and I'll do it, but you are no longer part of it. I'm trying to say last night was real. It's never been real for me before. I'm a different man from what I was when I got here last night."

"And this could all be part of the training, couldn't it?"

"Yes," he said. "It could."

Then why didn't he deny it? If he was stringing her along, he'd have to deny it. Unless he knew she'd think that. But why tell her in the first place?

"For God's sake, Allan, tell me the truth or lie to me, but stop *confusing* me."

"I don't want you confused. I want you suspicious."

"Suspicious? Of you?"

"Well, wary. Of me, of everybody. My attitude toward you isn't the only part of this mess that went into a new phase last night."

"What's that supposed to mean?"

"Never mind about that."

"*Damn* you, this is my mother we're talking about. It was my brother's fiancée who was killed."

"This," Allan corrected her, "is your *country* we're talking about. Your family is just the point of attack. All I can tell you is this: You made the right move when you went to Rines for help."

"I'm supposed to take your word for that."

"One of the things I like best about you is the way you bounce back from emotional upsets."

"You're wrong. You're no different than you've ever been. The ultimate wiseass."

"I won't argue with you. The thing is, the other side made a move last night and missed. And now I can begin to—"

The phone rang. Regina choked back some agitated words she had ready and went to answer it.

Allan followed her to the living room. "That could be for me," he said. "I told them I might be here."

Regina picked up the phone and said hello, then wordlessly extended the receiver toward Trotter.

He took the phone and said thanks. He didn't tell her to leave, so she stayed. And listened. It was *her* goddam apartment.

"Trotter," he said. "Secure from your end? Okay, check. All the way through, I'm on a regular phone."

He smiled at her while he waited.

"Okay. Good. What have you turned up? Well, then, who's your favorite possible?"

Regina looked at him. She could almost hear the sizzle of nerve ends firing in his brain. For the first time, she was seeing him completely in his element. She was impressed, and just a little afraid.

"Oh," Trotter told the phone. "Him. I thought he was a little too good to be true. What did he do, come on too strong to one of our friends on campus? One of our friends' friends?"

Trotter scratched his nose. "Sure, what the hell. If he bites, you'll know for sure. No, right away. No time like the present." He hung up the phone. "Did you understand that?" he asked her.

"Smarter for me to say no, isn't it?"

"Right. Although I don't think interrogation is what these people have in mind. They haven't so far."

No, Regina thought, just death.

Allan said, "I'm going to stick close beside you for the next few days."

"All—all right. Why now?"

"I started to tell you before. The situation now is such that I can begin to stir things up. It might start getting a little hairy."

"So you think I'm in danger."

He looked at her. "You've been in danger since the day you were born. It matters more than ever to me that I get you out of it. I hope you believe that."

Hope more than logic made Regina decide to believe it. And (she had to face it) she *wanted* him to care about her, as she had come to care about him, however little she understood him.

He asked her if he could make a phone call, and waited until she said of course before he started to dial. He pressed 1, then seven more digits, meaning he was dialing a number outside Kirkester, but within the 315 area code.

"You can learn the number on your next phone bill," he told her. "One way or another, this will be over by then."

*One way or another*, Regina thought.

Allan spoke to the phone. "Hello, this is Allan Trotter speaking. From the Kirkester *Chronicle*. I'd like to interview you for a possible feature article. We were thinking of calling it 'KGB—The Ultimate Terrorists,' and we thought your experiences as a victim of oppression would be a good concept to hang the article on."

Regina was impressed with how quickly he'd caught on to the jargon.

"No, sir. But I would be honored to meet you. I believe we have mutual acquaintances. When would be a convenient time for me to see you? . . . Not at all?"

Allan sighed a sigh that had so much *sincere* disappointment in it, Regina had to suppress a giggle.

"Well, sir," Trotter said sadly, "if you do change your mind, please call me at the newspaper. In case you do. Anytime, there's always someone there to take messages. It's not just a local paper, it's the Hudson Group. But I'm sure you know that. Thank you for your time." He hung up.

"Wouldn't talk to you?" Regina said. She assumed that it was part of this silly game they seemed to be playing for her to pretend she hadn't guessed it was Professor Smolinski at Sparta University he had been talking to.

"No, he wouldn't. Too afraid."

"Maybe he has relatives in the Old Country," Regina suggested.

"I'm sure he does, but that's not the reason he's afraid." He smiled slyly. Regina had never seen that expression before. "Still, that would make a good hook to hang an article on, wouldn't it?"

"What would?"

"Did you ever hear of anyone who was afraid to talk because he had relatives in America?"

"Now that you mention it, no."

"This concludes number seven hundred sixteen in a series of eight thousand installments of 'Why We Fight.' Tune in tomorrow for more."

Regina smiled. "I've never seen you like this. You seem more . . . real."

"The key word there is *seem*. Come on, boss, I've done my mischief for the morning. Let's go to work."

# PART FOUR

## CHAPTER ONE

General Borzov was in a bad mood. Something was wrong with the plumbing in this ancient building, and the hot water in his shower showed a disturbing tendency to disappear after three minutes, or just when he'd gotten his squat body thoroughly lathered up with the fragrant English soap Bulanin's successor in London got for him. There was no warning, either. One second, everything would be fine, the hot water stimulating the flow of blood to his brain, the scent of lavender pleasing his senses, and the next he was in Siberia, soaked and thrown into the cold. It was a technique still used as a punishment in many portions of the Gulag. It had the advantages of economy and of being able to be disguised as an accident. Borzov could swear to its effectiveness.

The shower didn't fail every time. If it did, he would simply give up the showers at the office until the plumbing was fixed, or take less time to wash. As it was, though, he had discovered a singular new form of Russian roulette. Sometimes, everything was perfect. This happened often enough to tempt him back under the water for the next possible freezing. When he did rush himself, and got out before the water turned cold, he always wondered if that time it had indeed been going to turn cold at all. The whole business was frustrating. Frustration was something Comrade Borzov did not react well to.

It was not wise, of course, to shoot or threaten a plumber whose worst crime was incompetence. Competence and sufficient loyalty and trustworthiness to allow him behind the walls of this building was perhaps too much to ask of one man.

Borzov never committed acts that could be foreseen to be unwise. That did not mean he was immune to error. As he looked over the latest reports from Smolinski, he realized just how little it meant he was immune to error.

His mistake was not in using Smolinski—that had been an experiment, a calculated risk. He was a Pole, and therefore under slightly less suspicion. He was a fanatical believer, and therefore safe to send into the West. The occasional agent came along who was vulnerable to temptation by the lushness of life in the West. Bulanin, for instance. Smolinski posed no such problem. Smolinski was intelligent, in his own way brilliant, and during his supposed time in prison he had been given intensive training, at which he had excelled.

Borzov, a student of the myths and legends of many societies, liked to think of the Pole as his Trojan Horse. The Americans would fawn over him; politicians and officials would climb over each other to be photographed with him. There would be some suspicion at first, but the Pole had been equipped with special bug-proof and interception-proof equipment, so that he should be safe. Borzov knew how they thought in the West. He did not understand it, any more than in his youth he understood what drew a fly to feces. But he learned that if the droppings were there, so would the flies be. In this case, no American agency would move against Smolinski without proof.

The proof was necessary because the Americans worked under a severe hardship—they could not count on anything remaining secret. Where Borzov might suspect a spy had been planted on him and order the man killed in the same week (sometimes the same hour), the Americans always worked with the specter of rampant journalism and political repercussions looming over them.

Borzov scratched his ear, though the itch he felt was inside his skull. *Almost* all the Americans acted that way. There were exceptions. The Congressman and those who worked for him. Borzov had resisted for a long time the idea that the Congressman was still active in the field. They had worked together against Hitler, and the General (as he was then) had been the most valuable of allies. After the war, he had been the most dangerous of enemies.

Borzov had rejoiced at the General's election to the Congress. But he came to realize that what he'd seen as the American's retirement had been simply a move to give himself more scope. Borzov told himself he should have been expecting it.

Then there was this "Trotter." Or "Bellman," or "Driscoll"—the names meant nothing. What mattered was that this young man had been trained by the Congressman, might be the old man made young again. His style was the same, the risks, the ruthlessness. And the *results* were the same. This young, real-nameless man had become a thorn deep in Borzov's insufficiently showered flesh.

And then he had turned up in Kirkester.

If there were two men in the world who could deduce what was going on in Kirkester, they were the Congressman and this "Trotter." If any agent could find and stop the man Borzov called Azrael, Trotter was the one.

The mistake had not been in wanting to kill Trotter. It was important to get him out of the way.

Borzov wanted control of the Hudson Group. He did not mean influence. Borzov and his colleagues had enough *influence* on the rest of the American press. When destiny was fulfilled, and the world was controlled by the Kremlin (whether or not the world became aware of it), thousands of American journalists would be unknowing Heroes of the Revolution. They were always ready to believe whatever Borzov instructed the handsome men the West was pleased to call "Soviet Journalists" to tell them. And anyone in opposition to the United States—*anyone*—from these Soviet Journalists, to that useful madman in Libya, to the anarchic terrorists who frightened even Borzov himself, to some worthless drug-addicted thief, would be given broadcast time and newspaper space to air their views, unchallenged, and usually uncommented upon.

Daily, the will of the people was sapped as men making millions of dollars sat in chairs and told their countrymen how corrupt they were, how weak, how foolish, how unjust. Some of these charges were justified. What did it matter if they *all* were justified? How did it serve the State to have them aired? It was amazing, impossible, that a government would allow it. That the Americans did was a gift Borzov was not about to let go by.

Because the prize, as always, was the collective mind of the American people. Their will to resist, their desire to strive actively for achievement. If the Soviet Union had been first to the moon, each day they would be reminded of the glory of it. If Chernobyl had been in America, five major corporations would have collapsed in an orgy of fault-finding and guilt.

But the conscious sympathizers and unwitting dupes in the American press were a constant, an advantage Borzov had come to take for granted. The Hudson Group, on the other hand, was necessary, or at least highly desirable, for the role it would play in one specific plan.

Important events were coming up. Decisions on arms control and grain sales and the proposed missile defense system that his (knowing and unknowing) friends in the American press had so successfully tagged "Star Wars," as they obscured its virtues and created doubt.

The woman known as Petra Hudson had kept the Hudson Group conspicuously apart from the sympathetic views of many of her most powerful colleagues. Borzov had not especially planned it this way, but he saw it was good. Because now, during this crucial time, Borzov would give the word, and the loud, influential voice of the Hudson Group would turn and shout down the men and policies it had cheered (most often alone) in the past. The rest of the American press would lose not a second announcing that a voice previously "ultraconservative" had "come to its senses." The people who had believed the old words would now either be persuaded or they would be confused and alienated, and they would cease to be factors. They'd join Borzov's most important army, those millions of Americans who had so lost faith in their country they no longer considered it worth the effort to vote.

Properly timed, the Hudson Group's turnaround could keep millions home during the next election. And Borzov had plans for the next election. Great plans. His masterpiece.

He slammed his hand on the desk. It all depended on this cursed woman. Borzov did not want to be forced to kill her children. That might drive her too far, lead her to kill herself. She was no good to him dead. Still, it might be that he had no choice.

He would try one more warning before he unleashed Azrael on the first child. If reports could be believed, Trotter would be a logical choice—he was supposed to be close to the daughter. Borzov assumed at least that the daughter thought so.

But Borzov would not risk Azrael against Trotter. Trotter was too good; Azrael was too valuable. Irreplaceable. It was a chance Borzov was unwilling to take.

Borzov wanted Trotter to die through ordinary channels. The thought amused him. Not so amusing was the realization that no one Smolinski might be able to muster would be able to succeed at the task. That was less important; at least Trotter would be kept busy.

But—and there was no way Borzov could have known this in advance—Smolinski was a coward and a fool. The first attempt fails, Trotter responds with a guess and bravado. Smolinski not only confirms the suspicions, he lets Trotter know *he* is frightened.

Smolinski had to be removed as soon as possible. That was in the cards all along, of course. The famous defector suddenly resurfaces in Moscow (in this case, Warsaw) and recants. The Western press always lapped it up the way a kitten lapped milk.

And *that* had been his mistake. He should have known better than to think a Smolinski would be a match for someone trained by the Congressman. Only Borzov was ever a match for the Congressman.

Borzov had trained himself to control his face, even in private, but he could feel his eyebrows climbing up his forehead. It *was* an interesting idea, to go to America in person and take charge of matters.

He sighed. It was also inadvisable and horrendously difficult, if not impossible. Besides, although he would kill to bring about the success of the mission he had entrusted to Azrael, he was not yet willing to risk dying or being imprisoned for it.

That degree of devotion would have to wait until the next American election.

# CHAPTER TWO

The Congressman put down the transcription of his son's latest report. He frowned, thought for a few seconds, then did something he almost never did—he called for the original tape and something to play it on.

The Congressman tried to remember how the Agency operated before automatic phone recorders. Mostly, it seemed, by-guess-and-by-God, with field agents dictating things to shorthand experts. Who could make mistakes. Who, even if they didn't make mistakes, wound up knowing altogether too much. The agents, of course, rarely had the leisure to write their own reports. It was frequently at the risk of their lives that they got to phones at all.

Now the calls were recorded by a machine at the Washington

end of an 800 number (which wouldn't turn up on anyone's phone bill). The machine could recognize enough English to obey priority code commands and channel the call to the Congressman no matter where he happened to be.

Then the tapes were brought to *one* government typist who had absolutely no interest in anything he typed, a strict eyeballs-to-fingers man who would have faithfully reproduced pig Latin from a tape, if the next higher civil service grade asked him to. He was no risk, especially since the Agency had a full-time man who did nothing but keep an eye on this typist. The reports and tapes were sealed by the typist in a steel box, handed to the Agency man, and delivered to the Congressman.

It was supposed to be a foolproof system, or as close to one as humans could get in a society that frowned on tongueless slaves. But now, the Congressman wanted to hear the tape. He wanted to know whether the typist had somehow been reached and was now feeding his unknown boss disinformation, or if his son had become suicidal.

From the sound of the tape, neither. Here the boy had deliberately blown his cover, or confirmed that it was blown, which was just as bad. He had let a suspected Russian agent know that they were on to him, which was worse. And he had fallen in love, which was ridiculous.

Love, or something like it, as the song said. Here it was, right at the end of the report, right after the part where he tells about that phone call to Smolinski.

"Operative VB subject sub prime one. No obstacle foreseen." Then, breaking code, Trotter's voice added, "Just thought you'd like to be the first to know."

VB. Abbreviation for the Italian phrase *volere bene*, meaning (literally) to want well, but idiomatically, to love. It might be important to an operation that somebody involved in it was in love with somebody. In love, as opposed to simply having it off (for which there was a totally different code word), meaning the person in question had a strength that proper action could bolster, if you needed him strong, or a weakness that could be exploited, if you needed to exploit him.

So there had to be a word for it, and the alphabet-soup boys in codes and ciphers had supplied one. The Congressman supposed it was a good one. It was impossible to forget, once you'd learned it. It was short and easy to hear over the phone.

But the Congressman had damn well never suspected an agent would use it in referring to himself.

Even when it *happened*, they never put it in a goddam field report. Even when it happened, once before, to his son.

The Congressman had sent his son into the field early. College campuses, radical groups. The boy had infiltrated one at a fancy Eastern university, and stumbled on a plan to plant a bomb under the steps of the administration building. Sort of a tribute to the plan some Columbia students years earlier had failed to carry out by virtue of blowing themselves up in constructing the bomb.

The Congressman's son's friends, though, had been more skillful, and the bombs had been planted. The boy was new with the group, so they hadn't told him in advance. But this girl he'd been sweet on, while not actually taking part in building the bomb, had been told where it was and when it was going to go off.

Well, there'd been no obstacle to the completion of that mission, either. The old man's son had to make the girl talk, and he had, and she had died. Turned out she had a bad reaction to the hypnotic drug the boy had used because he didn't have the heart to beat it out of her.

The Congressman blamed himself. It had never occurred to him that his son would be stupid enough to fall for a girl who was stupid enough to join a group of violent radicals.

What he'd forgotten was that while the boy had brains, and talent, and training, he also had a fully functioning set of emotions and hormones, and this had been his first chance to get any practice with them.

After that, his son had gone on the run, changing his name every few months. When the Congressman needed him, he had to go find him and force him to start the new mission. Only start it, mind you, because once his son got a taste of the action, there was no keeping him back. He was born to do this kind of work.

It was only the boy's damned pride and stubbornness (inherited, the Congressman knew, from the woman who bore him) that led him to keep up the pretense that he hated it all.

Until now. The Congressman was tired and light-headed, too tired to be doing this, really, but he rolled back the tape and played his son's report again. He didn't listen to the words—by now he practically knew them by heart. He was listening for tones of voice, for the attitude that shaped the words.

He was afraid to let himself believe what he was hearing. Or what he wasn't hearing.

There was no bitterness in his son's voice this time, no irony, or cynicism, or resignation, or any of the things the old man had gotten used to in these reports. There was not even the tone of hatred for him personally that the Congressman had become used to hearing, and it surprised him to realize how happy that made him. The Congressman had always told himself, and believed, that he had conceived and raised the boy as a weapon of war, unique in the world, as a gift to his country; that he did not need the boy's love or admiration so long as he had his respect and his fear.

And that, it seemed, had been fine, at least while there seemed to be no hope that the boy would ever feel anything for him *but* respect and fear.

But now. But now. It might be this Cronus business. The boy identified deeply with the children of Cronus, seemed to take a positive glee in fighting that particular operation and the bastards behind it. It might be because he'd fallen in love, and had some notion of slaying the Red Monster and saving the fair maiden and all she loved from its clutches.

Whatever the reason, there'd been a change in his son; from the Congressman's point of view, a change for the better.

"Just thought you'd like to be the first to know," the almost-happy voice on the tape said. The Congressman grunted, reached out and hit a button on the tape machine.

Had P— No, he never used the name the Congressman had given him. What was he calling himself now? The Congressman was upset with himself for forgetting. It was his pride that he never forgot anything.

Allan. That was it. Allan, um, Trotter. Lord, I must be getting old, the Congressman thought.

And that was the point, wasn't it? For security, the Congressman had handcrafted the Agency around himself. *His* Agency would be the one group defending the country that could *act* when action was necessary, without the long gavotte of procedures and clearances the other outfits had to dance. And, with one man making all the decisions, and everyone answerable only to him (who answered only to the President), there would be none of the faultfinding, ass-covering, or excuse-making that sapped an organization's efficiency and damaged morale.

Of course, that system had one inherent weakness. What happened when the man who was the foundation for this marvelous structure could no longer bear the weight? The day wasn't here yet, but it was coming. He was an old man, and he was starting to forget things. Like his son's current name.

His son. That was another reason his son had been born. The Congressman had seen this day coming years ago. Even during the late forties, when the Agency had been born, and McCarthy and his pals were getting wound up, and you couldn't spit in the District of Columbia without hitting a Russian spy—

God, that McCarthy was a bastard, the Congressman thought. Ruthless and stupid and, in the last analysis, the worst thing to happen to the United States since the Civil War because he had done something so crippling it endangered the very future of the world. *He had given anticommunism a bad name.* His own name, as it turned out. And the Congressman could think of no greater treachery to America than to make any attempt to expose its enemies suspect—

Where the hell was I? the Congressman demanded of himself.

Oh, right. Even in those days he had known there would be no dearth of dedicated, trustworthy, patriotic Americans who might, if anything happened to him, take over his Agency and run it to the best of their ability.

But who would have the ability? Who but someone with the capabilities *bred* into him? Who had been trained from birth in the ways nations maneuvered in the dark? Who but a child authored and raised by him personally?

The Congressman had never mentioned it to his son. The break between them had come too early for the subject to have been broached. And despite all the anger and accusations his son had flung at him, that was one thing he had never mentioned, either.

But it was there. That might have been what the boy was really running from all these years.

But now, there could be hope. He might be able to bring his son home. It would take thought and care. If this Regina Hudson was the reason, was it safe to leave her in the picture? A spy with a wife is a distracted man, and a vulnerable man. On the other hand, the Congressman's son, even distracted and vulnerable, would be worth the full-time dedication of anyone else the old man could think of. Even Rines, who was a distant second. Which reminded him. Rines should be here about now. They had a lot to talk about. Primarily, they would discuss whether they ought to do something about that weasel Smolinski before the Russians pulled him out and made a big propaganda thing out of him, or if they should just let him slide. The Congressman was inclined to the latter. As far as he could tell, the attitude of the American public seemed to be that if someone had a taste of American life and was still asshole enough to want to go back to Russia, he was too stupid to keep, anyway. It might be a little simplistic, but it was the kind of thing that helped the Congressman maintain faith in his countrymen. Still, he'd listen to anything Rines—

Music.

The Congressman could definitely hear music. Distant violins. He also detected a faint odor of melons.

Those two things went together somehow. Something he had read, something someone had told him. He was too angry to pin down the memory right now. What damn fool had put music on an official Agency report tape? He'd track them down, dammit—

The tape wasn't moving. He'd switched the machine off.

The music got louder and the smell of the fruit was sickening. What *did* those things mean?

And where was Rines?

And this damn new office was supposed to be soundproof. And clean. It was supposed to be clean. If he ever caught the person who left fruit here to rot, to stink up the place with a heavy, sickly sweetness that was beyond belief, he'd—he didn't know *what* he'd do, but it would be something drastic.

This might be secret, but it was a government installation. He was doing *important work here*, and nobody had the right to make it more difficult.

And then the lightning hit him, like Saul on the road to Damascus, and he was flung from his chair to the ground, and even before he hit, the voices started speaking, deep, resonant, demanding voices whose words were not understandable.

The Congressman wondered, almost abstractly, if this was the Voice of God, and if so, was he speaking Hebrew, or some unknown Heavenly language, or what. Then he remembered. Fruit and music. A stroke. A brain reacting to lack of blood, and he was having one, the lightning and the convulsion and the voices. Be funny if all Saul had was a stroke, wouldn't it? he thought.

Never mind, he told the voices. If you are God, let Rines get here before I die. Please.

# CHAPTER THREE

Tina called him up and asked him over for dinner. Joe said he'd be there. He was tempted to tease her about it, since he'd asked her out a couple of times already, only to be told it "isn't time yet," but something in her voice made him decide against it. If this was another step out of her depression over the baby's death, Joe Albright wasn't about to smartmouth her back into her shell.

He smiled at himself. Thinking like a social worker now. FBI— Friendly Busybodies Interfering.

He stopped smiling when he realized he should probably clear

**110**

this with Trotter. He did it because those were orders, and Joe had a healthy respect for orders. He wasn't sure how he felt about Trotter anymore.

Trotter had *murdered* that dude. He was very polite about it, sending Albright away so he could honestly say he hadn't seen anything nasty, but that was just a technicality. Wasn't fooling anybody. The guy might have been a Russian spy, and he might have been trying to kill Trotter, but Trotter had him down and helpless.

Sooner or later, Rines would have to know about this. If Rines told him to forget about it, Joe would have to see. He had no fondness for Russian spies, but these were not the rules they'd told him about when he'd joined the Bureau.

In the meantime, he'd do his job, watch his ass, and hope for the best.

Trotter wasn't home. Joe left a voice-code message on his machine. He wasn't at the office, either. Joe left a message there, too. Next he tried Washington, to let Rines know where he was going to be, and couldn't get him, either. It was beginning to be a drag.

Joe hooked up this electronic gizmo they'd given him and recorded a message on it. Trotter and Rines had little beeper things that would make it play back over the phone for them. They were supposed to be the only two people in the world who had devices that could make the right beeps, but Joe left the message in code just in case.

On the way to Tina's apartment, he passed a flower shop with a parking space in front. On impulse, he stopped, dashed in, and bought a mixed bouquet of daisies and something pink he didn't know the name of. "Here you go, Mr. Albright," the florist said.

Joe looked at him.

"Saw your picture in the paper. Welcome to Kirkester."

Joe thanked him and left. Tina let him in almost before he rang the door bell. When he handed her the flowers, she began to cry.

"These are tears of joy, right?" he said hopefully.

Tina nodded. She looked up at him, and he could see a smile behind the tears.

"Nobody ever gave you flowers before," Joe guessed.

"I used to think the only flowers I'd ever get'd be at my funeral," Tina said, and started to cry again. "Thank you, Joe. I—I—thank you."

"My pleasure."

"I'd better go put these in water," she said. She stood on tiptoe to kiss him on the cheek, then ran for the kitchen as if for her life.

Lord, Joe Albright thought, if I'd sent her a *bomb*, I wouldn't have caused so much commotion. Joe heard water running, more water than it took to fill up a vase. There was no noise for a while, then Tina came back looking as though nothing had happened.

"You like the flowers?" he asked.

She slapped at him playfully. "They're beautiful. But you made me do my makeup all over again."

"You're wearing makeup? You must be doing it right. I couldn't tell."

"You could tell if I didn't use it."

It occurred to Joe he'd like to find out for himself sometime. "Something smells good," he said.

"Fried chicken," Tina told him. "My granny's recipe. I hope you like fried chicken. I should have asked."

"Well," Joe said. "It's like this."

"Oh, my," Tina said.

"Are we alone?"

"Of course."

"No white folks around?"

"No, there's no white folks around, fool. What are you talking about?"

"If there's no white folks around, then I can tell you I *love* fried chicken."

Tina laughed, real and strong. It was the first time he'd ever heard her laughter, and it was a beautiful sound.

"You *are* crazy," she said.

"I like watermelon, too."

"So do I. I should have bought some."

"At this time of year it would cost a fortune."

"We'll get one in the summertime, then," Tina told him.

Joe said sure, but he knew he wouldn't be around Kirkester come summer.

"And," Tina went on, "we'll invite all the white folks we can think of. Come on, let's eat."

The chicken was delicious. So were the mashed potatoes and the gravy and the peas. He told her so.

"Apple pie for dessert. Cooking was the one thing I paid attention to when Granny tried to teach me."

The pie was the size of a Cadillac hubcap, but Joe, with minimal help from the woman who had baked it, put away two thirds of it before he got up from the table. Tina brought the pie and a big pot of coffee and said, "I'm glad you came over, Joe. You're easy to talk to." And she sat down and confessed to all her youthful indiscretions, and told him how it was all going to be different now, how Reverend Mr. Nelson had told her God had sent her baby as an angel to redeem her, and how she was going to live up to that.

Joe knew the details of Tina's pre-Kirkester life. That sort of thing was simple for the Bureau. This was the first he was hearing about Mr. Nelson's advice, though. Joe figured if that was what had been bringing Tina back to life over the last few days, then more power to the man.

"I realize there's only my word that I'm going to live up to it," she told him.

"Nothing wrong with your word."

"I mean, now that you know all about me . . ."

"Now who's crazy?" Joe demanded.

Tina went on as if she hadn't heard him. "Or maybe you want to make love with me or something."

"I'm in no hurry."

"Before, I would have made love with you five minutes after I met you. If I met someone like you, I probably wouldn't have made love with *half* the hoodlums I was with. Maybe none of them. But now . . ."

Joe put a finger to his lips to shush her. "Tina, don't worry, all right? If a man tried to make love on top of a dinner like that, the pleasure overload would kill him."

Tina tried to hold laughter in, but it leaked out in little hisses.

"You're a fine woman who *almost* messed herself up, but who got wised up. I like you. Besides, we've got to be friends. We're the only people in this town who can appreciate how weird it is to have all the white people be nice."

"We haven't met them all, yet," Tina pointed out. "But that reminds me of something I wanted to ask you about."

"Yes?"

"There's a girl at work. Sharon Piluski. She's not from the Program—her husband's in the Air Force, stationed near here— and she's going to have a baby."

"Good for her."

"Yeah. Well, we eat lunch together, and Sharon says she really doesn't know anybody around here, and she doesn't have any sisters or anything, and she doesn't know where her friends from high school are . . ."

"Yes?" Joe said again.

"She asked me to be godmother."

"That's great," Joe said.

Tina looked dubious. "Well," she said. "I *said* I'd do it. I couldn't really think of a way to say no."

"Don't you want to? It seems like an honor to me."

"I think she just asked me because—because my baby died."

"Even if that's true, she must also think you'd be good for her child. *I* wouldn't mess around picking a godparent for my kid."

"I think she's just trying to be nice."

"Nothing wrong with people trying to be nice. They keep trying, they might even succeed."

"That's not what I mean."

"What do you mean, then?"

"I don't know. I just—well, I can't back out, now, I guess." She sounded as though she hoped she might be wrong.

"Not unless you secretly hate this Sharon Piluski. Or is it you don't feel worthy to be godmother to a white baby?"

Tina was shocked. "That's a terrible thing to say!"

"Not a great thing to think, either."

"Well, it's not true. And I like Sharon."

"Then I don't see any way out of it."

"I'm jealous, Joe." Tina's eyes were wet. "I don't want a piece of somebody else's baby. I want my own baby back." She looked down at her hands, fascinated, apparently, by the way her fingers bent.

Joe knew that words wouldn't do it just now. He got up, walked around behind Tina, and gave her fatherly pats on the shoulder.

"Joe," she said at last, looking up at him. "The christening is next week. At the Northside Church."

"Mr. Nelson doing it?"

"Yes. Sharon's husband was raised Catholic, but he doesn't care. Sharon was Methodist, but she switched to the Northside when she moved here, I think maybe because of Mr. Nelson. Anyway, it's next week, I'll let you know just when—will you come with me?"

"Sure."

"It'll probably be business hours."

"That's okay, I'm self-employed."

Then the phone rang and made a liar out of him.

Tina said, "I wonder who that could be." She picked up the phone and listened for a second. "It's somebody named Rines," she told him with her hand over the mouthpiece. "Says it's important."

It damn well must be important, Joe thought as he took the phone, not only to call me here, but to use his right name.

"I take it you can't talk now," Rines said.

"That's right," Joe said.

"Okay, then, listen. Find Trotter. Tell him the clock has slowed down."

"The clock has slowed down."

"That's it. The sooner the better. He'll know what to do."

"He'd better, 'cause I sure don't." He said at least the last three words to a dead phone.

"What's wrong?" Tina said.

"The thing that's most wrong is I've got to go. A friend's in a jam, and I've got to go help him out."

"Anything I can do?"

Joe felt the sudden urge to kiss this woman, hard. He was able to whittle it down to a peck on the tip of the nose before he succumbed to it. "Feed me again tomorrow and don't worry. I'll tell you all about it later." *After I've had a chance to come up with a good lie*, he thought. The longer he stayed on this assignment, the less he liked it.

Tina said, "Be careful."

Oh, Joe thought, to hell with it. He kissed her again, a good one this time, apologized (though, to tell the truth, Tina did not seem offended), then went out into the night to look for the mysterious Mr. Trotter.

# CHAPTER FOUR

Wes Charles dropped Mrs. Hudson at the executives' entrance of the Hudson Group Headquarters and took off for the hills. Mrs. Hudson was doing it more and more lately, coming back to work after dinner and staying late. Okay—she'd always be there late Friday night, in case there were any late-breaking stories for *Worldwatch*, and she was needed to decide what was in or out of the magazine before it went downstairs to the printer. And she'd be around on Wednesday, before they locked up the soft-news stuff, fashion and movie reviews and stuff like that. But this was Monday, for God's sake, and as little as Charles knew about this business, he'd picked up enough to know that there wasn't a goddam thing that needed to be done on Monday night—this week's issue would be on the stands, and nobody would worry about next week's until tomorrow at the earliest.

But there she was, ringing for him twenty minutes after he'd taken her home that afternoon. Charles finished chewing his sandwich on the way up to see her. He knew she hadn't eaten anything.

It was as if she couldn't bear to be away from that place, like someone would blow it up on her if she didn't keep an eye on it.

Or, Charles admitted reluctantly, the fact that her son's fiancée had been spirited away from her as if by pixies made her nervous about staying home.

He supposed he couldn't really blame her. Charles had a long association with the outfit who'd installed the security system, and he had personally approved their plans. The problem was, he was too professional. Or at least he had approached that problem too professionally. After all that time protecting rich Americans overseas from Red Brigades and Baader-Meinhof types, and Mafiosi, he'd forgotten that someone could come at your defenses with something other than force. So all the sensors and alarms had been made irrelevant by sweet talk; by someone just *persuading* that girl to sneak out at night so she could be killed.

No wonder Mrs. Hudson didn't want to be there much anymore. The reminder of defeat, plus James Hudson, Jr.'s, floating around the place like a ghost, had killed any feeling of comfort Charles had ever felt there too.

He was supposed to drive back by the building at ten o'clock, although if previous nights were any guide, there was no guarantee she'd be ready to leave then.

Charles guessed he didn't really mind. Inside the building there were security guards carrying .357 Magnums. She'd be safe enough.

In the meantime, his time was his own. More and more he'd spent it driving up the country road to this spot, halfway up what in New York State passed for a mountain. It was nothing compared to the Alps, of course, but it gave a nice view. It was a good place to think.

One thing he thought about frequently was the fact that Hannah Stein hadn't been much older than Charles's own daughter, who was at a private school up in mountains of her own out in California. One of the reasons he'd taken the job in the States had been the idea that he could see Janie more often. It hadn't worked out that way. This was the worst of all possible jobs—boring, but still urgent—and he couldn't get away. And the one time he had, he and Janie had spent the time staring at each other, trying to think of something to say. It wasn't that she wasn't a good kid, or a friendly kid, it was just that she was now her stepfather's kid. Not his. All he had to talk about was the service, killers and kidnappers.

Looking back, he could see every link in the chain of decisions, all of them *his* decisions, that had made it happen this way. It was a shame you couldn't see it so well from the other end. He supposed some people did. Guys who hadn't made strangers of their daughters, for instance.

This was the time to take a deep last drag and crush the butt out brutally against the palm of his hand. It almost made him sorry he'd given up smoking.

He could feel the grin on his face, the one that grew there when he embarrassed himself with his maudlin stupidity. He took a look at it in the mirror. Aversion therapy. If he could see how big a fool he made of himself, he might stop doing it.

He saw something else in the mirror. Someone was coming down the road.

On foot. On this road, that was ridiculous. On a cold, humid, late October night, it was ominous. Still watching the mirror, Charles reached for his shoulder holster. He held the grip but did not draw the gun.

Whatever the walker was up to, it wasn't stealth. He crunched the gravel alongside the roadway so loudly, Charles could hear it through the rolled-up windows. As he got closer, Charles could even hear him whistling.

He could, of course, start the engine and pull out, but he was curious. Besides, everybody knew this was Mrs. Hudson's car, and if the walker was a motorist in trouble, he'd be making a PR problem for his employer.

The more he thought about it, the more he figured that it was more than likely a motorist in trouble. But long shots were what a security man was in business to protect against. He kept his hand on the gun.

The walker was closer now. Charles could hear him whistling. The walker stopped about ten feet from the car and stopped for a second, then moved toward the front window.

"Mr. Charles? Mr. Charles, is that you?" He walked up to the window.

Charles thought he'd recognized the voice; one look at the face told him he was right. He pushed the button and the glass rolled down. "I *thought* it was you. What are you doing here? Walking, no less?"

"I'm not sure. My engine stopped running. I wonder if I could trouble you for some help, or a lift back to town . . . ?"

Charles looked at his watch. More than an hour before he had to head back. He'd look at the car; it would make a change.

He hit another button. The electronic lock popped open; Charles unlatched the door and started to get out.

• • •

Roger pushed the hypodermic needle through the thick serge of Charles's uniform trousers into his meaty thigh. A look of surprise, then anger passed over the man's face before it lost all expression and the eyes drooped closed. Roger placed a hand on the driver's chest and guided him back into the seat.

Roger had thought long and hard about the assignment before deciding to use the hypodermic. The dossier on Charles showed that the man would *have* to be rendered unconscious before being killed. He was a trained professional. He'd put up a struggle. Roger had perfect confidence in his ability to handle Charles or anybody but—and this was the important part—not without leaving a trace.

And Roger would leave no traces. Not only did the nature of his current employment call for it, his own sense of the rightness of things wouldn't allow it. Azrael left no traces.

None that would be noticed, in any case. The Medical Examiner would find an extra puncture in the man's thigh, if he were conscientious enough to look for them in the very red face of the cause of death Roger would provide for him. It would be lost among the other punctures from the man's twice-daily vitamin shots. No one would look for a drug. The death would be a suicide.

Roger pushed a button with a gloved finger and unlocked the front door on the passenger side of the limousine. Then he took hold of the ignition key and twisted it, pressing Charles's foot on the accelerator as he did so. He left the foot where it was.

Next, he closed the door. He took a length of garden hose out from under his coat. He stuck one end in the tailpipe and the other in the window. He walked around the front of the car to the passenger side, opened it, and slipped in. He reached across the unconscious Charles to work the power-window button. He worked slowly, careful to close the window enough to hold the hose in place without pinching it closed and shutting off the fumes.

It was quite close inside the car by the time he was satisfied. He backed out hastily and took deep breaths of the cold air. But there was still one thing he had to do that would send him back inside the car, so the sooner he got to it, the safer it would be.

Stepping only on rocks or frozen patches of ground (Azrael left no traces) Roger climbed from the road up the slope to where a patch of week-old snow clung to the side of the hill. He took off his right glove, scooped up a cold, gritty handful and, moving just as carefully, returned to the car. He opened the passenger-side door, took a deep breath, and leaned in.

Roger thought he could see pinkness already in Charles's face, a pinkness that would ultimately deepen to the cherry-red of carbon monoxide poisoning. The man was asleep. He would simply stay asleep—forever.

Roger, however, had places to be. And God's clean air to breathe. He held his fistful of snow over Charles's thrown-back head and squeezed. Drops of water ran down the man's face and back through his hair. When the snow was gone, Roger gave a nod of accomplishment. He backed out the open door. He began breathing again and replaced his glove. Then he set the door to lock automatically and pushed it closed. He walked quickly back up the road, got in his car and drove home.

# CHAPTER FIVE

Smolinski returned to his cottage after his nightly four laps of the university pool. He saw that Mrs. Szczeczko had let herself in and out and done her usual marvelous job in between. She'd also left him fresh flowers, which she got from her son, who had a flower shop in downtown Sparta.

It occurred to Smolinski that he should arrange things so that he could spend more time talking to Mrs. Szczeczko. Not only did she openly worship him (coming out of retirement to clean for "such an educated man and a hero"), but she was garrulous about her brother's activities in what, after forty-five years away from it, she persisted in calling "back home." Since these activities consisted in large part of sedition, if not actual subversion, Smolinski owed it to himself to hear more about them. It would give the old woman a chance to speak fluent Polish, of which she was proud, instead of broken English, which embarrassed her, and it would give Smolinski the chance to find out just *how* her brother was getting this news to her in the face of postal censorship and radio jamming. At the very least, he wanted to find out if she was making it all up in an effort to impress him— then he could just ignore her.

Smolinski smiled half affectionately at her peasant loyalty and naïveté. He hung up his jacket, then returned to his desk, lifted the small vase, and smelled the flowers. They were yellow things, like daisies. Smolinski did not know much about flowers.

He checked the telephone machine for messages.

"Jersey," a taped voice said, and even if he hadn't recognized the voice itself, he would have known it was Mrs. Department

Chairman. The woman was a Doctor of Philosophy, yet was unable to grasp that the name should be pronounced "Yairtsy." No sounds alien to the American tongue. He wondered what Mrs. Szczeczko had suffered all these years.

He let Mrs. Department Chairman drone on. They were having a party. So soon? Smolinski thought. Oh. This time they would be getting drunk to benefit starving children in Ethiopia. It was amazing how Americans managed to feel guilty about that. The children in Ethiopia were starving because the revolutionary government wanted them dead—they would not fit ethnically in the Ethiopia the leaders envisioned. It was an effective and time-honored technique. Stalin used it in the Ukraine in the twenties. A man who must spend all day looking for a few grains of wheat for his family cannot spare the energy for insurrection.

He became tired of the woman's voice and punched a button. A student from his seminar, with a complicated reason her paper could not be in on time. This voice was much pleasanter. He had allowed her in the seminar solely because of her voice. He used it now for background music as he prepared a sandwich.

Smolinski was much happier with himself than he'd been after the phone call from Trotter. Then, he had been distraught. His first real test in the field, and he had met it with panic, running (figuratively) to Borzov over nothing.

For what could Trotter do to him? Who would believe him if he said Jerzy Smolinski had tried to have him killed? No one. And if there were danger of retaliation, Borzov would learn about it, and Borzov would protect him.

So. The thing to do now was to forget about it, put it behind him. He would redeem himself at the next opportunity. Borzov would be proud of him.

Smolinski returned to the phone machine in time to cut off the next message, a recorded message designed to sell him life insurance. That was as good an example as any of the American culture—one machine talking to another, trying to sell it something.

"This is the laundry," the next message said. "Your cleaning and pressing are done. They can be picked up immediately."

Smolinski dropped his sandwich on the floor. A slice of too firm tomato rolled under the chair. His mouth shaped *no* five times before he had enough breath to say it.

It wasn't fair. Not for one mistake. Or, he thought desperately, *perhaps* this *is the mistake. I must have heard it wrong.* Smolinski rolled back the tape and played it again.

". . . laundry. Your cleaning and pressing are done. They can be picked up immediately."

No mistake. He was being called back. They—Borzov—had given up on him as a field agent and were ordering him to return so that they could cash in his propaganda value at a press conference in Warsaw, announcing his disillusionment with the hypocrisy of Americ—

Even thinking about it made him sick. His new resolve would be all for nothing. He would have to leave now, make his way north, cross the border, and contact the cell in Montreal, who would take it from there.

If only he'd had more presence of mind when the damnable Trotter had called him. If only that fool had succeeded in *killing* him. Then he might never have gotten this message, the message that ended the dream and work of a lifetime.

Ten minutes ago, he was a man whose life was focused on a purpose—

Ten minutes ago he hadn't heard the message. He *hadn't been here*. What if he'd never come home tonight? More importantly, could he make it *seem* as if he'd never come home tonight?

He decided he could. Then he could carry his new plan forward, Trotter would be dead, and Borzov would see his worth. The plan was ready to go; his men were standing by. It would take one word in a telephone to set things in motion.

But not from this telephone. He hadn't been home.

Smolinski dropped to his hands and knees and found the fragments of his sandwich on the floor, each of which he ate. He would leave no food in the garbage that would show someone checking up on him by its state of freshness that someone had been here this evening. With his napkin, he wiped traces of mustard from the floor. He put the napkin in his pocket. He returned the answering machine to the record position. He got his coat from the closet and left through the back door. He climbed over a neighbor's fence and left on the other side of the block. He made his way to the nearest pay phone and put his plan in motion. Then he walked to a nearby shopping center where an automobile no one knew he had was parked, and drove toward Kirkester to see the plan unfold.

# CHAPTER SIX

"Thank you for this," Regina said.

Trotter laughed. "You're welcome. When I said I was going to stay close to you, that was all I meant. I had no intention of confining you to quarters."

He waited at the shopping center exit while cars went by. Allan had a new car now, a maroon Mercedes. He didn't tell her what had happened to the compact he'd been driving before. He was a very cautious driver. He let several openings go by that Regina would have scooted into. Heroically, she restrained herself from commenting about it. Instead, she said, "I really needed this."

"You have been a little tense," he said. He finally found enough space to suit him and pulled smoothly out into traffic.

"Of course I have. Nothing to compare with my mother, though."

"Maybe we should bring her to the movies."

"Not here," she said. "Here" was the Gastonville Plaza, a huge shopping mall forty-five miles, two creeks and a river away from Kirkester. "It would take too much time away from the paper. I'm beginning to think she cares more about the Hudson Group than she does about Jimmy and me."

Allan grunted noncommittally. "How did you like the movies?" They'd formed a resolution to take off and go to the pictures without deciding on a particular one. When they arrived, they learned that one of the mall's six theaters was showing a double feature of the original version of *The Thing* and *The Day the Earth Stood Still*.

"They were fun. How about you?"

"I loved *The Thing*."

"What about the other one?"

"Bullshit. Soviet propaganda."

"How do you figure that? Every time I think you're sane, deep down, you say something like this."

"Like what?"

"Like calling that lovely picture Soviet propaganda."

"Yeah, that lovely picture. Michael Rennie comes to Earth. We're supposed to admire him. We're supposed to admire him so much, they call him 'Carpenter' and have him die and rise again."

"I never noticed that."

"Ha. And then he brings this great message of peace. 'Surrender your sovereignty to a bunch of robots who know what's best for you, or die.' I believe the exact phrase was 'a burnt-out cinder.'"

"You realize you've ruined the movie for me."

"My heart bleeds."

She looked at him. "Not your heart."

"You'd be surprised."

"Anyway, the other movie was propaganda, too—'Don't trust them, they're monsters.'"

"Sure," Allan conceded. He grinned. "It's just propaganda I happen to agree with."

•   •   •

It never occurred to Smolinski to fear that his underlings would know he was disobeying orders until it was already too late to do anything about it if they had known. He was in a car equipped with special radio equipment with two men who seemed American enough to be fathers on television situation comedies. They had been in America for years, and had excellent records. One of them had as a cover an important job at *Worldwatch* magazine. They could have killed Smolinski in a second or subdued him and bundled him back to Borzov if they were so inclined. They were, however, perfectly content to take his orders. In the meantime they talked about college basketball. One of them, he was a Hudson Group employee, whose name was Mel Famey, a balding blond with a V-neck sweater vest and a bow tie, went so far as to ask Smolinski what he thought of the Sparta University team's chances for the coming season. Smolinski had favored him with a cold stare, and the man had subsided.

In between talks of "rejection" and "dribbling" and "steals" and "burns" and other unappealing topics, they managed to make their report.

Trotter and the girl had been followed to a mall some miles away. They had attended the cinema (Smolinski's companions said "movies") and were now heading back toward Kirkester. To reach home, they would have to pass the checkpoint where Smolinski waited—the Kirk River Bridge, a work of the early 1950s, a cantilevered construction in steel girders. Kirkester clung to the west bank of the Kirk River like a baby to its mother's breast. There was no way to travel east of town *without* going over that bridge. Smolinski's predecessor in this part of New York had known that and realized that the bridge could make a handy trap.

The trap had never been needed before now. Smolinski had found it ready-made and was delighted to use it to extend his usefulness to Borzov.

"How soon before they get here?" Smolinski asked.

The men had been talking about something called "reebs" and had to adjust their train of thought. The one with the mustache and the pipe, who was an English teacher at a regional secondary school, looked at his watch. "B unit just reported they'd crossed Hampton's creek. Make it about eight or ten minutes."

Smolinski tried to deny the excitement he felt as unprofessional but couldn't. He decided at least not to show it. He looked at the bridge, dark gray where the road lights hit the girders, of a darker blackness than the sky where it didn't. And if he put his forehead against the cold glass of the backseat window, below he could see the rippled surface of the Kirk River, like a shattered mirror, waiting to reflect a million images of the expression on Trotter's face when he realized he was plunging to his death.

· · ·

Trotter looked in the rearview mirror and said, "Uh-oh."

"What's the matter?"

"A car is following us. Has been for the last couple of miles."

"So," Regina said. "What does that mean?"

"It means I screwed up."

"Oh, God. No. No. I'm going to be calm. How did you screw up?"

"I had a little trouble with a guy. I told his boss I was on to him. That usually causes them to lay off for a while. They know that you know, and they have to figure you've passed it on. You become too hot to mess with, until they can think of something new."

"But this time it didn't work."

"No, dammit. It didn't. I wish I could figure out why. They must be nuts. Son of a *bitch*!"

"Allan," Regina said. "I'm being calm. I'm confused and afraid and I want very badly to scream. The *least* you could do is stay calm as well."

"You're right. I will."

"What are you going to do?"

"Keep driving. Hope they're just following us."

"*Just* following us! What if they jump us when we stop?"

"We drive onto your mother's estate. The security people will keep them from following. We can have armed men guarding us when we get out of the car."

124

Trotter had his eyes on the road, but he could feel tension coming off the young woman in drops, like rain.

"This really is what you do all the time," she said.

"Not all the time. Every time you say that you sound surprised."

"You act like it's routine."

"Keeping calm is important. You're doing very well."

"It isn't easy."

Trotter took a look at her. In a few seconds, he was going to have to tell her it didn't look as if it would be getting any easier.

•   •   •

Professional or not, Smolinski was gloating. They had passed the last turnoff, his man was behind them blocking off retreat, and the rest was ready. They—especially Trotter—were as good as dead.

•   •   •

"There are no more turnoffs before the bridge, are there?"

"No, we'll be able to see it—there it is now. Why?"

"Because I think they're probably going to try to force us off the bridge. Stay calm."

"*Stay calm? Allan, what are you going to do?*"

"I haven't decided yet."

"Haven't *decided*?" She grabbed his arm, ignoring him when he said, "Don't do that."

"Haven't *decided*?" she said again. "Allan, are you fucking *crazy*? You have to pull over! You have to fight them!"

"I thought you were going to stay calm."

"Not when you're going to let me *drown!*"

"I'm not going to let you drown. Anyway, I can't fight them."

"Why not? It looks like there's only one or two people in that car." She twisted around under her seat belt to look directly at it. He didn't bother to tell her to stop. Not only did he doubt she'd listen, but he realized there was nothing to be gained by trying to make the men in the car believe they hadn't been noticed.

"Yes," Regina said. "There are only two of them."

"They have guns."

It took her a few seconds to find her tongue. "You don't have a *gun*? What kind of spy are you? I'm going to die because—"

"You are not going to die for any reason. Now shut up and listen."

She shut up. He wasn't sure how much listening she was doing. She looked catatonic.

"You have to stay calm. No matter what they do, and especially no matter what *I* do, you have to *stay calm* or you'll kill us both. If you stay calm, I promise, I'll get you out of this."

She looked at him. She wasn't exactly calm, but at least she was quiet.

"Did you get that?"

"Stay calm," she said numbly.

"No matter what. Besides, it might be nothing. Then we can all go home and laugh about this."

"Laugh," Regina said.

Then he had no more time to spare for her. They were at the Kirk River Bridge.

•   •   •

Smolinski pushed the talk button on the microphone. Thrill-sweat had made his hand slick, but he held on long enough to say *now*. In minutes, he would be rehabilitated, and Trotter would pay for mocking him.

•   •   •

It shaped up the way Trotter had figured it would. The car behind him bottling him up, the car from the shoulder forcing him toward the rails, and—yes, here it was now—a truck pulled across the road at the other end to keep him from outrunning them. Not that that was much of a possibility. They were in gas-eating monsters with whole herds of horsepower under the hoods. His brain, as it often did in times of emergency, found something utterly trivial to worry about. Why did such a sturdily built bridge have such feeble guardrails? If they'd made the railings out of the same girders they used for the bridge itself, none of this would have been possible. Of course, if the bridge had been built that way, he would have been facing a different trap, in a different place.

Trotter forced his attention back to the current problem. He did a little side bumping with the car that was trying to force him off the bridge. Just a little. The idea was to make it look good without letting them do too much damage to the Mercedes.

He jerked them along for a while, but the time came when he'd have to get on with it. It made no sense to make a plan you were afraid to carry out. It was easier, of course, when you had no choice.

The time came sooner than he hoped (i.e., never). He was still pretty far from the opposite shore, and the water was deeper than he wanted to deal with.

But the time had come. He'd have to live with it. Or die with it.

**126**

"You're a brave girl, Bash. Remember what I said about staying calm?"

She nodded from behind her hands and drawn-up knees.

"Okay, then, hold on tight." With that, he cut the wheel sharply to the right. The car smashed the barrier, scraped bottom on an overhanging girder and pancaked down into the river.

• • •

"Watch them!" Smolinski said. Instantly, the other cars stopped. The basketball fans drove Smolinski to the scene as four men with guns went to the railing and watched the car.

"Anything?" Smolinski said when he arrived.

"Nothing," one of the men said. "Probably knocked out when they hit the water."

"Keep watching."

"Of course."

They watched until the car sank, which was a much longer time than Smolinski had anticipated. The motor had stopped, but the headlights remained on, making a swooping ramp of light for Trotter and the young lady to follow to the bottom.

"We'd better go," one of the men said. "It's late, but somebody's going to come by."

"Put your guns away. Then we are simply motorists who stopped to see if we could help."

Smolinski watched the lights below the water with a thin smile on his face. Then the lights went out. Very good, he thought. Bravo. Show's over.

"All right," he said. "Well done, men. *Now* we can go home."

# CHAPTER SEVEN

Trotter was not at his apartment, and he was not at the Hudson girl's apartment. Joe Albright had not been content with phone checks to those two places—he took his behind out into the night and checked in person, just in case something had happened. There was a certain amount of risk in that, of course. He wasn't supposed to know Trotter or Regina Hudson—hell, he *didn't* know Regina Hudson—and sneaking around prominent citizens' houses after dark was a good way to change the minds of a lot of townspeople about the wonderfulness of having a black businessman among them. And a pickup truck with your name and address printed on the side is not the perfect infiltration vehicle.

He wished he knew what the hell was going *on*, the particular color and consistency of the shit that had hit the fan back in Washington. Rines had told Joe (before he had so graciously hung up on him, cutting off questions) to *"Find Trotter!* No matter what."

But did "no matter what" include blowing cover? If Trotter was somewhere that took real looking to find, the best thing to do would be to visit the local cops, show them his FBI decoder ring, and ask for some cooperation. On the other hand, for all he knew, that would ruin everything. So he'd better stay in the Salvage/ Reclamation game for the time being.

Besides which, he didn't *want* to blow his cover. Tina would take it wrong. She'd be hurt; she'd think his relationship with her was just a ploy. It wasn't. It hadn't been even at the start. Keeping Tina from further hurt now came right after Duty, Honor, and Country on his list of priorities.

So. Where was Trotter, and how was a humble Salvage/Reclamation man to find him? The thing to do was to get back home and hit the telephone, because they sure weren't going to let him into the places he had to go now.

He had his list of calls to make, and he had his cover story—a weak one, maybe, but it might get by. It was all he had.

Any more thinking on the topic, he decided, would only make him nervous. He turned on the radio in the truck just in time to catch the beginning of the ten o'clock newscast.

"Shit," he said. He didn't turn it off—a man in the field can't afford to scorn *any* information—but he wouldn't have minded a song or two before the news came on.

"Tragedy continues to stalk the Hudson Group," the announcer said.

"Now what the hell?" Joe asked irritably.

The radio answered him. "Weston Charles, driver and bodyguard to Petra Hudson, chairman of the communications conglomerate, was found by State Police . . ."

Joe heard the rest of it and shook his head. Now they'd killed the bodyguard. That ought to do it. The radio said suicide, but then they'd said the other ones had been accidents or natural causes, so what the hell. And there was a kicker.

". . . and Captain Petersen, while confirming that Charles's head appeared to be wet, would offer no theory as to why. Mr. Charles served in the United States Army—"

Who pours water on his head before he eats a gas hose? It didn't make sense.

Joe smiled in spite of himself. He was starting to remind himself of Trotter.

The smile went away. Trotter was this way after the Stein girl turned up dead on his hall steps. Her hair was wet too.

This was something he would be very interested in. Joe would tell him about it, right after he told him about Rines. If, of course, he found him at all.

There was a travel advisory on the radio as Joe pulled into his yard—railing out on the westbound side of the Kirk River Bridge, drive carefully. Joe promised the announcer he would, then snapped off the ignition. He took the stairs two at a time and got on the phone.

Trotter wasn't at the *Chronicle*. According to the guard at the front gate, he hadn't entered the grounds of Hudson Group Headquarters at all. The guard had trouble understanding why anybody would be checking with *him* because one of the reporters had a chance to buy an antique clock cheap, even if it did have to be first thing in the morning. Joe didn't try to explain it to him because it seemed pretty lame to him, too.

Joe pressed on. It was a bad time to call the Hudson residence, perhaps, but what the hell. Reporters did it all the time, as did cops, of which he was one. His trouble, he decided as he dialed, was that he was too much a method actor. He was supposed to be a Salvage/Reclamation man, so he automically *thought* like a Salvage/Reclamation man.

He asked whoever answered the phone (light Spanish accent, probably a maid) if by any chance Mr. Trotter was there.

"Mr. Trotter? No, he's not here. Sorry. They tell me to keep the line open for the police. I hang up now—"

Joe was already shrugging and trying to think of someone else to call when he heard a different voice, a man's voice, some distance from the phone, say, "Wait!" He heard the girl grunt, as if she'd been pushed away from the phone.

"Trotter?" the man said. "Is this Trotter?" If he were any angrier, he would choke.

Joe made his voice calm. "No, it isn't. I'm just looking for him. My name is Joseph Albright. Who is this?"

"Looking for him, eh? So am I. You tell him I said—"

"If I tell him what you say, I might as well tell him who you are."

"What? Oh. Jimmy Hudson. *James Hudson, Junior*! Tell Trotter I know him for what he is! I know he killed my Hannah, and now he's killed Mr. Charles, and he'd better kill me next, because I'm going to make him *pay* for it! I don't believe in violence, but I'll find proof, and when I do, God help him!"

Joe replaced the phone gently. Things were getting very weird, and it all had to do with Trotter. And the earth, it seemed, had swallowed up Trotter and the girl.

There was only one phone call left to make. He'd have to call Rines and tell him he'd failed. Maybe he'd get lucky. Maybe, after he'd made his report and let wiser brains go to work on this mess, maybe the earth could be persuaded to swallow *him* up.

# CHAPTER EIGHT

Trotter didn't know if it was control or shock that kept Regina from screaming when the car hit the water. He found out as soon as the river lapped over the top of the roof.

"Oh, my God," she screamed. She started scrabbling for the door handle. "We've got to get out of here!"

"We will." He made sure the electric locks were closed. Thank God for luxury cars. "Now shut up and save air."

It worked for about a quarter of a second. Then a stream of bubbles erupted from the trunk, and the weight of the engine pulled the nose of the car the twenty feet or so to the bottom. The buoyancy of the air in the passenger compartment left them facing down at a forty-five-degree angle. The thump brought new screams out of her, without words this time.

The worst thing about being in a situation where someone panics (however justified the panic may be) is that it forces you to keep your own fear hidden. Trotter hadn't done this because he was looking forward to it. It was just that the alternative was worse.

Right now, he was afraid Regina was going to use up all the oxygen, and they'd either suffocate or have to leave the car too soon and be shot.

"Shut *up*," he commanded. "Dammit, Regina, I know what I'm doing!" *Would I lie to you?* he thought.

It had no effect at all. He hit her. Punched her hard on the left shoulder, twice.

She shut up. She sat rubbing her shoulder and looking at him in the bottom-reflected glow of the headlights.

"You done?" he asked quietly. She looked at him. "Because I'll knock you out if I have to."

"Kill me," she whispered. "Please. I have nightmares about dying like this."

"You won't anymore."

"Of course not, I'll be dead."

Trotter started to take a deep breath and stopped himself. Shallow breaths would do. He looked at the seals around the edges of the windows. There was a slow, tiny leak. This was a well-made car.

Regina was starting to whimper. He almost wished she'd start screaming again. He could hold it against her when she screamed.

It was inevitable. Talking wasted air, but he was going to have to talk to her.

"I'm going to unlock the door now," he said. Regina's head came up; she had a kind of wild hope in her eyes that died when Trotter went on to say, "But the doors won't open. Water pressure."

"And we'll die."

"We will not die." It was ridiculous. She was starting to sap *his* confidence. It occurred to him he would feel better punching her again, or punching something, but he decided it would be counterproductive.

He hit the switch in the console to his left and unlocked the doors. It wasn't until he'd done that he remembered the water might have shorted out some of the circuits.

Which reminded him of something else. "I'm going to turn off the headlights now." He could feel water coming through the window, coating the inside of the door like a coat of paint and soaking his sleeve.

"What difference will that make?" Regina said.

"It will leave us in pitch blackness. Don't scream, just keep listening." He turned out the lights and surprised himself with how right he was. It was darker than the inside of a black velvet bag, and it suddenly seemed colder. Trotter suppressed a shiver. Keep talking. Had to keep talking.

"Water coming in on your side?" he asked brightly.

"Y-yes."

"You won't believe it, but that's good. Now, Bash, the reason we're down here is that this is the one place they can't follow us. They think we're dead now, probably thought so the second the lights went out."

"That's why you—"

"That's why I turned the lights off. Now, I figure we had about fifteen minutes of air when we came down here—"

"How long ago was that?" The voice quavered, but the question was relevant, and it showed maybe a little trace of hope.

The radium slashes on Trotter's watch were the only light in the world. "Not quite five minutes."

"Don't lie to me."

"I'm not. Honest. Now. I'm figuring they've gone away by now up there, and talking cuts our time down a little, so we'll start getting out of here right away."

"You know how?"

"I know how. If Mary Jo Kopechne knew what I know, Ted Kennedy would be President by now."

"That's sick. You're sick."

"But accurate. Now do what I tell you. Unbuckle your seat belt and climb over into the back seat." He heard the click and the rustling. She kicked him in the head going over in the pitch blackness.

"Excuse me."

"It's all right. Now I have to let water into the car. Can you swim?"

"Hell of a time to ask. Yes, I can swim."

"That's good, but we could have done this even if you couldn't. Now, as soon as enough water is in the car, the pressure will equalize and we can get the doors open. The air will be trapped up where you are, so you can keep breathing until the last second. Okay?"

"Okay," she said, as if she had a choice.

"I'm going to open the front windows, now," he said.

Five seconds later, Regina said, "Go ahead."

"I changed my mind," he told her. Which was true. He changed his mind because the circuit that operated the power windows *had* shorted out.

Regina said, "Oh, God."

"Regina, please." Trotter started thinking rapidly. The first decision he came to was that he was going to have to try to break one of the windows. Which would be, of course, specially hardened safety glass. The second decision was that if he couldn't do it, he would put Regina out of her misery so that her last minutes wouldn't be filled with gasping and terror.

Breaking a window. Leverage, and something to hit with. He could hear a perceptible trickle now. Water was coming in, but not fast enough to save them.

What could he use? The seat-belt buckles were hard enough,

but didn't pack weight enough to do the job. He'd powder his hand before he could punch through, especially with the pressure reinforcing the glass.

Regina was being incredibly brave back there. Either that, or she had fainted.

"Bash?"

"I'm okay," she said in a small voice.

"Everything's under control," Trotter lied. Well, thinking was getting him nowhere. The effort of brute force would use up the air and kill them faster, but you had to go out doing *something*. It would have to be the seat-belt buckle. Trotter felt for the button, pressed it, and the seat belt rolled away. As it did, the forward tilt of the car brought him sliding forward. He put a hand forward to stop himself. He bent a finger painfully against the steering wheel, then finally braced himself against the windshield.

He felt the cold glass against his fingers and called himself an idiot.

He slid across the center hump into the other bucket seat. There was more water on Regina's side than there had been on his—maybe her window hadn't been quite as tightly closed. Because Regina was smaller, his legs were cramped. That was good, too.

Trotter worked his legs up over the dashboard, sank down low in the passenger seat, braced himself, and began smashing the heel of his shoe into the windshield.

Again and again he pistoned his right leg forward, trying in the dark to hit the same spot each time. He was starting to feel short of breath, but he decided it was from effort.

On the twentieth blow he heard a sort of creaking. On the twenty-fifth he heard a crack, and two strokes later his foot broke through to the cold of the Kirk River.

The water poured in. Trotter kicked a few more times, making the hole bigger, but soon he had to stop. He scrambled back to join Regina. He had to yell over the rush of the water. "Breathe deep!"

"What?"

"*Breathe deep*! No sense leaving any oxygen behind."

Now she was yelling something. She had to say it twice before Trotter could make it out—"Shoes off!" An excellent idea.

By now, the water was lapping the top of the front seat. Trotter reached down and found the front door handle, pulled it toward him, then leaned his shoulder against the door. It budged one grudging inch, but that was enough. More water began to pour through, and the door swung open.

He and Regina yelled at each other to take one last deep breath. Then he said, "Hold my hand." It took some groping, but the hands found each other. Trotter felt his way through the doorway, then guided Regina out. Hand in hand, they kicked to the surface.

# PART FIVE

## CHAPTER ONE

"I'm surprised you didn't freeze to death," Fenton Rines said. He pointed at a pile of brown and green and white that sat on a plate near the television set. "Mind if I have some more of this? I've been too worked up to eat."

"Eat it all," Trotter told him. "Room service runs till midnight, and it's government money, anyway." He'd raised his head to look; now he eased it back to the pillow.

Rines was somewhat at a loss. With the Congressman down, the only reasonable move to make was to find Trotter. He'd thought of going to the President, but—and this was a ridiculous situation—he didn't know how much the President knew. The Agency (meaning the Congressman) reported directly to the President, but Rines had gathered he didn't report much besides results. *If* the President knew that FBI Special Agent Fenton Rines had been moonlighting for the Agency, it would have been no trouble to get in to see him. If he *didn't* know, though, that would mean going through channels, four layers or more of functionaries, most of whom owed favors to some newsman or other, or would like a newsman to owe a favor to them. This was not the time for the existence of the Agency to be revealed to the

# WILLIAM L. DEANDREA

press. And it really wasn't the time for the word to get out that it had, through Rines, been using the FBI as a sort of farm team.

Which left Trotter. Who couldn't be found, or at least hadn't been the last time Rines had spoken to Joe Albright. And there was the operation in progress. Trotter might be missing because he was out chasing something, or he might be missing because something had caught him. Which would leave the operation exactly nowhere. Albright didn't know enough about it. Rines made his excuses in Washington and caught a plane north.

He was in-flight when Trotter turned up at Albright's place soaking wet and shaking like a paint mixer from the cold. Rines had suspected that might happen and had left an underling at the phone with orders to arrange a meet. Rines had phoned back to Washington when he arrived, and was glad to know Trotter was still around. He was even more gratified to learn that he'd holed up under another name at a businessman's motel near the airport. A place with room service open until midnight, which delivered really excellent nachos.

He munched away at corn chips and cheese and mashed avocado and sour cream and looked at the Congressman's son. Rines had always known the young man was strange. From what he knew of his background and his relationship with his old man, it was hard to see how Trotter could have turned out any way *but* strange.

But Rines hadn't been prepared for the reaction his news brought. Trotter reacted, at first, like a son. Like anybody's son, like Rines himself, when he'd heard of his father's condition.

"A stroke?" Trotter said. His face showed nothing but concern. "My God, I'd better get down there."

He was actually reaching for a jacket when Rines said, "And do what?"

Trotter stood there, holding the jacket.

"Besides," Rines went on, "he's in intensive care. And—"

"And intensive care visits are restricted to immediate family," Trotter completed for him. "And it's a well-known fact that the Distinguished Gentleman has no family." He walked calmly to the closet and replaced the jacket. Then he slipped out of his shoes and lay down on the bed. "I've got nachos over there by the TV," he told Rines. "Help yourself."

And he hadn't shown a trace of emotion since, expect perhaps a vague amusement. He asked how bad the stroke was (pretty bad) and asked what the chances were the Congressman could come back (unknown).

"Is he going to babble?" Trotter had asked.

"Babble?"

**136**

"You know, talk without realizing what he's saying."

Rines was quiet for a second. He'd seen and done a lot, but the realization that he had just heard a son ask if his father should be killed before he inadvertently spilled something embarrassing, in exactly the same tone of voice he'd ask a pharmacist for a bottle of aspirin, took a little digesting.

"I doubt it," Rines said. "It happened in his office. I found him. He was a mess. He couldn't keep drool back, let alone talk intelligibly."

"All right, then."

"Who's in charge now?" Rines wanted to know.

"Huh? You are."

"Oh, come on, Trotter—"

Trotter was amused. "I'm serious. The only operation I know about is this one. I don't know anything about the rest of the Agency's personnel, what they've done, or what they're good for."

"You could learn."

"From whom?"

"*I* could teach you that much."

"Which means you already know. I've got a job to do. Not my father's. You hold it together until the old man gets well."

"Assuming he does," Rines said. "What happens if he doesn't?"

"Then Knox County is going to have to hold a special election, and you're going to have to have a chat with the President."

"Look,.I'm serious about this." Rines didn't like that little note of panic he heard in his voice. He decided to try again. "I don't like the implications for the Bureau. If a reporter gets hold of this, it could be Watergate all over again."

"You're the one who spent three years finding out what makes the Congressman tick."

"You're a big help, Trotter."

"Just think of me as Fred Dean, all right?"

"Who?"

"Fred Dean, of the San Francisco '49ers. He'd come into the lineup only to rush the passer in long-yardage situations. *I* come into the lineup to bust up the Russians when they're trying to work a Cronus operation."

"And to hell with your country."

Trotter smiled. Rines was a trained and experienced man. He had a gun on his hip. He was standing, and Trotter was lying on a bed. It all meant nothing. He saw the smile and remembered that this young man was dangerous.

Trotter spoke, very matter-of-fact. "That kind of shit didn't work when my father pulled it on me. It won't work for you, either."

Rines decided to forget it for now. "Made any progress?"

"My usual kind."

Now Rines smiled. Trotter might not be exactly sane, but he could be charming. "In other words, chaos."

"I think we've gone beyond chaos this time. We're dealing with pure pandemonium. We've got two sets of Russian agents, working, as far as I can tell, at cross-purposes. We've got the subject's daughter stashed away under an assumed name at a hospital, and according to Albright, the son would shoot me on sight, except he's too civilized. And we've also got a couple of corpses with inexplicably wet hair."

"Apparently yours got pretty wet, too. I'm surprised you didn't freeze to death." Rines got another helping of nachos.

"It's all government money, anyway," Trotter said, lowering his head again to the pillow. "Actually," he went on, "the water itself wasn't bad. Or, it wasn't as bad as the air on the wet body was. It took me half an hour to get a car to stop. Thought we were going to lose Little Bash to hypothermia."

"Little Bash?"

Trotter's smile was as warm as his last one had been chilling. "Never mind. In-joke."

"So you're going to let everybody think you're dead?"

"Missing, anyway. Just for today. Rest up. I'll try to keep Regina out of the way a day or so longer."

Rines nodded approval. The ability to bring back a daughter who had been feared dead would be powerful leverage to use on Petra Hudson. "I don't think you can keep it going longer than a day or two," Rines said.

"Neither do I. The hospital's seventy-five miles away from here, but the farther you get from the big cities, the less distance means. The Hudsons are too well known for real safety. I should have punched her in the face instead of the arm."

"Why?" Rines did not like the idea of women being hit. Not for any reason.

"So there'd be a bandage on her face and no one would recognize her."

"Why did you hit her at all?"

"She panicked and wouldn't listen. Relax, Galahad. It was to save her life." Rines made a noise. "Besides," Trotter went on, "I paid for it. She came out in a bruise, and the cold air made it seize up when we hit the surface. I had to haul her in by the chin like a lifeguard half the width of that goddam river."

"Think it's time to brace the mother?"

Trotter sighed. "I guess so. I hoped to put Azrael out of business first, but he—or they—have been too much for me so far."

"The sooner the better, if you ask me."

"Tomorrow afternoon," Trotter said. "Promise."

"What about tomorrow morning?"

"I've got a plan for tomorrow morning. Something unprecedented for me."

"What's that?"

"I'm going to simplify things a little."

# CHAPTER TWO

Trotter walked around Smolinski's neighborhood a few times. There was a newspaper on clips under the mailbox, and white showed through the window in the box itself.

Good, Trotter thought. Everybody who was likely to be coming to Smolinski's had already been there. Unless UPS showed up with a delivery or something, Trotter could feel reasonably confident he'd be able to do what he wanted to do without interruption.

Not that it was going to take all that long. Screw the silencer on the end of the .38 he'd borrowed from Albright before driving to Sparta this morning, through the yard of the vacant house-for-sale on the other side of the block, over the corner of the fence, in through the back door or kitchen window (whichever was easier), find him, pull the trigger. Once would do it. Twice to make sure. Two minutes, tops, and that was allowing a full minute to find one man in a three-room house.

So why was he still casing the neighborhood? It wasn't caution. The plan was made; the more time he spent on the street, the greater chance someone would remember him. And while he'd been careful to efface himself as far as the citizens were concerned, he'd been obvious enough to attract some attention from any of the Pole's professional colleagues, assuming any had been around.

There had been no response. It came as a minor surprise; even with Trotter (as far as Smolinski could tell) dead, there should have been someone around protecting him. Trotter wasn't the only spy America had. Besides, with someone as new as Smolinski, with such a visible cover, it only made sense to have someone nearby to wet-nurse him, if necessary.

No wet nurse. Trotter didn't care. It gave him one less thing to worry about.

He kept walking around the neighborhood. He wasn't holding up out of reluctance. He didn't enjoy killing, but he'd always done it when it was the best thing to do. And he didn't have any qualms about killing Smolinksi in particular. Trotter hated that bastard on every conceivable level. He hated him as a man, both because he worked for the Russians and because in doing so, he had betrayed his own people. The Poles, if you asked Trotter, were the most remarkable people on Earth. Victims of geography and history, they had spent hundreds of years enslaved by one bunch of vicious scumbags or another but still maintained their faith and their identity as a people. It didn't seem likely, but they deserved to be free someday. Bastards like Smolinski kept backing that day deeper into the future.

He hated him as a professional. Trotter hated sloppy work, even if the work was designed to kill him. A second-rate gunman, followed by a trap that by its very nature was less than foolproof, was very sloppy. And Smolinski had broken one of the unwritten laws, one of the hypocritical-but-necessary accommodations that had been reached to make it possible to keep delaying the start of World War III. The rule Smolinski had broken was simply this: You do not kill an enemy agent unless you have something to gain by it. "Something to gain by it" did not include arranging for there to be a smaller number of enemy agents. Down that road lay war. It was too easy for the enemy to retaliate.

Just as, Trotter thought, I'm about to retaliate now. If I get around to it.

Trotter hated Smolinski on a personal level, too. He heard the cowardice when he'd phoned the man; he'd seen his complete disregard for Regina's life. Dropping the hammer would bring Trotter no joy, but it would be a cleaner world as soon as Smolinski left it.

It was his father. He was hesitating because of his father.

Or, more correctly, because of the *absence* of his father as anything but a lump in a hospital bed.

Because every rotten thing Trotter had ever done before, all the lies, deceptions and violence, he had been able to blame on the Congressman. He'd used people, and abused them, and maimed and killed them, but deep down where the real *he* lived, the little boy with the name the man never used, he could say his heart was clean. All the rotten things he'd done had been done because the old man had forced him to, or in an effort to keep the old man from forcing him to do things even worse. It was his mouth telling the lies, his body making the love, his fist smashing the face, his finger pulling the trigger, but it had never been his *responsibility*.

Trotter estimated that over the last thirteen years, since he'd first tried to get out from under, he had spent less than two full days, total time, in the old man's company. But he'd always been there, a monkey on his back, a voice in his ear, saying, "You'll be back, son. Can't help it. Might as well try to make an octopus sing as for you to try to walk away from what you were born to. It's in your blood, boy. It's your destiny; you couldn't stop if you wanted to."

Except—and this was the thing—except *now, he could*. If he wanted to.

If he wanted to, he could keep walking until he saw a cab or a bus or a train, and take off. Rines wouldn't look for him—he'd be too busy trying to handle the Congressman's job. Even the thought of foisting the Agency off on Trotter wouldn't be an incentive for Rines to find him. Nobody was going to trust a man with the kind of power the Congressman had once wielded after he walked out in the middle of an operation.

For the first time in his life, since *before* his life, Trotter's fate was entirely in his own hands. If only, he thought, mine were the only fate.

Trotter went through the yard of the vacant house. He got barked at by a dog in one of the nearby yards but aroused no human's interest. He went to the corner that touched the corner of Smolinski's yard, jumped, caught hold, and pulled himself over. There was a small stoop under Smolinski's back door. The storm door was open; the wooden door behind it locked.

It was not a good lock. This was a safe neighborhood, and it was more important to fit in than to be barricaded in the house. One of the standard ways to find amateurs (terrorists, bank robbers, counterfeiters, drug dealers, etc.) in a suspect neighborhood is to see who's got the best locks on the house. The smart ones, and the trained professionals, used what everybody else had. If there was really anything inside that had to be locked up, you built a safe in the back of a closet or a vault in the cellar floor.

That wouldn't work, though, if they were after something you couldn't keep in a vault. Such as your life.

Trotter unzipped his jacket and took the gun and the silencer from an inside pocket. He put them together close to his body, using the loose flaps of the jacket to screen him, in the unlikely event someone was looking. He tucked the gun in his belt, took out an L-shaped piece of stiff, thin plastic, slipped the lock and went inside.

He looked around and listened. There was nothing to hear. The kitchen looked like a kitchen. In the dish rack to the side of the stainless-steel sink was a cup, saucer, spoon, and something that looked like a vase.

It was all very tidy. Trotter could hear Smolinski coming home the other night—"I tidied up Trotter, now I'll tidy up the house." Trotter got the gun ready and began walking quietly through the house.

The whole place was tidy. A mother would be proud.

Oops, Trotter thought. Spoke too soon. Through a doorway, he could see sheets of paper almost incandescently white against the dark wood floor. He hugged the wall alongside the doorway, then popped in, crouched low, gun ready.

Smolinski was sprawled across the desk. His left arm was straight out, as if pointing at something. His right arm was clutched to his chest.

Softly, Trotter said, "Get up." No response.

He tried again, a little louder. Still nothing. He walked across to the desk and poked Smolinski with the silencer. He did not move.

It could be a ploy. Trotter doubted Smolinski had brains enough to come up with it, but it could be. Play dead—get your would-be attacker to want to know if you're alive. If he wants to take your pulse or feel your temperature, he's going to have to take off one of the gloves the October weather and the desire to leave no fingerprints have undoubtedly caused him to wear. If he uses the other hand to remove the glove, the gun has to waver from you, at least for a split second. If he pulls the glove off with his teeth, chances are his eyes will roll up with the effort for that split second. It may not be much, but it's more than you had, and sometimes, a split second is enough.

Trotter was not giving out free chances today. The gloves would stay on. He took a handful of Smolinski's intellectual-long blond hair and pulled his head up sharply. One look at the face was enough. For instance, no one in the world was a good enough actor to stay unblinking with his hair being pulled and pencil shavings clinging to his eyeballs. Trotter lowered him gently to the desk.

Smolinski was dead. How convenient. Looked like natural causes, too, a heart attack while he was cleaning his pencil sharpener—the cup had fallen to the floor when Trotter raised the head. The posture, the face, everything looked like sudden heart failure.

Trotter didn't buy it for a second. He bent close to Smolinski's mouth, but facedown in a pile of pencil shavings, there wasn't much to smell but pine and graphite.

**142**

Another remarkable coincidence. The Russians developed a little toy back in the fifties that was a big hit with their East German and Bulgarian attack dogs. It was a little glass tube that shot a mist of cyanide in somebody's face. Once the bitter almond smell dissipated, there was damned near no way to tell the victim hadn't succumbed to a heart attack. Safe for the operator, too, provided you swallowed a good dose of milk or olive oil beforehand and took the antidote right after you used it.

No smell, no proof.

Trotter was thinking what to do about it when he noticed Smolinski's hair. For some reason, it had stayed in the shape of the inside of a fist. It was as if Trotter had grabbed a handful of bread dough. Not a good idea to leave that behind.

He was brushing the hair down roughly with a gloved hand when he heard the jingle of keys from outside. He ran quickly to the window alongside the door, hooked the curtain aside, and took a look.

What he saw was a dumpy old woman wearing a shapeless coat between her babushka and opaque stockings and sensible shoes. She tried a key. It didn't work, and she cursed. In Polish.

The cleaning lady. Trotter had checked her out. It wasn't her day to be here. Damn.

Or maybe no damn. A plan blew to fullness in Trotter's mind like an inflatable raft. He hoped the old woman's heart would take it. He took another look, and decided she seemed healthy enough. He saw the reason she was having so much trouble with the keys was that she was encumbered by a huge bunch of yellow flowers.

Trotter went on tiptoe back to the desk and propped Smolinski upright. He ran back and stood alongside the door.

She was taking forever with those keys. Trotter was tempted to open the door for her, but he got over it.

At last he heard the tumblers click. The door unlatched, and he heard her wiping her feet assiduously on the welcome mat. She had her head down, making sure she got every speck of mud. And she was speaking. Polish, a language in which Trotter was not fluent. Still, it was related to Russian, which he did speak, and he'd picked up a bit of Polish during his travels, so he got the gist of what she was saying. She was sorry she couldn't make it before, somebody was sick, the flowers probably died, new ones, would only be a minute, busy man.

Then she stepped in the door. He watched her eyes. At the *instant* she saw Smolinski, after she saw his face, but before she could think, He's dead, Trotter put a bullet in Smolinski's forehead. He'd been dead for a while, so there wasn't much blood, but there was enough. The body pitched back against the chair, then forward to the desk again. When it hit, Trotter fired again, putting a hole in the top of Smolinski's head. That one didn't bleed at all.

Even if he had spilled *oceans* of blood, the old woman's reaction couldn't have been any more drastic. She screamed, sank to her knees, beat the floor with hands made leathery from a million acres of dirty floors.

Trotter screamed at her in Russian. "Silence!"

He raised the pistol and pointed it at her forehead. *"Smert Spionam,"* he said, which meant "Death to spies" and provided the words for which SMERSH was an acronym. SMERSH, as a separate organization, no longer existed, but the policy did, and every Polish refugee would know the phrase, or be able to figure it out.

The old woman had. She stayed on her knees, made the Sign of the Cross, and spat. Trotter assumed only the spittle was for him.

He wanted to hug and kiss this old woman, and tell her she was worth a hundred Smolinskis. Instead, he smiled coldly at her and spoke more Russian. "Tell them," he said. "Tell them no one escapes the KGB."

She understood KGB, all right. Trotter went out the front door. He dropped the gun in Smolinski's hedge so the cops would find it, and not some little kid, and walked calmly back to his car.

On the way, he assessed his day's work. They'd do an autopsy. They'd know soon enough the bullets hadn't killed Smolinski, but they might not be able to decide what had. They'd know damn well *something* had gone on. It would make the media. The Russians had killed the heroic defector. Smolinski would wind up serving the cause of freedom, anyway. That was worth a smile.

Trotter got to the car (a Dodge Aries K, this time) and went to take off his gloves to get the keys from his pocket.

There was something yellow on one of the fingers of his left glove. He looked closely at it. A flower petal, like the ones on the flowers the old woman had dropped on the floor in panic. But how had it gotten on his glove? He'd been nowhere near her. Or the flowers.

He pulled off the gloves and noticed that the left glove was slightly tacky, as though something had been sprayed on it. He sniffed, and got a faint, sweet smell. There was the vase in the sink. She said she'd brought *new* flowers today. The vase in the dish rack was *empty*. And all Trotter had touched was Smolinski's head.

That really called for a smile. It was his style to stir things up, but he hadn't realized just how well he'd been doing it. He had them killing *each other* now. Because the stickiness came from Smolinski's hair, and it got on Smolinski's hair because someone poured water from a flower vase on him. And who did things like that?

The killer the Russians called Azrael. The Angel of Death had, so to speak, come home to roost.

# CHAPTER THREE

"You could have started a *war!*" Joe Albright said. He looked at Trotter. "You can sit there smiling at me, man, but you could have started a fucking *war!*"

Rines's voice came from the front of the truck. "Albright . . ." Like a teacher warning a school kid.

Joe shut up. It was too much to take. Super-secret organizations that used the FBI as errand boys. Science-fiction layouts. The inside of this truck looked like a condensed version of NASA control in Houston. The outside of it looked like a moving van, and it was parked right now in a sea of identical moving vans in back of a warehouse not far from Albright Salvage/Reclamation. Trotter told him it had been the Congressman's pride that this little number had been purchased with the profits from hamburger joints.

It was pretty obvious, what with all Trotter had told him, that Joe's days as a nice, everyday, bank-robber-chasing, dope-dealer-finding FBI man were at an end. What was coming now wasn't certain, but it was a damn good possibility, after what *else* Trotter had told him. He'd set it up to look like the KGB had come and killed this beloved political refugee on American soil? And bragged about it? It was a wonder the missiles weren't already flying. They would be if Albright didn't know anything but how Trotter had made things look and he had access to the button.

And Rines was in charge of this shindig now that the Congressman—and, of course, Joe now knew which congressman it was—was out of action. He was (ostensibly) Trotter's boss, but Joe could see it was a lot more complicated than that. Every time Rines told one of the technicians (and what a bunch of zombies *they* were) to do something, Rines would sneak a look at Trotter like a base runner looking for the steal sign. Trotter had given him nothing but nods so far, but Joe knew nobody was gonna stop Trotter from doing what he wanted, if he had the notion it was the right thing to do.

The control-room truck was, apparently, the ultimate in bugging equipment. It was hooked into a satellite, he wasn't sure how. What it accomplished was to draw a circle around Petra Hudson.

The setup was what Joe had figured all along—somebody trying to force Mrs. Hudson into doing something. Trotter and Joe had been talking. Trotter had said he was impressed with the setup.

"I called for it yesterday," Rines said.

"Before you talked to me?"

Rines smiled. Joe had been surprised to see it. Hadn't thought a smile would fit Rines's face, somehow. "I knew how that was going to turn out. I also figured the best time to make our move right after the next demand, and I wanted to be sure to know when it happened. So I called for the Congressman's little toy."

"And it came?"

"Oh, sure. The old man had told everybody who counted in the Agency that if anything happened to him, they should take orders from me. Or you."

"One of the reasons I've always hated him is his penchant for thinking of everything."

"Pitching you in without water wings, I know." Rines tightened his lips, then said, "Her bodyguard's being killed has made it easier for us—she stays at the office now. We've got any phone she could conceivably get to covered, and we've got computer descramblers if she somehow finds a coded phone. We're intercepting her mail, and if she gets a telegram, we'll know about it before she does. We're getting photographs of anyone she meets and running checks on them right away."

"What if somebody passes her a note?" Joe had found himself asking.

Rines gave that smile again. Joe suppressed a shudder.

"We've got a man inside," Rines said. "A plumber. There was suddenly a lot of trouble with the plumbing yesterday. How did you think the bugs were planted?" He hadn't waited for an answer, which made Joe just as glad. Instead, he turned to Trotter and said, "I only hope we don't wind up sitting in this parking lot for three days waiting for the Russians to move."

"They won't," Trotter said. "They thought taking care of

Smolinski would remove a problem for them. I put it back in their laps. With the heat on about that, and, for all they know, Regina dead, they're going to want to get the Hudson Group sewn up as soon as possible. They've got to figure they're going to need it."

And that's when it had hit him. Trotter had "dumped it back in their laps." He had probably made a lot of Americans good and mad. *Too* goddam good and mad. And all Rines was worried about was a junior Special Agent saying "fucking" in public, if a bunch of zombies with headsets plugging their ears and their eyes glued to green scopes counted as public.

"Don't worry, Joe," Trotter told him calmly. Even *he* had an earplug. "There won't be a war."

"Maybe not. But the press has hold of this already—"

"That's why there won't be a war. Listen to this." He pulled the earplug from his ear, wiped it thoroughly on his pants, and handed it to Joe. Joe wasn't crazy about the idea of a used earplug, but he decided Trotter looked clean enough, and stuck it in.

He expected to hear terse voices speaking arcane codes in reassuring tones. What he got instead was the local all-news radio station. ". . . doubtful the KGB did in fact commission Smolinski's death. The Soviet news agency, TASS, as well as official Polish government sources, say that Smolinski was executed by the CIA, who were afraid he was going to redefect. No U.S. Government source who would comment on the charges could be found. In Europe, American allies urged caution—"

"Enough?" Trotter asked.

Joe pulled the plug from his ear. "Sure," he said. "You knew this was going to happen?"

"As well as I know the sun will come up in the east tomorrow. It used to be you got a couple of days before the media tore the guts out of the American side of anything. Now you've got a grace period of maybe two hours. If that. I refer you to the Libya raids. The American planes hadn't landed yet, and we were getting Russians on network shows telling us what bastards we were. And, my, wasn't there a lot about Qaddafi's daughter. I just thank God the public has enough brains to know that if we *were* as corrupt and evil as most of the media makes us out, bastards like Qaddafi would be dead and these high-priced reporters would be in jail."

"But in this case," Albright pointed out, "they're right. Sort of."

"No, they're totally wrong. It was still the Russians who killed him. I just brought things out into starker relief. So they couldn't ignore the truth completely and say Smolinski committed suicide in despair at the state of American culture or something. This way, at least, we've got one person—this Mrs. Szczeczko— who is *sure* the KGB did it, and a lot more people who think they *might* have, because the media had to spend an hour or so acting like they really believed it."

"It hardly seems fair. They make such a big thing out of being impartial."

"Come on, Joe. Did you ever meet a reporter who didn't have his mind made up about any issue you could think of? Also, there's more money in bad news. That's what this is all about, Joe. Petra Hudson has kept the Hudson Group papers clear of the bandwagon. They're a 'conservative voice.' The idea has to be for Borzov to swing them left at the right time."

"And this is the right time."

"Damn soon."

"Why?"

"Something in the works. Something big."

"What could be bigger than this? I see figures that say the Hudson Group subsidiaries reach almost a hundred million people."

Trotter gave him a bland look. "Scary, isn't it?"

Joe never got the chance to answer. One of the technicians said, "Mr. Rines." Joe had to admit he did not sound like a zombie. He sounded like a robot.

"Put it on the monitor," Rines said.

". . . at last ready to agree to perform your duty?" The voice on the monitor could have belonged to the technician's brother.

"Where—where is my daughter?"

"Mrs. Hudson, you still have your son. For the time being. You personally have been spared because you can still fulfill your duty, but our patience is not inexhaustible."

"You son of a bitch! You've killed my daughter, do you think I care what you do to me?"

"There is still your son."

Joe had to admire both their techniques. Joe knew (now) that Regina Hudson was tucked safely away in a hospital, but Mrs. Hudson didn't, and the accusation was an attempt to get confirmation. The caller was pretty sure Regina *was* dead, but he was admitting nothing.

"You have thirty seconds, Mrs. Hudson."

Rines said, "Can we trace this call?"

Trotter's face said why bother. "New York," he suggested. "Washington. One of the embassies. They're not going to make a call like this from anyplace the government can raid."

"New York or Washington look like good guesses, Mr. Rines," one of the technicians said. He punched a few buttons. "South and east of here, at any rate. We'll have it for you in a few minutes."

Petra Hudson was taking every one of her thirty seconds. Everybody in the truck waited with her. Finally, she said, "I'll do what you say."

"Good, good," Trotter said.

The robot voice spoke from New York or Washington. "You will receive instructions." There was a click, very loud, over the monitor, as the connection was broken. Joe thought he heard a sob from Mrs. Hudson before she hung up, but he wasn't sure.

Joe turned to Trotter. "Okay, I'm just a simple little FBI man from the backwoods of the Northwest, but I don't see what's good about it. She just said she'd do what they wanted, didn't she?"

"It's *why* she said it, though. It means she'll do what *we* want."

Joe thought it over for a second. "Not if anything happens to her son. You'd better keep an eye on Junior."

"We're watching him," Rines said. Joe thought, God, what a set of rabbit ears. "Junior," Rines went on, "is being watched by six men. He's safe as a church."

"I hope so," Joe said.

"In fact, he's *in* a church."

# CHAPTER FOUR

"Mr. Nelson?"

Will Nelson gave the bolt one more turn with the big-bladed screwdriver, then slid out from under the pew. "Oh," he said, "hello, Jimmy. I'm just tightening up the benches, you know, or they creak. I could barely hear my own sermon last Sunday."

Jimmy Hudson did not smile. "It—it looks like a big job."

"I don't mind. Mike was going to help me. Do you know Mike? Helps out here part-time."

"I've seen him around."

"But he had a chance to go over to the lake and help some fellow get his boat in for the winter. Seems to me he's about a month late, wouldn't you think? The pay was half again what the church could afford to give him, so I told him to go ahead. Besides, it's kind of fun sliding around on the marble floor. Undignified without a good excuse."

"I'd think it would be cold."

"Cold it is. Come on over to the house, I'll make us some hot chocolate, and you can tell me what's on your mind."

Jimmy looked miserable. "I don't want you to go to any trouble. And I don't want to take you away from your work."

Will put a hand on the young man's shoulder. "Look. For one thing, it's no trouble. I want some myself. For another thing, I'm done with this section. I'll get to the rest some other time, or when Mike gets back. And, finally, the Scripture says, 'Whenever two or more of you are gathered in My Name, there I am among you.' It doesn't say anything about pews, creaking or otherwise. People are the business I have to attend to first. I can tell by looking at you that you've got something on your mind that's so heavy, it's mashing you flat. Am I right?"

"I wanted to get your advice," Jimmy admitted cautiously.

"Then come over to the kitchen and I'll give you as much as you want."

The house was right next door. Will had always thought it was the kind of accommodation a congregation with their head on right provided for the preacher. Everything in it was well built and well cared for; none of it was fancy. Too many places tried to impress—the world? God?—tried to impress whoever with their prosperity as indicated by the sumptuousness of the preacher's house. Others seemed to get the idea that their minister should be a living symbol of the mortification of the flesh. The people of Kirkester realized that their spiritual leader was simply a human being with a job to do. Fanciness was unnecessary; poverty-for-show made the job harder. Will Nelson's stay in Kirkester was going to be over soon—nothing definite, but he'd had a letter from Mr. Nethercott, the regular preacher, saying that his son was much improved, and that he might be able to start thinking about coming home in a month or so. Will would hate to leave. He liked to think he'd accomplished a lot here.

Still, he knew it wouldn't have been possible without the good work Mr. Nethercott had already done here. And he knew when he'd first come the work would only be temporary. But he'd always remember the town with affection.

He took Jimmy's jacket and hung it up in the hall closet, then led the way to the kitchen. He liked the kitchen, too. Big and homey, with a solid, black-enameled wooden table in the middle of it. He told Jimmy to sit, got cocoa powder and sugar and milk, measured, mixed, and put the pot on the stove over low heat.

"My wife is doing her weekly visiting," Will said. He stirred with a wooden spoon.

"I'm sorry to miss her."

"She'll be back soon."

Jimmy Hudson looked at his hands. Will decided to let him get to the topic in his own good time. In fact, he decided, it might be a good idea to give him a little while to think about it.

"Jim," he said. "Would you mind watching the pot for a few seconds?"

"I wouldn't mind, I just wouldn't know what to do. The cook makes all the hot chocolate at my mother's house."

"You're a college boy, right? I think you can master it." Jimmy came over and joined him at the stove; Will showed him. "See? Figure-eight, then around the edge, keep the spoon touching the bottom of the pan. If it starts to steam, give a yell."

Jimmy took over. Will watched him for five seconds, then said he was a natural, which elicited a smile from the young man. Will took the stairs two at a time, went to the bedroom and changed the jeans and plaid shirt he'd been working in for a pair of dark gray wool trousers, a black jacket, and his dog collar with a royal blue yoke. Then he looked in the mirror and thought about the demands of his ministry. He'd always known what his duty was, and now his duty was to take a risk, if it meant helping Jimmy Hudson.

"Mr. Nelson!"

"I'm coming." When he got to the kitchen, he sniffed and smiled. "Smells good." He got some marshmallows and put them in cups. He put the cups on the table, then poured.

"Sit down, Jim," he said. He slurped some chocolate and melted marshmallow off the top of his cup. "I had to put on my preacher suit in case anyone shows up."

"Are you expecting anyone?"

"Not a soul. Why don't you tell me what's on your mind."

Jimmy took a sip from his own cup. "Hot," he said.

"That's the idea. Hot chocolate."

"You sound just like my father. I think. I don't remember him really well, but I seem to recall his saying things like that. Or maybe it's just that right now I feel like a kid."

"And what's wrong with that?" the Reverend Mr. Nelson wanted to know.

"I don't feel happy like a kid or innocent like a kid. I'm upset and afraid like a kid."

"And angry, too."

"Is it that obvious? At school, I have a reputation of being cool."

"It's not *that* obvious, I just have a lot of experience."

"And I have a lot of anger. And hate."

"Hatred of whom?"

"Allan Trotter. I don't suppose it's much of a surprise."

Will sipped his chocolate. "Why do you think you hate him?"

"It's not that I think it, Mr. Nelson. It's a fact."

"This is where I'm supposed to tell you that hate is a serious business."

"Don't you think I know that? That's why I've *come* here!"

Will smiled, just a little sadly. "They don't hand out magic wands with this job, you know. But I'll help you all I can."

"He killed Hannah," Jimmy said.

"Only if your sister is lying."

Jimmy's voice was harsh. *"For all I know he's killed my sister, too!"*

"What do you mean, Jim? What happened to your sister?"

"I don't know. She's disappeared. They both have."

"It could be something as innocent as an elopement."

"God forbid! And I'm not blaspheming when I say that."

"Of course not."

"I don't think anything he *does* is innocent. I saw him looking at Hannah that night at dinner. He got her to sneak off the grounds, and he killed her."

"And left the body on his own front stairs? Besides, your sister says she was with him the whole time."

"Then he *had* her killed."

"Why, Jim?" Mr. Nelson asked softly. "And by whom?"

"I don't *know* why! It's driving me crazy. I think this Trotter, or whoever he represents, is doing things to drive my mother insane. You wouldn't believe what's happened to her."

Will picked his words carefully. "She has seemed to become distracted over the last few months."

Jimmy looked ruefully at him. "Well, in the past few days, she's seemed to become insane. Ever since Charles killed himself. She won't come home from the office. She hardly eats at all." He made a noise in his chest, something between a cough and a bark of bitter laughter. "Maybe," he said, "that's what's happened to Regina. She couldn't take it anymore, and she ran off. If she could only see what a wreck she's made of Mother . . ."

"Should I see your mother?"

"I don't think she'd let you in."

"You could take me in."

"To the grounds, yes. I doubt she'd see you. I'm not even sure she'd see *me*. I mean, I've tried, but not too hard. All I'd be able to talk about is that murderous *Trotter!*"

Will Nelson sighed. "As I said before, no magic wand. I can't open you and take the anger and hate out, or the fear or confusion, either, if it comes to that. I suppose it does no good at all to point out that the police have investigated, ruled it an accidental death, and cleared Mr. Trotter."

"Not a bit of good. If he had an alibi, he also had an accomplice."

"Any candidates?"

"How should I know? Maybe it's that junk man everybody is making so much fuss over. The black man. Albright. He was trying to find Trotter the other night."

Will sighed again. There was nothing more he could say, except the classic, all-purpose clerical advice: Be strong and pray. It always sounded so trite, a fact Will found all the more maddening in the face of its proven efficacy. He himself was a living testament to the power of strength and prayer. When he had been troubled, he had striven to endure, and had asked the Lord for help. And he had endured, and he had found his way to this ministry. When he had been confused, the Lord had made things clear. Be strong and pray. Advice that could change a life, and so often it provoked only scorn, or anger.

"Be strong and pray," Will said.

This time neither scorn nor anger but despair.

"Don't you think I *try* to be strong?" Jimmy Hudson cried. "I can't sleep for fighting. I fight the urge to get up and find Trotter and kill him with my bare hands, and I fight the cowardice that says the only reason I don't is that I know he could tear me apart without breaking a sweat. I fight the despair over my mother. I fight the voice that tells me Hannah might not . . . be . . . might be in . . ."

"In hell?" Mr. Nelson asked softly.

Now James Hudson, Jr., did seem like a little kid. He put his face in his hands and sobbed. "Not for anything to do with *her*! That's the worst of it. Just—just on a *technicality*! She was an angel on earth, Mr. Nelson, but because of that man—"

"Shh. Jimmy. Quiet. You don't have to worry about it."

Jimmy looked up at him. Tear tracks glistened in the fluorescent light, but there was a wild, skeptical hope in his face.

And that, Will thought, is the advantage of making tough decisions in advance. This was what he'd foreseen; if he'd put off his decision, he'd have to hesitate and make it now, and his words wouldn't carry the authority and comfort the boy needed.

"You wouldn't have had to worry in any case, you know. The Lord gives us our parents; He doesn't punish us because of whom He's given us."

"But Hannah had been coming to me for instruction."

"What?"

"She wanted it to be a surprise. She used to drive in from campus. I thought the whole business was a little frivolous, but she explained that it was a gift to you. The surprise, that is. The conversion was for herself. I baptized her."

"You did?"

"It doesn't become a man in my position to lie, Jim."

"But her parents . . . you let her be buried."

"Her parents had to deal with losing her. Why burden them with something like this at the same time? The One Who counted already knew."

"Why didn't you tell *me*?"

"Frankly, because it never occurred to me you'd have any doubts that a young woman who, as you put it, was an angel on earth would have any trouble being one in heaven."

"Thank you, Mr. Nelson."

"I should have told you."

"And I shouldn't have doubted."

"You're a little young yet to be perfect." He clapped the boy on the shoulder. "Are you going to be all right?"

"I guess. But nowhere near perfect."

"It takes time. Drink your chocolate. It ought to be cooler by now."

Jimmy drank his chocolate. Will made him promise to call again, as often as he liked, to phone any time of the day or night, if Jimmy needed him. He showed him out.

When he came back through the house, Will saw that the TV set had turned itself on to The Weather Channel, a high-numbered channel on the tuner of the local cable system.

Neither Will nor his wife watched The Weather Channel, but sometimes it just popped on. Donna thought it was funny, one of those electronic mistakes that no one can explain and that would be too much bother to have fixed. Will thanked God for the millionth time that he had found Donna.

He turned off the set. He was glad it hadn't happened with Jimmy there. There were explanations, but not to have to explain was best.

Will got a fleece-lined car coat from the closet and went back over to the church. He climbed the steps to the tower room. In a closet up there, behind some spare choir robes (which reminded him: Sunday, he'd have to urge the congregation to take a greater interest in the choir) he found the transmitter. He took it out, placed it on a small table by a window, and switched it on. It was already tuned to the proper frequency.

He waited for his leader to bounce and scramble between satellites and earth stations, through wires and waves.

This must be important, he thought. Again. They weren't supposed to beam the summons to that special device in the television set at this time of day, except in the direst of emergencies. And two of the direst emergencies in one week was quite a lot.

A few seconds was enough. He put the headset on, pushed a button, and said, "Azrael. Responding to Control."

They insisted on being called "Control," but he used them as much as they used him. More. They helped him with his purpose; he was thwarting theirs.

"Azrael." The Reverend Mr. Will Nelson was impressed. Borzov was making this transmission in person.

# PART SIX

## CHAPTER ONE

His name had been Roger Brude. Of course, it still was, but not to the World. Not even to Donna. It was vanity to seek recognition, or even appreciation, and pride was a Deadly Sin. Even in a time as sinful as this, a man who tried to live a good life, to follow the Word, to help others, could not avoid being noticed. Temptations to pride would be all around.

That was why Roger lived his public ministry under the name of another, the man or (as Roger was convinced) the angel, who had shown him the end of his confusion. It was the closest Roger could come to the kind of tribute his late friend deserved—a whole life lived in his name.

Roger had been born in West Virginia, but he had lived all over as a child—as far north as St. Paul, as far south as San Antonio. His father was a bookkeeper with a knack for finding employment at firms that were about to go out of business or be swallowed up in mergers, with his father's job being ground up in the belly of some already overstaffed corporate accounting department. Dad would get a severance check and a reference, and the family would move on.

When he was younger, Roger would cry at night over these

157

dislocations. He was always the New Kid, and the New Kid was always the enemy. And they would try to make him fight.

It was sinful to fight. Roger knew that. His mother mentioned it repeatedly, read it from the Book. It was a sin to fight, except when you fought for the Lord. It was discussed at length around the family table, the one that had covered more distance, it seemed, than a space shot, and there was really no way he could construe making the other kids stop tormenting him as fighting for the Lord.

"The Lord was spat upon," his father would say around a mouthful of meat loaf. "And reviled. He took it. He forgave, and even blessed, His tormentors."

"Don't talk with your mouth full, dear," Mom would tell Dad, then turn to Roger. "But your father is absolutely right. The whole thing is, we have to try to be like the Lord."

"But He was *God*. He was *perfect*."

"We still have to try. Do you think your father likes it that none of his jobs seems to last more than a year? That worse bookkeepers keep getting the promotions, men ten years younger—even some *women* now—are making more money than your father does, just because they've been lucky enough to stay in place and build up seniority? Do you think he likes not being able to buy us a house because he has to keep moving around the country like a fugitive because of bad luck and bad timing? Do you think he likes that?"

Roger had thought the question rhetorical, but his mother pressed on. "Do you?"

He turned to his father. "Do you, Dad?"

Dad's mouth moved a lot before any voice came out. When it did, it sounded strange. "No, son," he said. "I don't like it, especially."

"Of course he doesn't," Mom said triumphantly. "Only a worm could *like* that kind of treatment. But your father is a God-fearing man. He doesn't go around beating up the boss every time he gets laid off. He doesn't grab him by the collar and scream about how unfair it is, even though it is, of course. He goes on, doing the best he can. You know why that is, don't you, Roger?"

"Because our reward is in Heaven."

"Because our reward is in Heaven. Worldly things don't matter. God is the only Judge that counts, and Heaven and Hell is where the real justice is done."

So the family kept moving, and he was still the New Kid, and they still tried to get him to fight. And he would run away, so they marked him yellow and continued to torment him, or ignored him completely. Or he would give in to sinful human nature and fight them. And most of the time, he would win.

That was both the glory and the pain of it. Because he was actually quite good at this fighting stuff. He was a big kid, and strong and healthy. Mom said he reminded her of his father. Dad had never looked especially big before, but Roger took another look, and guessed that Dad would be pretty good-sized if he would pull his shoulders back a little and stop letting his head slump forward the way it did.

Roger had good posture. Teachers always told him. They seemed more impressed with his posture than with the good marks he got in school. A's in everything except math. Roger didn't want to be good in math. If you were good in math, they might try to make a bookkeeper out of you. Roger honored his father, but he'd had enough of that life already.

But he had a good body, and a good brain, and fast reflexes, and things that hurt other kids, caused them physical pain, had to hit Roger a lot harder before they hurt him.

And when they taunted him enough to make him forget his parents and the Lord and fight anyway, he just *didn't care* anymore. He already *knew* he was sinning. He knew every bruise he got would bring a scolding ("He that spareth the rod hateth his son") so he would do whatever it took, and he would win.

That's when the real pain started. Because even when he won, he never won anything. Sure, the other kids would accept him, would want to "be his friend," but what was that? What good was a friend who cost you part of your chance at Heaven? Who wanted the respect of a fool who would only respect someone who was willing to hurt him?

Roger grew up alone, except for Mom and Dad, of course. Then the accident happened, and he lost them, too.

It was Roger's junior year of high school. They were living in Pennsylvania at the time. They'd been there over two years, longer than Roger could remember every staying in one place. They'd been there because Dad had run out of places to go. The factory closed down, and there wasn't another job to be found. Dad collected unemployment; they scrimped, and they got by. But the unemployment was almost up, and the prospect of Welfare faced them. As Mom said, unemployment was bad enough, but Welfare would be a disgrace. Roger worked at a hamburger joint after school, but he couldn't help much.

One hot night, while Roger was at work, Dad and Mom went out for a ride, probably to get some air. They'd sold their air conditioner to avoid temptation, with electricity so high. A ride in the car was about the only way to cool off, and with gas the way it was, even that had to be restricted.

A policeman came and pulled him out from behind the grill. Roger had never been so embarrassed. He hadn't done anything wrong, at least not what the police thought of as wrong.

But it wasn't that. The policeman told him Mom and Dad were dead, crashed into the abutment of an overpass on Interstate 70. It was kind of a mysterious accident, since witnesses said they didn't swerve to avoid a hazard or anything, just swerved from the lane into the concrete piling.

Roger was sure he knew what it was. Something had broken in the car, the brakes or the steering. He told the cops, and asked them to find out what it was, to save other people from crashing.

They said they looked, but they didn't find anything wrong with the car. They started trying to tell him about his father, but Roger got very upset, and told them not to try to slough their incompetence off on somebody else. He apologized later. Maybe the flawed part had been burned up in the crash. He was sure the police had done their best. He consoled himself that Mom and Dad had found True Justice at last, and all the bad luck would be made up for, and all the striving for goodness would be taken into account.

Now he had to face his own life. He was completely alone, now. Well, never completely. He summoned his strength, and he prayed, and it came to him that as soon as school was done, he would join the Army. Yes, he would be fighting, but he would be fighting for Freedom. Fighting for the Lord.

He did very well in Basic Training. He requested to be sent to Vietnam. He met Will Nelson soon after he got there. They were assigned adjoining bunks. But something special happened. Will just seemed to fall into treating Roger like a friend, as though Roger had grown up next door to him in Chicago.

They talked a lot, about their lives and families. Will was a recent orphan, too. That is, his mother had died years ago. His father, a policeman, had been shot by a drug dealer. He'd been working his way through college (there were no other relatives to go to for help) when the low number came up in the draft, and he decided to go and get it over with. "Save something up, get GI benefits, cut down on the work hours, stay awake in class for a change."

Will seemed to take things with a stoicism that would have been impossible for Roger without the Lord's help. Will claimed not to believe in the Lord.

"Whatever happens, happens," he would say. "My father had plenty of chances to go into private security, but he insisted on staying a cop. You put yourself out on the street between the pushers and fucking crooked politicians, you're asking to get shot. Like the kind of idiot who'd volunteer to come to Vietnam." He'd grin at that, since he'd told Roger he'd volunteered himself. Roger reminded him. Will said, "Maybe I feel like shooting somebody myself," and laughed.

Then came the night patrols, one particular night patrol. They were supposed to tempt the enemy out of hiding. There was a reason for that, but Roger never learned what it was.

"We're dead," Will had said, smoking a last cigarette before they pulled out of camp.

"You think that way, we will be," Roger said.

"This is a suicide mission. I won another lottery." Roger had tried to protest, but Will went on. "You know, I bet we've cost the government something like a hundred thousand dollars each in training, equipment, pay, transportation, and food."

"So?"

"So, when someone is willing to spend money like that to set you up to be killed, you're better off dead if you ask me."

Roger asked him, as a friend, to stop, and Will, as a friend, did. The serg                and they went on patrol.

They            ey tempted the enemy into attacking. And it *was* a su        ion. Fire came from alongside the path; fire came fro            of trees, from in front of them and behind them. R             t three times. He went down, lost consciousness, and

He *must* have died—either that or he'd come so close no one could tell the difference. Because it was routine for both sides to cut the throats of anyone who managed to survive the killing fire. Will had been spared. He was sick and confused, but he was alive with his throat intact.

His only coherent thought had been to find Will. He had to do it by dog tags because several of the corpses had no faces, and one had no head. Somehow, Roger got to his feet and staggered back toward camp. He would have stayed with Will, but the many creatures of the jungle who grew fat on death were beginning to work, and Roger didn't want to wind up on the menu by mistake.

He was found, after a few days, field-treated, then transferred to a hospital ship for surgery and flown back to the States for recuperation.

And counseling. They gave him counseling. A lady doctor, sympathetic, but somehow too sincere, told him not to worry about his guilt feelings. She said survivors of incidents like this often felt guilt.

Roger smiled and nodded and thanked her for her help, but the idea of guilt had never occurred to him. He had been dead, or hopelessly close to it, but he had been spared. Only God had the power to do something like that. God had saved him for a purpose. He didn't know yet what the purpose was, but strength and prayer would lead him there in God's own time.

People came around distributing Bibles to the men in the hospital. Roger was happy to see them—his own had been lost in the jungle. He had a dream once of it taking root, fertilized by the essence of his buddies, and converting the Communists by the miracle of itself. Roger knew how silly that was as soon as he awoke. He was alive. How many miracles did he want?

In any case, he had a Bible, and he read it, and in *Exodus*, he saw it. The Lord sent the Angel of Death among the Egyptians and took the firstborn son of each household. And he saw more. The Angel of Death visited not only the Egyptians, but the Philistines, and others. Individuals as well as groups. *Every individual, in fact.*

Some background material reminded Roger that in non-Biblical Hebrew (and Islamic) lore, the name of the Angel of Death was *Azrael*. "Help of the Lord," it meant. It was Azrael who greeted each soul as it left the body and escorted it to Judgment. And it was Azrael who was sent to perform the merciful harvest of souls when God's great Plan said they were ripe. Roger did not believe that the firstborn of Egypt suffered when Azrael called. That would be cruel, and God was Good. They had simply been taken to a better life, perhaps Heaven itself, even though they were not of the Chosen.

Death today was so cruel.

And then he knew why God had spared him.

Will had prepared the way, with his talk about money being spent to get people killed, and the inevitability of death in those circumstances.

It was a truth so blazingly obvious that Roger had almost been blinded by the realization of it: *When someone is so determined to have someone dead that he is willing to sacrifice money and his immortal soul to see it done, the death in question is part of God's plan for us, and is therefore inevitable.*

What was needed, then, was someone who *understood* this, who treated it as the holy mission it was. Who executed the Will of the Lord with compassion and mercy. Who delivered the soul into the Hand of the Lord without suffering and without judgment.

"That ye be not judged," Roger whispered.

What was needed was a modern avatar of Azrael.

And he had been chosen.

He would accept the honor, but not in his own name. When he was released from the hospital, he went to Chicago, to the Bureau of Records. He knew Will's birthdate, he knew his father's and mother's names; it was easy to get a certified copy of Will's birth certificate. He became Will Nelson.

Roger stole nothing from his only friend's life but his identity. He did not try to get transfer credit from Will's old college when he enrolled in a different school. He didn't even use his friend's high school record—he told the admissions officer the transcripts had been lost and took a battery of tests to make up for their absence.

He kept to himself, pretty much, except when he was cultivating the criminal element on campus—the drug dealers, the gamblers, the pimps. He made much of his Army training. He intimated he was insane and acted in a way to back up the claim. Soon, he was introduced to some of the big boys. He was offered a commission. There was a student, a distributor, who was skimming the profits. He was to be put in the hospital and taught a lesson.

"I'm not a teacher," the new Will Nelson said. "And I'm not in this business to leave witnesses."

The bravado impressed them, as he'd known it would. He was handed another commission, across the river in the next state, someone who had skimmed more deeply, and for a longer period of time, and who had already been warned once.

Azrael had paid him a visit. He had rendered the man unconscious with chloroform, then he'd done what he could to help him on his way before putting him in his garage with the motor running. The authorities said suicide, in fear of his associates. The job was done so smoothly, in fact, that even Roger's employer had his doubts. Roger convinced him, and his ministry was born.

He met Donna about the same time. Donna was a home ec major. Roger saw her as a tangible sign from the Lord that he was following the right path. She understood him, and she made him happy. Once he met her, he was never lonely again. And she was a good woman, a wise woman. She was good enough so that when Will (for he was coming to think of himself now as Will—he was Roger to himself only while engaged in Azrael's work) had to leave campus over a weekend on one of his increasingly frequent business trips, he never wasted a fraction of a second worrying about her. She was wise enough to know she never had to waste any time worrying about him, either. By the end of sophomore year, they were engaged.

Before long, he started working for the Russians. He wasn't sure how they learned about him. He suspected that someone in the drug business was working for them. He suspected, in fact, that the Russians had a *lot* to do with the drug business, that they thought by pouring poison into America, they could weaken and destroy her.

It was this kind of situation that gave the new Will Nelson an occasional small glimpse of the machinery of God's plan. Will felt sure that just as one of the effects of pesticides was the breeding of super bugs, the ultimate effect of the flood of drugs would be to breed super Americans, by killing off the morally weak, the foolish, the self-hating.

So Roger worked for the Russians, through college, the seminary, and all during his open ministry as substitute pastor for churches all over the country. They paid well, better than the criminals did, and every time Will wrote out a check for his tithe, it amused him to think the Communists were underwriting so much of God's work in America.

It was a good life, and a fill-in pastor had a lot of free time to enjoy it. It gave him more time, too, to do his hidden work.

This particular assignment had posed certain problems. It would involve his being on the scene for several months, perhaps longer. Control had told him it could be as much as a year. How could he arrange to get Mr. Nethercott out of the way that long? Will didn't think it was in the Plan for him to be killed. If it was, it hadn't been revealed yet to the Reverend Will Nelson. Will had used some of his extra time to examine the whole situation, Mr. Nethercott and his family. He found out that Mr. Nethercott's son had been selling cocaine at a ski resort. It occurred to him to tip off the local police and get the boy arrested, but that was chancy. Would Mr. Nethercott take a leave of absence to see the boy through the trial? Would he disown him? Or something in between? Will did something he rarely did and discussed the situation with Control, which (he presumed) had led to the boy's horrible skiing accident, which had lured Mr. Nethercott away for months to stay at his bedside.

Lord, they were ruthless. It was that kind of ruthlessness that relieved Will's conscience about using them, fooling them into helping God with the Plan.

This had been, he decided, his best mission ever. Usually, to the extent someone honored by being allowed to go about the Lord's business could, he felt sad. He was always sending to judgment filthy, corrupted souls who had no chance to repent and make amends for their wrongs. He did what he could for them, but the Lord was a stern judge.

But in Kirkester, the joy of serving the Lord was magnified by the knowledge that Azrael had been summoning souls destined directly for Heaven (the two children; Hannah Stein in the first grace of her Conversion). Even the young man under the car was the most venial of sinners. The only soul he was sure he'd consigned to hell was that of Smolinski, who was a spy, a traitor, and a murderer.

Personally, then, he was pleased with his work. Control seemed anxious over the larger operation (it had something to do with Jimmy's mother, but Will didn't know exactly what), but that concerned him not at all. If the plotters of the Kremlin were finding themselves in difficulties, it could only be because they were being thwarted by a Plotter greater than they could ever be.

"Is that all?" he asked the transmitter.

"You confirm your mission accomplished? Without complication?"

"Any complications were added later. You insult my competence."

"My apologies."

Will smiled. He would have thought the roughly accented voice that spoke to him at times like this would have choked over an apology, but the man had gotten the words out almost as if he meant them.

"Your apologies are accepted."

"Thank you. Hold yourself in readiness."

"I am always ready." Will said it proudly. He was doing the Lord's work. He *had* to be ready.

"Again, my apologies." He was getting positively good at it, Will thought. "I may contact you again as soon as this evening, your time."

"I'll make it a point to be here."

"The mother has at last promised to cooperate."

"I don't know what you're talking about."

"You know more than you show." It sounded, amazingly, as though Control were talking through a smile. "The mother," he said again, "has promised to cooperate. If she reneges, the son will pay."

"I will be ready," Will assured him. They broke transmission. Carefully (he did everything carefully) he put the radio back in its hiding place.

He went downstairs to the church itself. He knelt at the altar and said a prayer of thanksgiving. Jimmy was such a *good* young man, caring and God-fearing. The Lord would surely forgive the anger and hate he felt after the loss of the girl he loved. When Azrael called on him, he would do it with more joy than ever. Not only would he be sending another good soul to its reward in Heaven, he would be reuniting Jimmy with his lost love.

The knowledge that he was the instrument the Lord had chosen to bring this about filled him like a cloud of light, and he bowed his head and was humble before the Lord.

# CHAPTER TWO

It was two o'clock in the afternoon when Allan came to get her. If she'd known he was coming, she wouldn't have bothered choking down another god-awful hospital lunch.

It was miserable to be in the hospital, especially when you weren't very sick. It was even worse when you were hiding out at the behest of the FBI (or whatever) and you couldn't have any visitors or phone calls.

The minute she saw Allan, she sprang out of bed and went to the closet where she kept her things. She paused with her hand on the handle and looked at him, but he just raised his eyebrows as if he were wondering what the problem was.

She told him. "You are really springing me, right? You didn't bring flowers, so I figured it isn't just a visit. Unless you're not the type to bring flowers."

"I'm the type. Too many women I know wind up in hospitals."

Regina realized that that didn't really answer her question, but she decided to pretend it did. She slid back the door and got her things.

"The nurses are just going to let you sit here and watch me dress?"

"They don't know you're leaving. Do you mind?"

"I don't mind."

"You could always draw the curtain."

"It's a little late for that," she said, and pulled her hospital gown up over her head. She felt ridiculously happy, even happier when she saw that someone had seen to it that her clothes got washed. She smelled her dress, like an actress in a fabric softener commercial, then threw it on the bed. The other night, he'd screwed her brains out, then told her it was good to be alive. Fear was misery, but having it relieved was an incredible high. Incredible. She'd never felt like this.

"Have we ever done it in the daytime?" she asked him.

He smiled at her, a knowing smile that said he'd seen this kind of reaction before, not that Regina cared. For her it was brand-new, and she was going to enjoy it.

"No," Allan said. "Usually we're working in the daytime."

She looked pointedly at the bed and wiggled her eyebrows. It was the kind of impulse that is succeeded almost before it's over by the suspicion that you have just made an incredible ass of yourself. Regina had thought she'd trained herself out of them.

Fortunately, Allan took it the right way, laughing and shaking his head regretfully. "We're working this afternoon, too," he said.

"I thought the coast was clear."

"It's not that the coast is clear; it's that we've finally got as many ships in the water as they do."

Regina found her bra and shrugged into it. "Fasten me up?" she asked brightly. She came over to where he sat, and he did it. "You've had practice," she said.

"How do women do this when they're by themselves? Are you all double-joined, or what?"

"Not me. I put it on backward, then twist it around."

"That must be fun to watch." He kissed her back softly, then put his hands on her hips and turned her around.

"This is going to be a tough afternoon, Bash. Are you okay?"

She was thinking that Allan was the only person besides her father who could call her by that silly nickname without her resenting it, but she said, "My shoulder still hurts, Mr. Macho. Can't you see the bruise?"

"I'm sorry about that, but that's not what I meant. Can you face something unpleasant this afternoon?"

"How unpleasant?"

"Rotten."

"Allan," she said. "Darling. After our little impromptu submarine ride, I think I'm ready. We're not going back in the river, are we?" That last wasn't banter. It came to her that he was perfectly capable of it.

"No," he said. "This could be worse than going back in the river."

"Not if you're claustrophobic," she said with feeling.

"Well, your claustrophobia is safe, I can say that much." He kissed her belly, stroked her bottom. "Come on, get dressed before I like this too much."

There was a beige Ford van pulled up at the main entrance of the hospital as they left. "That's for us," Allan aid. The side door slid open, and Allan helped her inside, assisted by a black man.

"I know you," she said. "You're the fellow we did the article about. Mr. Albright."

"Call me Joe," he told her.

"Or Special Agent Albright," said a voice from the front seat. Fenton Rines.

Allan climbed in and closed the door behind him. Regina

looked at him and said, "I see what you mean about having a lot of ships in the water."

Allan smiled at her, got her seated in one of the swivel chairs, took one himself, then asked Special Agent Albright if he had everything. Albright wiggled a pen in front of his face like Groucho Marx and said, "I've never had any complaints so far."

Rines made a noise. "This country is in a lot of trouble."

"I guess this is the payoff," Regina murmured. Allan had his head down in a folder, looking at documents with TOP SECRET all over them, and didn't hear her.

She nudged him. "Is it?"

"What? Oh, no. Rines is just a tight ass."

"I'm not talking about jokes! I asked if this is the payoff."

"Sorry. Sort of."

"What do you mean, sort of?"

"This is where we talk to your mother about what's been troubling her—"

"You found out?"

Allan went on as if she hadn't said anything. "—and what we think she ought to do about it."

"Are you telling me you can *fix* it?"

"We can make it stop," Allan said. He spun his chair around and took her hand. "Look, Ba—Regina, I mean—I told you this was going to be tough. You're going to find out some things about your mother you would prefer not to know."

"Why are you building up the suspense? I'm a newsperson, remember? Inverted pyramid. Give me the biggest news first."

"No," Allan said.

"No? Why not? You can't make hints like that and then not tell me."

"If you hear it from me, you won't believe it."

"Who am I going to hear it from, then?"

"Your mother." He gave her hand a squeeze, turned the chair around, and spoke to Rines. "You have any trouble getting these things out of the old man's files?"

"Hell, no," Rines said. "I keep telling you, I'm the Lord's anointed."

"Wait a minute!" Regina demanded. "*What* is my mother going to tell me?"

"You'll hear it," Allan assured her. He went on before she could give him her opinion of him. "If I tell you, you'll call me a liar. If I could have arranged things so that you never found out, I would have. But it's rare when you can do what you want to in my business. Now leave it alone."

Regina had principles about taking orders from men, but Allan

Trotter had been kicking dents in them since she first met him. She resented it, but when he had that burning-dead look in his eyes, she didn't think there was anybody, woman or man, who would defy him without thinking it over very carefully.

Still, she wasn't going to let him shut her up completely. "What do you mean, 'sort of'?"

"As I said, it's rare when you can do what you want to do. I wanted to get the Russians off your mother's back—"

"It *is* the Russians, then."

"Oh, that's right, you doubted it, didn't you? Yeah, it's the Russians. We can get her clear of them. But I haven't been able to find Azrael."

"Who?"

"Exactly. The Angel of Death. The assassin. The slick bastard who killed Keith Smith and Lou Symczyk and Clara Bloyd and Hannah Stein and Wes Charles. That man, or woman, or team, has been just a little too good for us."

All trace of humor was gone from Joe Albright, now. "We don't even have a goddam corpus delecti, let alone a killer. Even if we knew who it was, he'd probably walk. Or she. Or they."

"You're thinking like a law officer, Joe."

"That's what I am."

"Not anymore. You're a soldier. A counterinsurgent. International power games leave no time for niceties."

"I'm not sure I like this," Albright said. "Nobody asked me if I wanted in on something like this."

"We were all drafted, Joe," Allan said.

Rines said, "You're talking in front of a reporter, you know." He sounded like someone remarking on the weather.

"I—I made a promise," Regina said. "I haven't forgotten."

"I wasn't worried," Allan said. Regina was not reassured. No matter what they felt for each other (and it was definitely *something*, though Regina knew by now it would take a lengthy essay to characterize exactly what), she knew that if the promise she had made to Rines somehow *did* slip her mind one day, she could very easily become one of the "niceties" there was no time for.

The van's dome light went on. Joe Albright said excuse me, reached across her, slid back a panel, and took out a telephone receiver. Looking at him, Regina thought that he made much more sense as a "Special Agent" than as a junk man. He seemed to be hating this as much as she was, but he grunted it down and did his job.

"Uh-huh," he told the phone. Rines probably would have said "Roger," or "Ten-four," or something equally official-sounding.

She had given up trying to predict what Allan would do in any situation whatsoever.

"Uh-huh," Albright said again. "Where is she? Okay. Got the place watched?"

Allan made a spiraling motion with his finger. Albright nodded. "Get the helicopter up, too," he told the phone. "We'll be there in less than ten minutes."

He put the phone back and slid the panel shut. "She left the office and went home."

"It figures," Allan said. "Now that she's capitulated, the pressure's off."

"She thinks," Rines says. "Does this change anything?"

"Makes it better for us. Oh, psychologically, it would probably be better inside the edifice she built with her own efforts. Remind her of what the Russians are trying to take away from her. But I don't think it'll make that much difference. She knows what she's accomplished. Besides, we'll get her away from the KGB mole in her organization."

"There's a KGB mole in the Hudson Group?"

"Of course there is," Allan said.

"Who? I know all those people! Who is it?"

"That's something else that's missing from the payoff."

"If you don't know who it is, how do you know there is one?"

"Because the Russians are vicious but not stupid. Look, you may take my personal word for it that there are CIA moles in *Pravda*, TASS, *Izvestia*, even *Krokodil*, and they have a lot less influence there than the major outlets do here. Do you seriously think the Russians are going to let the American press make plans unmonitored? Do you think they're going to let themselves be *surprised* by the American media?"

"Why doesn't somebody *find* them, expose them?"

"If the government exposes them, it's a witch-hunt," Rines said. "Anybody else is a crackpot."

"But if they get to be influential . . ."

Rines said, "Ha!"

"Don't listen to him, he's bitter. I wouldn't have it any other way. Freedoms are not free, and a certain amount of having our own shoelaces tied together is the price we pay for Freedom of the Press. It's worth it."

"The old man would wash your mouth out with soap," Rines said.

"I was practically quoting him," Allan retorted. "Besides, that's the reason we fight for this country. Where there's freedom, there's hope. Maybe someday, a reporter with enough brains, balls, guts, and perseverance will come along, find the bastards, and get it into the newspapers. I didn't say they *all* worked for the KGB, you know."

Regina asked him who the old man was, but he just smiled and said maybe he'd tell her someday, and went back to his papers.

Regina fell silent, half wishing she understood what the hell everybody was talking about, half fearing that the understanding would come all too soon.

# CHAPTER THREE

Trotter's emotions were always mixed by the time they got to this part of an operation. There was something liberating about having the masks off and the credentials flying. Rines hit the guard at the gate with the weight of the Federal government, left Albright with him to make sure he didn't phone the house, and the van sailed onto the grounds. It was signal for the gun lap of a race—strategy had (or had not) put you in the position you wanted to be in, but strategy was over. Now it was who was the fastest and the strongest. Now it was who wanted it most. Trotter liked that. It could be brutal, but in its way it was honest.

What he didn't like was the knowledge that even if everything worked out right, if he had been smarter and quicker and tougher, he still was a loser. Because no matter what, Allan Trotter could not be allowed to survive this mission. Too many people knew who and what Allan Trotter was for the Congressman's son to be able to afford to keep him around anymore. Already he felt the identity beginning to dry on him and crack like a snake's skin. The Congressman's son was ready to shed Allan Trotter, and with him, another year of his life. He was tired of it. A man reaching thirty should have *some* kind of past he was willing to claim. A childhood to look back on. An achievement he could tell people about.

Not him. If he lived through the next few days, he would soon be wearing another name, carrying a made-up past, facing an indifferent future.

The van stopped. Rines was saying something.

"I'm sorry, what did you say?"

Regina said, "He said it's not too late and are you sure you want to go through with this."

"That what you said?"

"That's what I said," Rines admitted.

"Did you talk to the President?"

"He talked to the *President* about this?" Regina said.

Rines ignored her. "Yes, I did."

"What did he say?" Trotter asked him.

"The *President*?"

"Yes, the President. Your mother is an important woman. You knew that when you went to Rines in the first place, so don't act as if you're finding it hard to believe now." He turned to the FBI man. "What did he say?"

"He left it up to me." Rines sounded miserable. "The old man had told him about me, by the way. He said I was the one on the scene, but he would back me all the way."

"Nice of him. But he thought it was a good idea, didn't he?"

"Yes, he thought it was a good idea, but what the hell does that mean? He doesn't know anything about this kind of work. When you discover an enemy operation in progress, you don't blow the whistle on it, dammit—blow the whistle, hell. You're talking about sirens. Bursting bombs and a symphony orchestra!"

"And the Mormon Tabernacle Choir," Trotter told him. "The bigger, the better."

"But if you take the enemy operation and *don't say anything*—"

"You can infiltrate and create disinformation and maybe double some of their people. That's what the book says. I know what's in the book. You may remember I learned the craft from one of the *authors* of the book."

"What's wrong with the book?" Rines demanded.

"Nothing's wrong with the book, as far as it goes."

"What does that mean?"

"It means, it only goes as far as *spies*. If the whole world were like Russia, there would never be any reason to go outside the book. Everything would be secret, we'd win a few, they'd win a few, and World War III would never happen, because we're all having so much fun."

"But?" Rines said.

"Didn't my father teach you anything?"

Regina said, "Your father?"

Trotter felt panic. He couldn't believe what he'd just done.

Rines saved his life. Without missing a beat, the acting head of the Agency said, "Code name, Miss Hudson. Please forget you heard it." To Trotter he said, "Yeah, he taught me a lot."

"Yeah," Trotter echoed. He was still catching his breath.

"Didn't he teach you the Russians absolutely cannot hurt us without our help? Didn't he tell you that all that bullshit about the people running things in this country is the truth?"

"I never doubted it."

"So all we have to do is give the people a decent chance to do the right thing."

"Granted. But why does that make this the only way to go?"

"Because we've got a chance to show the country what fucks we're up against. We'll have proof of their wrongdoing that does *not* involve an American traitor. And—and this is the most important part—we win a big one, and we let the public *know* we've won it."

"All right, you've got me convinced."

Trotter smiled. "Are you sure? I've got more if you're not."

"Guess who you remind me of," Rines growled, then smiled. "Like what?"

"Like we pull the plug on Cronus forevermore. They wouldn't dare try to use it again."

"What's Cronus, for God's sake?" Regina said.

"That, my dear, you will find out in a very few minutes." He took a deep breath, held it, then released it as a sigh. "Let's go inside."

A maid let them in. Rines waved the magic wallet, found out Mrs. Hudson was in the drawing room, then told the maid to go do the laundry or something.

"The laundry was done this morning, sir," she said.

"Then go polish the washing machine. You want to be out of earshot."

She looked at Regina, who said, "Go ahead, Wanda, it's all right," as though she really believed it. Wanda went.

Regina showed them the way to the drawing room. Trotter told her to wait outside with Rines and listen. Then he walked through an open archway into a beautiful, tasteful white room. Petra Hudson was looking out the window, absorbed, apparently, in the way the wind blew dead leaves across her tennis court.

"Mrs. Hudson?" he said.

She turned to him. Her head moved as slowly and heavily as the door of a bank vault.

"So it's you," she said. "I thought it might be."

"Did you?"

"It crossed my mind. I could see you weren't a fortune hunter, and you were too—what difference does it make?"

"I'm interested. Please go on. May I sit down?"

"As if I had the right to say no to you. All right, I'll go on. I suppose this is part of the punishment. You were too *calm*; you were too in control. My daughter is a very wealthy young woman, and I am"—she gave a little laugh—"I *was* very powerful in my own right. If you and Regina were truly in love, you would have felt at least a *little* nervous. Or, if you'd come from the kind of background that would have allowed you to handle the situation with ease, I would have heard of you."

She looked out the window again. "I tried to keep her away from you, but what could I do? I was trapped. There was no way out."

That was the most encouraging thing Trotter had heard all day. If she'd held out this long believing there was no way out, she'd fight like a tiger once he'd convinced her there was.

"You used my daughter dreadfully, didn't you?"

"I used her," Trotter admitted.

"She loved you. She may not have known it herself, but she loved you. Does that make you feel good?"

"You used her father. He undoubtedly loved you."

"I was following *orders!*"

"Of course you were. You, me, Eichmann, Lieutenant Calley . . ."

"Did you make her suffer before you killed her?"

"She didn't suffer," Trotter said.

Petra Hudson closed her eyes and took a breath. "Thank you. I'll give you that much. The ones you killed didn't suffer."

"No," Trotter said. "They didn't, did they?"

"Are you surprised about it? Didn't you mean it that way? Don't worry. You made the living suffer enough."

"You could have prevented it," he told her. "You could have prevented all of it."

"*Don't you think I know that?* Don't you think I lay awake at night thinking about it? Hating myself? Knowing I was inviting the day when the same thing would happen to my friends and my children?"

"It had to go pretty far before it affected you."

"You have no right to say that to me. You're the one who did the killing. Remember, young man, I had the same training you did; and mine was under *Borzov*. It takes a long time to get over expert training in ruthlessness."

"I guess a woman who would come to a foreign country, seduce a man and bear him children, knowing all the time they might be used as weapons against him, would have to be fairly ruthless."

She leaned forward, as though preparing to bite his throat. "*Yes, she would.*"

"Still, your part in Cronus died with your husband. What you

**174**

were asked to do was no more than your duty. Yet you let those people die rather than do it."

"I was trying to save my *own* life. Self-preservation is something else that dies hard."

"Your life was in no danger. As long as you do what you're told, you're in no danger now."

She looked disgusted; at him, at herself, at life in general. "You wouldn't understand."

"Try me."

"*I built something*! Damn you, *I* built something! I took over when James Hudson died and built that company! I built it to be strong, and honest. And because I *owned* it, I knew there would be no committee overseeing my decisions. I could appoint the best people to jobs they could do well—I didn't have to go out of my way to surround myself with incompetents so that I would shine by comparison. I was free to hire people who could do the job I needed them to do, without regard for their ideologies. I set the policy for the Hudson Group, but not for its employees. I was a free woman, leading free men and women, *and it worked!*"

"You became a capitalist."

"Yes, I did! Tell that to Borzov; tell it to the Chairman; release it on TASS! But you won't, of course. You wouldn't dare. The Americans are right, Mr. Trotter. You are wrong. When I think of the Russian people—"

"The Soviet people."

"The *Russian* people, damn you! When I think of the Russian people, their patriotism, their pride, and I think of what they could do if they were free, it makes my heart ache."

She looked at him. "What are you grinning at?"

"Until this very moment, you never looked Russian to me."

"You look it to me. That was something else that made me suspect you."

"My mother's side of the family is Russian." She turned away from him but he kept talking. "You hate me right now, don't you?"

"Forever," she said.

"And you hate Moscow."

"Yes."

"You'd fight back, if you could."

"When I was young, you made my life a mockery. I redeemed it, but now you have come to make it a mockery again. If I could, I would kill you all."

"Well, you can't kill them all."

"There is no need to tell me."

"But you can fight them."

"How could I fight you?"

"Not me, them."

"What—what are you talking about?"

"I'm on your side."

"Liar."

"I'm not the KGB man you were waiting for. I'm not KGB at all. I'm an American agent."

"*Liar!*"

"You may have heard of the Congressman?"

"No."

"The General, then." He was the General when she would have heard of him.

"He was a legend. Borzov himself respected him."

"That's who I work for. And I tell you this: You can fight them. And you can win. And you're going to."

"You've ruined everything! You've doomed my son, and me, and my life's work!"

"Not after we've beaten them. They wouldn't dare."

"You can't beat them."

"You're having a lot of trouble with your pronouns lately. Not me. You. It's so simple, you've probably never thought of it."

"It's insane!"

"You haven't even heard it yet."

"It's insane, whatever it is. And whatever it is, it won't bring my daughter back."

Trotter scratched his nose. "Well, that *I* can do." He looked over toward the archway. "You can come on in now, Bash."

# CHAPTER FOUR

"No! I won't! Let me go, damn you!" Regina's voice.

The woman known as Petra Hudson had been a regular churchgoer since the early 1950s (because James Hudson was, and it was her mission to be perfect for him) but only now did she feel there might be any reality to the concept of a merciful God. Her daughter was alive. Somehow, the men in Moscow had become convinced she was dead, and at death, they were experts. Petra Hudson did not deserve to have her daughter alive. But here she was.

"Just let her see you." This was a man's voice Petra Hudson didn't recognize.

"I don't want to see her."

"Then close your eyes. Come on, you started this, honey. Am I going to have to carry you?"

Since Trotter had come into the room, Petra Hudson had been shooting emotions like drugs. Surprise to find him there at all. Hatred of him. Defiance. Disbelief when he told her who he was and that her situation wasn't hopeless. Shock at learning Regina was alive. Relief. Guilt. It had left her numb. Only two coherent thoughts could fight their way to her consciousness: *I don't blame her for not wanting to see me* and *How could it possibly be her fault?*

She had no time to wonder about it, because Regina was standing there. She didn't have her eyes closed; she couldn't have closed them if she'd wanted to. The loathing pouring out of them would have burned her eyelids off.

"Regina," she said.

She turned to the white-haired man with her. "She's seen me. Can I leave now?"

"You keep a room here," Trotter said. "Wait there."

"I'm never spending another minute under this roof."

"Regina, darling." Petra Hudson was almost startled at the sound of her own voice. She had never had to beg before. She was never so far out of control of things that begging was relevant. She'd known it would be like this. Her life, her life's work (which was the same thing), the respect of her children, or their lives. As soon as the messages began, she had known she was going to lose them. She realized now that she had defied Moscow because something in her thought it could deal with *losing* Regina or Jimmy more easily than it could with their rejecting her. A selfish part of her. A stupid part.

"Regina, please," she said again. "I—I didn't know what to do. You couldn't have wanted me to give *in* to them."

"You betrayed them, too. You betray everybody. Them, America, Daddy. And Jimmy, me—you betrayed us the minute you *conceived* us! How could you—"

"That's enough," Trotter said.

Regina turned on him without bothering to stop the loathing. "You had me dragged in here, damn you."

Trotter's voice stayed low. "No, damn you, you had *me* dragged in here. If you don't want to see little white crawly things, don't ask someone to turn over a rock."

"But I never knew—"

"Well, you sure know now. You went to Washington asking people to help your mother. Turns out she needs it more, and maybe deserves it less than you had in mind. Too bad. We're not going to shoot her because you changed your mind. This is the big leagues, Bash. It hurts when you get beaned."

He didn't wait for an answer. He spoke to the white-haired man. "Take her to her room, okay? Then get Albright up here to baby-sit her."

Petra Hudson had given enough orders to know that the white-haired man didn't especially enjoy Trotter's sending him away, but all he said was, "Right. I'll be right back."

When they were gone, Trotter went back to his chair and sat. He gestured for her to sit, too.

"All right," he said. "Are you ready to talk strategy, or do you have to cry or something first?"

"Do you have to enjoy this so much, Mr. Trotter?"

Trotter said, "Who, me?" but pain crossed his face.

"It doesn't matter. I did all my crying when they first told me to hold myself ready to run the Hudson Group the way they told me to. I knew all this would happen."

"You didn't know your daughter would happen."

"No. No. I thought they would kill her. She found you in Washington?"

"She found someone who found me. She was worried about you. She idolizes you."

"Nonsense."

"Don't tell me nonsense. She does."

Petra Hudson took a deep breath. The world didn't hold enough air. "Well, she doesn't now, does she? Mr. Trotter, never put yourself in a situation where there's nothing you can do."

"You could have done what your daughter did."

"Come to you? I may not be much of a mother, but I'm not a fool."

"We had to sit around letting people die, letting the Russians put enough pressure on you until you were ready to break. If you'd come to us, we could have devoted our time to catching this bastard who's been killing children in your town."

"She'll never forgive me for letting those people die."

"Stop feeling sorry for yourself. Let's talk about how we're going to save the Hudson Group for you."

"Save it for you, you mean. Instead of planting articles and editorials for the KGB, I'll be planting them for the CIA. It doesn't matter if the strings go to Moscow or Washington, Mr. Trotter. I'm still a puppet."

"No, I've got that one covered, too."

"Oh," she said. The sarcasm was fueled by exasperation. This young man had all the answers. "What are you going to do? Submit to brain surgery? All of you who know my secret, you're going to have the cells that store the knowledge removed, how nice."

"No surgery. And again, I'm not the one who's going to do it. You are. You're going to make it impossible for anyone, from any country, to blackmail you over this."

"And save me from the Russians?"

"That's right."

"Very simply, I ask you, how?"

"It is simple. Two words."

"Yes?"

"Go public."

"Go *what?*"

"Public. Go public. You own a big whistle. Blow it."

"On myself?"

"On the KGB slave masters who deceived you into coming to America as a spy and who would not let the past die."

"And go to jail for the rest of my life."

"Aside from coming into the United States under false pretenses, have you ever committed a felony?"

She knew why he asked. Part of the training for the Cronus Project had been in various ways to dispose of rivals, ranging from gossip to murder. Murder was recommended—that way the rival would have no chances to win the man back. "No," she said. "Fortunately, James was a bachelor."

"Okay. Did you in fact ever do any spying for Borzov? Or anybody?"

"No. They tried to keep contact with the Cronus operatives to a minimum. I never heard from them until—until all this started. Sometimes . . ." She closed her eyes. "Sometimes I could forget all about it."

"You committed no crimes; you did no spying. You are the mother of two American citizens. Your charity work is legendary. You're a major employer. You have tried to put the past behind you, make it up to America for deceiving her that one time, so long ago, though you had no choice at the time but to do it or be killed."

"You sound like a press release."

"Just trying to channel your thinking in the right direction. You are a heroine. Lots of Americans work their way up from nothing—you worked your way up from minus one thousand. You built an important business and did great American things, all the while looking over your shoulder for the KGB.

"And something else, the most important thing from my point of view. You will tell them about the Cronus Project. I'll back you up with all the documentation we've got."

"How much have you got?" Impossible. It was ridiculously impossible. But there was something about this young man that made you forget you had already reached decisions other than the ones he wanted you to make.

"A decent amount. Enough to make somebody with an open mind think. Enough to make most of the op-ed regulars at certain non-Hudson Group newspapers purple in the face trying to deny it. You'll hold press conferences. You'll testify before Congress. You are a very persuasive woman, and it will only help that you'll be telling the truth. The idea is to let people know, the way you know, what we're up against. You'll make them look bad."

"And what about when someone asks me about letting innocent people die because I didn't do anything about it? How will that make me look?"

Trotter raised his eyebrows. "Look, Mrs. Hudson, I know you've been through a lot here, but you don't want to lose your journalistic instincts entirely. They won't ask you."

"They won't? Why not?"

"Because Borzov has outsmarted himself, him and his ace assassin. *All those deaths were accidents or suicides.* All anybody has to do is check the police reports. Sadness over the deaths, and the realization that nobody's children were safe, even without the KGB in the picture, has given you the courage to make your confession, but implications of anything else are cruel to all concerned."

Petra Hudson was surprised to hear herself laugh.

"What's so funny?" Trotter demanded.

"You said it would be easier because I would be telling the truth."

"You'll be telling the truth about everything important. The situation you were in, the fear for your children. You'll be telling the truth about Cronus."

"If I go along with this—"

"Go along with this? This is Christmas morning for you, Mrs. Hudson."

"Perhaps I'm ungrateful. It is a better offer than I've had from Moscow, and I suspect I have as little choice in the matter. Very well, *when* I go along with this, of course I'll tell the truth about Cronus. How I was mad to agree to it; how a man, or a woman without a child, can never know the sheer inhumanity of it. But with everything involved here, why is the exposure of Cronus in particular of so much importance to *you*?"

He showed her a twisted grin. "If I ever own a newspaper, maybe I'll go public, too."

# PART SEVEN

## CHAPTER ONE

So here I am again, Regina thought. Sitting in Mother's chair, at Mother's desk. Where she had been when Cronus had come into her life, bringing in its wake the trip to Washington, and Mr. Allan Trotter, and the KGB, and the bottom of the Kirk River, and a killer called Azrael who left no traces.

And the truth about Mother. Almost a full day later, and Regina still couldn't formulate a coherent thought about it. Mother wasn't Mother—well, she was, but she was more—and what that "more" was was a lie—but she's still the woman who tucked me in at night and taught me . . .

The thoughts went round and round, going nowhere, ending only in shudders or tears.

She looked at the beige phone on the desk as though it were a reptile that could bite her. Since she touched it last time, she'd been scrambling desperately for footing on the glare-ice surface of the Cold War. With, she decided, a pronounced lack of success. She kept getting these little shoves. The death of her brother's fiancée and Mr. Charles. The fact that her own existence was the result of a Russian plot. Falling for Allan Trotter.

Damn him, anyway. Who the hell did he think he was? She

thought about that for a second and decided she didn't care to know the answer. It was more relevant to ask, what the hell was he up to?

Because this was his doing, her being here today. He'd choreographed the whole business, though the public would never hear his name in connection with it. He'd somehow gotten Mother to put herself on display; he'd told Jimmy the news when he'd come home, speaking gently, like a big brother. Nothing like the macho professional act he'd put on for her, slapping her with words after the worst shock she'd ever gotten in her life.

Not that it had done any good. Jimmy had dissolved into instant hysterics, directed at Trotter. He hadn't made a lot of sense, but Regina had gotten the idea that Jimmy hated Trotter for trying to get him to believe that Hannah, one of the two most wonderful women in the world, was dead because of the actions of his mother, the other one.

Regina, who had been escorted (dragged) from her room by Albright, just so she could be there for the show, envied her brother's strategy. He latched on to one small part of what they were trying to tell him, refused to believe it, and never even let on he'd *heard* anything else. Of course, he hadn't had the disadvantage of hearing it from Mother's own mouth during a time she had no conceivable reason to be lying.

And that, she thought suddenly, was undoubtedly the reason he'd set things up that way. So she'd have no *choice* but to believe it. He'd let Jimmy fool himself, the bastard, but *she* had to take it right between the eyes. She almost wished Jimmy had killed Trotter when he went for him. He had certainly wanted to, and he ran at the young man from Washington with such rage, Regina had screamed in spite of herself.

And once again, she felt like a fool. Because she should have known that her brother had as much chance against someone like Allan Trotter as he would against a flamethrower. Even less. Because Trotter ducked one fist, and took hold of Jimmy in such a way that he was as helpless as a quadriplegic. Trotter had just held him there until Jimmy had cried all the violence out of himself and collapsed. They got a doctor in for him, then put him to bed.

Jimmy was still in bed, but he was here now, in the family suite on top of Hudson Group headquarters. Mr. Trotter had decided (or had planned all along) to move everyone here for "the duration." Safer, he said.

Regina had made the mistake of asking him for the duration of what.

He smiled at her and worked whatever sneaky spell it was he

had over her, and the next thing she knew, she was sitting at this desk.

This time, she wasn't just watching the phone. (She looked at it again—it sat there silent and treacherous.) She was, for the next few days at least, the Publisher of *Worldwatch* magazine. The place was in a quiet frenzy—the magazine was being remade, but only a handful of people knew exactly into what. For instance, Regina had told the Art Department that her mother's picture would be on the cover, but not why. Makeup was junking articles left and right, making a sixteen-page hole to be filled at the last minute. The special edition of the magazine went to bed tonight, hit the printing plant tomorrow afternoon. What Regina had found herself in charge of was doing almost a whole new issue in one day, an issue that would make the scrutiny she'd received as the daughter of a mere rich and powerful woman seem like indifference by comparison. Trust Allan to put her on a spot like this.

This kind of madness had happened before—disasters, assassination attempts, things like that. The difference was that at those times, everybody *knew* what the urgency was about. This time they could only guess, wondering at the same time why the place was lousy with polite and helpful, but absolutely taciturn, FBI agents.

The people at *Worldwatch* were experienced and better than competent. They were getting the job done, but there were still a million decisions the Acting Publisher had to make. The intercom (*not* the telephone, thank God) had gotten so much use, it was hot to the touch. It was only quiet now because Regina had asked for a moratorium. She had to concentrate, she said, on writing the Letter from the Publisher. And what the hell was she supposed to say? Regina thought of changing her name and running away.

And while she couldn't formulate a comprehensible opinion about her mother, she knew for certain she didn't envy her at this moment. Petra Hudson had spent hours past, and would spend hours more, spilling her insides for selected employees. The reporters, writers, and researchers were told to treat this like any other story; to scoop up the woman's guts and serve them up still steaming on the pages of her own creation.

It was all happening *too fast.* She needed to talk to somebody, but when she tried to think of someone she could talk to, the only one she came up with was Allan. And to hell with him.

All she could do was lose herself in the work. God knew there was enough of it. She cranked a fresh sheet of paper into the typewriter. Maybe she'd take a page from Mother's book and spill her own guts, tell the world how she was feeling.

She took a deep breath and hit the keys. What the hell, she thought as she felt a smile twist her lips. At least we're going to sell a *lot* of magazines.

# CHAPTER TWO

Elizabeth June Piluski began to cry when the Reverend Mr. Will Nelson poured the water on her head. Tina Bloyd shushed her gently and stroked the baby's golden fuzz with one finger of the brown hand that supported her head. Elizabeth June stopped in mid-bleat and started to coo.

Mr. Nelson was saying prayers, and Tina was answering on the baby's behalf, and grandparents and friends were standing around being proud.

Joe Albright was as proud as any of them. After all her doubts, Tina was terrific. She was a natural with babies. She even seemed happy. Things had been so busy, Joe had been afraid he wouldn't be able to get away from the Hudson Group in time to keep his promise to be at Tina's side. Ordinarily, Joe could get so wrapped up in his work, he could forget private-life promises he'd made to *anybody*. There was, for instance, a famous birthday his mother would never let him hear the end of. But something in him was extremely resistant to the idea of breaking his promise to Tina, and he was glad when Rines and Trotter had let him out of there in time.

Trotter, in fact, had done more than let him go—he had come with him. He was here now, sitting in the back of the church, though God alone knew what he was waiting for. Somehow, Joe doubted he was praying.

It might be, Joe thought, that Trotter was having woman troubles of his own. Rines had told him how Trotter had dressed Regina Hudson down last night; Joe had heard her sobs for himself while he was guarding her room.

Joe had had his suspicions about this one from the beginning. Meeting Miss Hudson yesterday had clinched it. These two were strips of Velcro—get them anywhere near each other and they'd get tangled together so tight it would take a real effort to pull them apart. That they were apart at all came from fear. She was scared shitless of him (for which Joe couldn't entirely blame her), and he was scared to death he was losing his edge, going soft in some kind of extremely youthful old age.

Joe was sorry for the girl—Trotter was a lot of things, but Joe doubted he'd be much good at spreading happiness—but it was interesting to see Trotter going through this. It proved that he was at least a little bit human.

Joe was a lot more human. Now that (in Trotter's words) the masks were off, he had been scared about how Tina would react when she found out the Salvage/Reclamation business was not his true calling. He'd told her this morning when he'd come to pick her up.

"The FBI?" she had said. "No kidding?"

He showed her his credentials.

Tina had packed a lot of living into the last few years, and it was easy to forget she wasn't too far out of her teens. That she'd get bowled over by something like this.

"The FBI," she said, "wow. I knew you weren't any junk man."

It was better than the hostility he'd been expecting, but Joe felt obliged to defend his former work. "Salvage/Reclamation," he told her. "It's honest work."

"Of course it is. I just—you always seemed to me like somebody who'd do something important. What are you—no, I can't ask you what you're working on."

No, Joe thought, you most certainly cannot. Masks might have been off (although he doubted that Trotter's own mask ever came off, unless he had layers of them, an onion-head of masks that got you no closer to the real him no matter how deep you cut into him), but they weren't revealing *everything*. Now that he was more than just an FBI man, it was okay to tell her he was an FBI man. It was definitely not okay to let her know what they'd made him now. He didn't know the words for it, anyway.

He didn't want to lie to her. Instead, he told her a misleading truth. "I usually work drug cases."

"I knew it was important. I suppose when you're done here, you'll go back to wherever . . ."

"Portland. Oregon, not Maine." He smiled with delight as he saw the sadness on her face. "But I doubt I'll be going back there. I think I'm about to be transferred East." Probably Washington. Now that he knew so much about this goddam Agency, he was sure Rines would keep him close. "I'm a licensed pilot," he went on. "I'll be able to get up here whenever I've got time off. If you want to see me, that is."

"Joe," she said. "You're smart, but you're *dumb*."

"How's that?"

"Of *course* I want to see you. You saved my life. You and Mr. Nelson. When my baby died, I was ready to give up, kill myself, or go back to what I was, which would only be killing myself slowly. Mr. Nelson kept me keeping on long enough for you to show up."

He started to say something, but she cut him off. "Let me go on, Joe. I'm not putting pressure on you. I'm not dumping responsibility for the whole rest of my life on you. But whatever happens from now on, you came along at the worst time of a not very good life and made me happy. And now that I know that's possible, I'll never get so far down again."

"I've been making me happy too," he told her. He looked at his watch. "Hey, we'd better go get that baby baptized."

Now the baby *was* baptized; Mr. Nelson said something about everlasting life, and a bunch of people said amen, and it was over. There were smiles all around, and the mother insisted Tina carry the baby from the church. Good luck or something.

Joe followed, still happy, still proud. Then he saw Trotter, in the last pew. Joe's first reaction was irritation. What is he still here for, are we Siamese twins, or what? Then he got a good look at Trotter's face.

It struck Joe that he may have been wrong before. This could be what Trotter looked like under the last mask. It was not pleasant to see. Trotter had the staring eyes and slack jaw of a man who has slipped with a saw and is now looking at pieces of his body on the ground.

He was going to say something, but Trotter pulled himself together enough to give Joe an angry look and shake his head no.

All right, Joe thought. Be that way. He caught up with the woman he loved and her goddaughter and helped them down the steps of the Northside Church.

# CHAPTER THREE

Trotter was a monster, conceived in cold blood and dedicated to cold war. He accepted it; he didn't like it. He knew it was part of what made his father value his services so highly. The Cronus Project, for instance. The idea of recruiting a woman to bear and

186

raise a child as a pawn to be sacrificed was so monstrous, no one but a monster could have figured it out. The fact that he was not alone, that the people who came up with the plan and those who carried it out were monsters, too, was not a comfort.

But if Cronus had been bad, what he'd been thinking of since he'd seen the water hit the brow of Elizabeth June Piluski was a nightmare. After all he'd seen in his life he still had trouble bringing himself to believe it. All but two of them. He could be sure of all but two. Louis Symczyk was uncheckable, but possible. The police reports Trotter had been getting clandestinely had included photographs showing a sink in the garage. But the other one, the baby . . .

Trotter crashed the christening party. It was easy enough—people were coming and going all the time, all he had to do was walk through the door with a smile on his face. He didn't know how he was going to find out what he wanted to know without causing mass hysteria, or even if he needed to know so badly he didn't care what happened. He just knew he needed that fact. Not for proof. It wouldn't *prove* anything. Trotter just wanted something to confirm him in his belief of something he hated believing in.

A man with his tie loose and his shirt sleeves rolled up stood behind a makeshift bar and insisted Trotter have a drink. Trotter took it, got out of the man's sight, and put it down. He walked around from room to room, smiling, agreeing that the baby, at whom he had yet to get a good look, *was* the cutest little thing in the world—and looking for Joe Albright.

Or Tina Bloyd. Trotter did not want to spring this on Tina without Joe's being there, but he had a strong suspicion he'd do it anyway, if he got the chance.

He didn't have to worry. He was making a second circuit of the ground floor when he saw Albright coming down the stairs. Joe did not look as happy as a man who'd been given a day off in the middle of an important operation usually did.

Trotter caught him at the bottom of the stairs. "What's the matter, Joe?"

Albright looked at him with equal proportions of irritation and surprise. "What the hell are *you* doing here?"

"Confirmation," Trotter said.

Albright smiled in spite of himself. "You mean baptism."

"That too. What say we take a walk?"

"Okay, but not too far. Or if you're really dragging me off, I'd better tell Tina."

"A short walk will do it." They went back out into the early-afternoon chill.

"Which way?" Albright asked.

"Toward the school. At least we'll have the wind at our backs."

"It'll be in our faces coming back," Albright said, but he went along.

It wasn't a bad walk, as far as walking went. The dryness of the air the last few days had gotten rid of the snow without putting the town through slush and mud. The sky was bright blue, and the wind sent dry leaves all around them, scratching secrets on the pavement as they walked.

They walked a block and a half in silence. Finally, Joe Albright said, "You want to talk, or is this just a sight-seeing trip?"

Trotter kept walking with his head down, watching leaves. "In my whole life," he said, "there is only one person I've ever asked the permission of to do anything, and you are not him."

"No," Joe said. "I suppose this Congressman you and Rines can't keep yourselves from talking about is him. God knows you don't care what Rines says. What about it?"

"I'm asking you. Now."

"What is this, a test? You should have sprung your goddam tests before you let me know all this secret bullshit."

"I've got to talk to Tina Bloyd about her baby's death."

Joe stopped in his tracks. "And you're asking my permission?"

"I guess I am."

"Then, no way."

"Joe—"

"You giving orders now? I'm not saying I'll follow them if you give them, but if it's on a permission basis, then no. That woman got through a tough day, but she fell apart at the party, just went to pieces. I'd just come downstairs from getting her to lie down. Doctor who delivered the Piluski kid was there, fortunately. He got his bag from his car and gave her a tranquilizer. I'm not going to go getting her all upset again."

"One question. All I need is the answer to one question."

"You go to hell, Trotter. I've seen you Agency people in operation, now, so don't try to jive me with this 'permission' crap. If you want to ask her a question—under drugs or torture, even— you'll do it. But you will never, *never*, you motherfucker, get me to say it's okay. If that's the test, I flunk. Have me shot."

"Then you ask her."

"Are you crazy? This is a woman trying to stay *sane*, and I happen to be in love with her."

"Other people's kids died, too. With more still on the menu, maybe. Can't you just ask her one thing."

"Let's hear it."

"Ask her if the kid's hair was wet."

Albright started to laugh. He laughed aloud. Cars passing by in the street slowed down to try to see what the big black guy was laughing at.

"Hey," Trotter said. "I may not be proud of it, but I don't think it's *funny*."

"You will in a second," Albright promised. With an effort, he stopped laughing and caught his breath.

"Trotter," he said, "you have to be the smartest son of a bitch alive. Or the luckiest."

"I don't feel like either at the moment."

"You won't have to ask your question."

"You know the answer?"

"I do. And I'm probably the only one who does. They got back to the house after the christening, and the baby was asleep. They put her in the crib, but when the guests started showing up, of course they all had to see how cute she was, so they trooped through there in shifts. It got to the point where there were so many, Tina was taking them through as well as Sharon. One time, she came out shaking like a dog shitting peach pits. I asked her what the matter was, and she said the baby was going to die. She was really upset about it. I kept her from making a scene, got her into the john with the doctor—it was the only place we could have a little privacy. He said she was just overexcited, gave her the shot, and told me to put her to bed.

"The shot took awhile to work, so I waited with her upstairs. I got tired of telling her the doctor said the kid was just fine, so finally I asked her why she thought the baby was in danger. Guess what she told me?"

"I'm not in this for the fucking suspense, Joe. What?"

"Because little Elizabeth had drooled, the way babies do, and there was a big wet spot near her mouth. I told her all babies drool, but she wouldn't hear it. She said babies must drool in their sleep before they die, because when she found her Clara, there was a big wet spot on the sheet all around her head. It had almost dried, but it was still there."

"That's it, then," Trotter said. "Where's a phone?"

"Back at the party, I guess. I don't remember passing any en route."

"Then maybe a store or—wait a minute. You said the doctor who delivered the Piluski kid was there."

"Yeah. Do you think I'm making it up? He gave Tina a shot, remember? I thought this drooling business was part of a pipe dream. Apparently you don't."

"No," Trotter said. "I don't. So the doctor was there. What about the minister who performed the baptism?"

"He was there, at least for a while. I didn't see him after Tina got upset, but I was in the can and then upstairs."

"Then let's just see if he's still there before we use the phone. I've heard an awful lot about the Reverend Mr. Nelson, and I think the time has come for me to meet him face-to-face."

# CHAPTER FOUR

The Piluski home was filled with smoke and loud voices by the time they got back, to say nothing of body heat and liquor fumes. Joe Albright couldn't see how these people could care much about the baby they were supposedly celebrating when they made the kid's environment so rotten. There was so much shouting and loud laughter, Joe was amazed that Elizabeth's mother was able to hear the baby cry—it had to be more ESP than actual hearing.

They didn't find Mr. Nelson at the party. The consensus seemed to be that he'd gotten a phone call (though hearing the phone would be an accomplishment all its own) and rushed out somewhere. Trotter kept asking people where, nearly shouting himself hoarse to do it.

Joe knew that there was probably some complicated national-security reason Trotter was not taking a step that seemed perfectly obvious to him. At the risk of making a fool of himself, he decided to risk suggesting it. He leaned close to the Agency man and said, "Why don't you call the church?"

"What?"

"Call the Northside Church. That's where he probably went, and if he didn't, he probably told his wife where he was going."

Trotter nodded solemnly. "And you wanted to know why I didn't call."

"Gotta learn sometime."

"Okay. I didn't call the church because I'm an asshole. Great idea. Now where's a phone?"

That led to another series of questions shouted at random partyers. It turned out there were three phones—one in the living room, one in the kitchen, and one in the main bedroom upstairs, the one Joe had put Tina to sleep in.

The party had, as this kind of party often did, spilled out into the kitchen. Joe was ready to forget the phone there and lead Trotter upstairs. Instead Trotter picked up the phone and handed it to Joe to dial. Joe decided to feel flattered—he had been spending time at the church, so Trotter assumed he'd memorized the telephone number. Joe was very happy that he had. He finished pushing buttons, said, "It's ringing," and handed Trotter the receiver.

There were still a lot of people around. They were paying attention to a woman in a low-cut dress who was using the process of getting ice cubes from a tray as an excuse to put on a show. That was a pretty good attention-getter, but they could still hear things. Trotter apparently didn't care.

Wrong again. Trotter took the receiver and walked its extra-long cord right out the back door, closing it behind him. Nobody even noticed.

Trotter came back a few seconds later looking sick. "His wife says he's gone to hold Jimmy Hudson's hand."

"So? He'll do the kid good. He did wonders for Tina, helped her deal with the loss of her baby."

"It was the least he could do. It was his job."

"So it was his job. He did it very well, turned her around when she touched bottom."

"I don't mean that. I mean it was *his job*. He killed Tina's baby, he killed all of them, and I've got to warn Rines before he kills Jimmy Hudson and ruins everything."

"But I *know* him, Trotter. He's absolutely sincere. He's a *good man*."

"That's the worst kind. Go see how Tina's doing."

Joe's mouth went dry. "You don't think—"

"No, I don't. No leverage to be gained in hurting her now. Just go up there, see to her, and get on the phone. Hurry up."

Joe went. He pushed people aside and sprinted, like a man desperate for the bathroom.

As he climbed the stairs Joe was thinking, this is going to kill her. She had forgiven herself for her baby's death because Will Nelson had shown her why she should and made her believe it. If she found out he was a spy and a murderer, that he had in fact *caused* the death he had helped her get over, it would all collapse—faith, hope, confidence, everything. Nothing would be left but bitterness, and Joe couldn't blame her. He felt pretty bitter about it, himself.

Tina was still sleeping soundly. She seemed more peaceful now than when he'd left her. She looked very innocent and pretty, like a woman redeemed. No, like a woman who'd never *needed* to be redeemed. How much of that was him, he wondered, and how much of it was Mr. Nelson?

He stood looking at her for a few seconds, aching for her so much that he almost forgot to pick up the phone. She moaned softly as the receiver left the hook but didn't awaken. Joe smiled.

The smile deepened when he heard Rines's voice over the phone saying, "Oh, he's been and gone already."

Trotter's silence was eloquent with surprise. "And everybody's okay?" he said at last.

"All Hudsons present and accounted for. He showed up at the gate, said Jimmy had asked for him. They checked with me, and I told them to send him up. He saw Jimmy in company of one of my men—"

"Thank God for that," Trotter said. "By the way, Albright's joined us."

"Hello," Joe said quietly. "I don't want to wake her up."

"Wake who up?" Rines demanded.

"Don't be a goddam prude," Trotter told him. "Go on. He saw Jimmy Hudson . . ."

"Jimmy asked him for reassurance in a general way, nothing specific, or I wouldn't have let Nelson go, got it, and left."

"Are you sure?"

"I sent Swinton to see him off."

"Check," Trotter told him. "Ask Swinton exactly what he said and did."

Rines sounded resigned. "Right away," he said, and put Trotter and Joe on hold.

"This stinks, Joe," Trotter said over syrupy music.

Albright wanted to ask him if it had ever occurred to him he might be wrong, but that might wake Tina. He grunted noncommittally.

"If I'd been less timid about my conclusions, we could have nailed him on the scene. And I should have thought of him long ago. He got here just about the time the murders started. He's close to the Hudsons; he *got* close to the others after the deaths. He's the one who'd think of baptism. Why else do you *wet* somebody's *head*? What a mind; what a sick, brilliant mind. I should have been on to him days ago—should have seen it would take a friend of the family to lure the Stein girl off the grounds. The Congressman would have my balls for hemming and hawing like—"

The music cut off. "I can't find Swinton," Rines said. "He didn't come back."

Trotter cursed; Rines said it went double for him. Albright thought, the man is scary, but whatever this business takes, he's got it. It was a very low-percentage operation to laugh at one of Trotter's conclusions.

"What do we do now?" Joe said, forgetting about Tina for a second.

"Joe?" she said sleepily. She lifted her head, looked around for him, smiled when she saw him. She reached out for his hand. He let her have it. She lay back down, still smiling.

Trotter said, "Yeah, what do we do now? Joe, you get down to the church. Don't go in. Just try to spot if he's there, and tail him if he comes out. If he doesn't come out, wait for one of Rines's men. Rines, have you got a tame Federal judge around here?"

"Friendly, at least."

"Friendly enough to give you a search warrant for a church on not much?"

"And the warrant says what?"

"Who cares? This is never going to be a court case. The idea is to get in the door, and defuse the local cops if Mrs. Nelson is there and wants to call them."

"She could be, um, persuaded not to call." Joe could hardly believe his own voice. Was he really volunteering to go into a woman's house and beat her into submission? Or was he just playing devil's advocate? He wanted to believe the second, but he was honest enough with himself to know he wasn't sure. This spy business was insidious. From things Rines and Trotter had let slip, Joe gathered Trotter had been doing this kind of work all his life. Joe was beginning to understand how he got so weird.

"Goddammit, Joe!" There was real anger in Trotter's voice. "You said you had to learn sometime, so learn this now: *We don't hurt people for practice.* Got that? We're fighting swine, and we're covered with plenty of our own pig shit, but we are American enough not to have sunk that low. Yet. Okay?"

"It's better than okay. Lets me off the hook."

"It won't always. Get moving."

"I'm sending two men," Rines put in. "Maybe three. I want to make sure they get there."

"You're sure Swinton is dead?"

"Dead or crippled. He wasn't a plant."

"You never know," Trotter said. "I'll be out there right away."

Rines grunted and hung up. As Joe replaced the receiver, he thought of the background checks Rines had run on prominent local citizens. The one on Nelson had come out absolutely clean. No, he thought, you never *did* know.

"Tina, are you all right?"

"I'm fine now. I'm sorry about blowing up that way."

"It's okay. Everything's going to be okay." He said it as if he

**193**

meant it. He had no problem sounding as if he meant what he said next. "I love you, Tina."

"I love you, too, Joe."

"I've got to go do some work." And may you never find out what it is, he thought. "I'll call you later." He kissed her and left, to go hunt the Reverend Mr. Will Nelson.

# PART EIGHT

## CHAPTER ONE

Roger sat in the office of Mel Famey, Senior Editor of *World-watch* magazine and KGB agent, looking down at Mr. Famey's corpse, telling himself the truth. Telling himself many Truths.

Faith. Faith was the important thing. To a man of Faith, anything was possible. God did not try us beyond our strength. It raineth even on the just as on the unjust—it *had* to, otherwise the unjust would have an excuse. But Roger knew that the trials God sent did not depend on your righteousness. No one was more righteous than Job, but Job suffered more than anyone.

Everything that happened was God's will; it was all a part of the working out of the Plan. God could have lifted His Hand and brought the Plan to fruition instantly, but it was reflection of the love He felt for Man that He chose to work His will through men.

Roger bowed his head and prayed for Faith to accept the Will of the Lord, and to know what to do.

Because God had a new task for him. That had been made obvious by the events of the past few hours. Or perhaps it was just a new phase of the old plan. Whatever it was, it would require changes in the life he had made. It would mean giving up Donna. It would mean he could no longer be Will Nelson. So be it.

*Not my will be done*, he thought, *but Thine*. The Lord was demanding no easy sacrifices, but Roger could draw one consolation. The Lord must now feel that Will's memory had been sufficiently honored by Roger's dual ministry. He was cheered by the belief that he had brought the name of his only friend to the Lord's attention, and that Will rested happy in the bosom of the Father.

As for Donna, he would miss her terribly. But she was a good woman, a pearl beyond price. She would find a place; she would continue to serve the Lord.

As would he. Roger's ministry was not over, just the phase of it that had seen him using the Russians to his ends.

They had *turned* on him. They were so blind to the workings of the Lord that they had thought they could kill him.

Worse than that, they'd tried to use a confused, innocent soul like Jimmy Hudson to get to him. Apparently, some information Control would find very embarrassing was about to be released by Jimmy's mother. Of course, Roger had known she must have *something* to do with Moscow, or they wouldn't have devoted so much attention to her, but Borzov (during another panic-stricken radio message early this morning, before the christening) had gone into excruciating detail about it.

Roger hadn't listened. He had no interest in their evil purposes, he just wanted to know the next soul Azrael was to bring to judgment. He said as much.

Borzov had turned cold and terse. "You will receive instructions."

As he had, instructions relayed unknowingly by Jimmy Hudson during a plea to his pastor for help. "Could you please come out here? I—I'd really appreciate it."

"Of course I'll come," Roger—still Will Nelson, then—had said, but the boy was talking again before he'd had a chance to hear the words.

"Not just for me, either," Jimmy had gone on. "Mel Famey is working on a story about my mother—he'd like to talk with you, too. To get your viewpoint. He told me to say you might serve as a control on the sensationalism—you could help tone it down."

And that was it, the words *control* and *tone* in the same sentence. Roger had known there was a Russian agent inside at the Hudson Group. Now he knew he was this Mel Famey, and that Borzov required a face-to-face meeting. Famey, Roger had to admit, had been quite resourceful, taking advantage of the opportunity to avoid making personal contact through an obviously monitored switchboard.

*Tone* also meant it was to be a secret meeting, but from the security he had been subject to when he spoke to Jimmy, that was not going to be possible if he simply honored Mr. Famey's request for an interview. He had no intention of speaking about the soul of a member of his Congregation for public consumption, which was all he'd have been able to do with an FBI man present.

Instead, when he'd finished with Jimmy (and he thought he'd done the boy some good—Jimmy had the will to holiness, but he had not yet learned to subjugate his emotions to that will), he ostentatiously spurned the invitation to be interviewed and allowed Special Agent Swinton to drive him to the gate.

Roger felt terrible about Special Agent Swinton. Granted, it was the Will of the Lord that he die, but he seemed a man of such *quality.* It seemed almost wasteful for his part of the Plan to have been simply an obstacle for Roger to clear before confronting his destiny. That, of course, and as the source of a gun.

But that was how it worked out. As Swinton drove his car through the woods that hid Hudson Group Headquarters from the highway, Roger told him there was an insect on his collar.

"Odd for October," Swinton had said, and tried to brush it off.

"No," Roger said, "you keep missing it. Let me get it." Once Roger's hands were that close to a man's undefended throat, even a *trained* man's undefended throat, the outcome was almost a certainty. Roger rendered Swinton unconscious, gained control of the automobile, pulled off to the side of the road, trickled a few drops of water from a vial in his pocket on Swinton's forehead, and finished him.

Then he removed his clerical garb and replaced them with Swinton's shirt and jacket, taking as well his revolver and identification. He had no intention of using either—the identification would have done him little good in any case, since he looked only superficially like Swinton—but the Lord was guiding his actions.

Roger turned the car around and drove back to the building's rear parking lot. He found a use for the gun amost immediately, shooting the lock from a loading-dock door and going in that way. Again, the Lord was with him. No one heard the shot, and no one saw him as he made his way through the busy pressroom and upstairs to the editorial offices. He had spotted Mel Famey's office when he was there before. It was down at one end of the corridor, the other end of which held the executive offices and the entrance to the Hudson family suite.

He opened the door and walked in. Famey jumped.

"We were to meet," Roger told him.

Famey's beard twitched. "Yes," he said. Roger was wondering

what the man was so nervous about when Famey's hand came up from under his desk with a gun in it.

Roger dropped to the floor. While he was falling, he heard the spitting sound of a silenced revolver. He took Swinton's gun from his pocket and fired once. Famey fell backward from his chair. His head thumped heavily on the floor.

Roger turned and faced the door, his brain working madly. The shot, the crash of the body—an army of FBI men should be here any second. He couldn't shoot it out with all of them, and he couldn't think of a way to explain the gunplay, either on his part or Famey's.

No one came.

A masterpiece of modern architecture. Roger's memory supplied him with the phrase from some old magazine article he'd read while preparing for his stay in Kirkester. No expense spared. All offices soundproofed for maximum working efficiency.

Roger offered a short prayer of thanksgiving. Barring a telephone call, he would have a few minutes to sort this all out.

He went and looked at the body. There was no obvious wound, but there was a dark pool of blood around Famey's head. Roger tilted the body with a toe to see underneath. He saw a ragged exit wound in the back of Famey's neck. He'd shot the man through his open mouth. Roger had once heard an emergency-room intern describe that phenomenon as a "hole in one." It had seemed completely tasteless at the time, but now it struck him as rather amusing, and he began to giggle.

As soon as he recognized it as a nervous reaction, he made himself stop and think the situation over.

Now he had done that, and accepted the new life God had in store for him. The first thing to do was to get out of this building—he had nothing more to do here; nothing more to do in Kirkester, now that he knew the Russians had turned their treachery on him.

He could not count on getting out of here as easily as he'd gotten in—he only knew one way off the grounds, and that was through the heavily guarded, all-vehicles-searched front gate. He needed some kind of safe conduct, and the answer to that was at the other end of the hallway, where the Hudsons were.

There was just one thing here he still had to do. The dead man at his feet may have been a would-be murderer and a traitor to his country and to God, but he was still a human being with a soul. Roger couldn't just leave him and still be true to his ministry.

But there was a problem. He had used all the water he'd

brought with him on poor Swinton, and there was no source of water in the office.

No source of *pure* water, at any rate. There was a coffee machine and a pot of black coffee. It was hot, but Famey wouldn't feel it, and in the eyes of God, it would all be the same.

# CHAPTER TWO

Roger felt strange as he made his way down the corridor, exposed. Before now, back to Biblical times, the Angel of Death was known to man only by the results of his works. That was only fitting. "The Lord works in a mysterious way his wonders to perform" meant simply that He kept His own counsel and revealed His instruments only rarely.

This, it seemed, was to be one of the times. It was an honor. Roger had to remember that. The Lord was good to him far beyond his desserts. There was no need to be nervous simply because he had grown unused to face-to-face confrontations since Vietnam. The Lord would make plain to him what to do.

And he did. As soon as Roger presented himself at the locked, soundproofed door of the Hudsons' family suite, he knew what to do.

•   •   •

"I *know* it's all for my own protection!" Regina told Rines. "And *don't*, please, remind me that I came to you for help. I remember, and I appreciate it."

"What's the problem, then?" Rines wished Trotter would show up. They'd phoned from the gate that he'd entered the grounds already, how big *was* this goddam place? Granted, with security checks and everything, it would take a little longer, but he should have been here by now. He was needed. Rines wasn't fond of the fiction of Trotter's not being the one in charge, but he was willing to play along. Knowing what he knew about the Congressman's son, Rines figured it was just Trotter telling himself, for the sake of his sanity, the kind of lie nobody but the teller has to believe.

It was more or less working; everybody who counted knew Trotter was in charge, but they almost automatically pretended to defer to Rines. Except Regina Hudson wouldn't play. Anytime Rines told her to do something, she wanted reasons. Rines, to his own surprise, had enough pride to have become sick of giving her the one reason that always worked: "Trotter said so."

So they were having an argument. "You were brought here from the office for your own safety, Miss Hudson," he told her.

"I have work to do."

"There's a telephone; there's a computer terminal. What else do you need?"

"An explanation." She had been standing to argue; now she flopped down in a chair. "That's all," she said wearily. She looked miserable and scared and very young, and Rines realized she had been using the anger to keep the rest of it from showing.

"We think—" What the hell. "*Trotter* thinks we know who the Russians' hit man is, and we have reason to believe—"

"*Who?*" she demanded. "*Who is it?*"

A buzzer went off just as Rines opened his mouth. He held up a hand, asking Regina to wait, and went to the intercom. "Yes?"

A voice croaked, "Swinton, I . . ." There was a click as a finger slid off the talk button.

"How the hell did he get up here?" Rines asked the room at large. Nobody had any specific answers, but since Rines and the man with him both knew he'd never gotten off the grounds, Swinton had to be around somewhere. Rines drew his gun and stood to the side of the door. "Wish they had a TV camera here or something."

Regina said they never thought they'd need one in this part of the building.

Rines smiled at her. "No need to sound so apologetic. I wouldn't have, either. You stand there, so you'll be behind the door when it opens, okay? Not that I expect anything to go wrong, but why take chances?"

Regina nodded dumbly and took her place at the door. She'd been doing everything dumbly lately. Rines and the man who'd brought her upstairs weren't saying anything, but it was obvious that they suspected the man on the intercom *might* be the killer. The person Allan *thought* was the killer. Which was good enough for her.

A small part of her wanted to see the face of someone who could kill children merely to give someone negotiating leverage. That was probably the last of her "news instinct," shocked by so many personal scoops that it had shrunk to something considerably smaller than everyday curiosity. The rest of her wanted to run away somewhere and forget any of it ever happened.

Regina pushed herself back against the wall as Rines told his man to open the door.

Regina had noticed over the last day or so that except for Rines (who was older) and Albright (who was black), it was impossible for her to tell the FBI men apart. The one with his hand on the knob was a Xerox copy of the ones in the main corridors who were duplicates of the ones at the entrance. It wasn't that their features were identical, though they did all seem to be handsome without being striking. It was more an attitude, as though the Bureau had somehow cornered the market on all the Boy Scouts who'd grown up taking the oath seriously.

Rines's man undid the lock and turned the knob. Then things got confusing.

As soon as it was unlatched, the door lurched open. Rines's man instinctively pushed back against it. Regina, behind the door, could see nothing, but the man said, "It's Swinton," and let the door open the rest of the way. Regina gasped as a limp body spilled out across the floor. Rines's man lowered his gun and bent to help, and the body on the floor rolled over, raised a gun and fired twice.

Regina screamed and tried to claw her way backward through the wall. There was no third shot. She was still in one piece. He hadn't shot her.

She was still trying to grasp the concept when she noticed that the barrel of the gun was pointing directly at the middle of her chest. Above the gun was the face of her pastor. She thought absurdly, *Jimmy is going to be so disappointed*, and began to giggle.

"Please be quiet, Miss Hudson. I don't mean to harm you."

It was the voice from the church steps, the quiet sound of concern and reassurance that had made him so popular. Regina stopped giggling. In the presence of that voice, in these circumstances, nothing was funny.

He got to his feet, keeping the gun trained on Regina all the time. "Are you all right?" he asked.

"Why don't you kill me and get it over with?" How odd, she thought. What she'd intended to say was *don't shoot please don't shoot*.

"If everyone behaves intelligently, there'll be no question of anyone else getting killed. I need you alive." He gave her a small encouraging smile. She'd seen him smile that way at Sunday school students. "I didn't even kill this gentleman. Mr. Rines, I think. Control said Rines. I didn't kill you, did I, Mr. Rines?"

A voice came from the other side of the door. "Go to hell."

Regina continued to surprise herself; in spite of the spot she was in, she had room for relief at knowing Rines wasn't dead. And she could take her eyes away from the gun long enough to notice the look of pain that flashed over Mr. Nelson's face when Rines damned him.

He shook it off. "Well," he said, with an air of decision. "I was hoping to find your mother, but I think you'll have to do. Come with me, please." He gestured with the gun. Regina found it very compelling.

She took two steps out from behind the door, then stopped. The man who had opened the door was writhing on the floor in agony. One hand was trying unsuccessfully to stop the redness pulsing from his belly. The other hand clutched tightly at one of Rines's hands, the one on the end of the arm with the big red stain surrounding a small black hole.

The young man was whispering. She hadn't been able to hear him behind the soundproof door. "The jacket and the hair," he said. "Swinton's. Just like . . . *Swinton's*, sorry chief, jacket . . . hair . . ." Then he made a rasping noise and both hands fell limp.

Regina said, "Oh, Jesus," and started to cry.

Nelson's voice was soothing. "It's all right. I promise. Remember, 'My Kingdom is not of this Earth, but my Father's, which is in Heaven.'"

Nelson bent and picked up the guns the FBI men had dropped. He stashed them safely in various pockets. Then he went to the small desk in the room and poured some water from the pitcher into a Dixie cup. Still keeping the gun trained on Regina, he knelt beside the dead man (who, Regina knew now, had *not* been a cookie-cutter creation but a human being, unique and irreplaceable). Nelson turned the body faceup, closed its eyes, and trickled water on its head.

"I baptize you," he said, "in the name of the Lord, and humbly beseech him to forgive you your sins, and to take you to be eternally happy with him in Paradise."

"Oh, my God," Rines groaned. "All the *wet hair* . . ."

Nelson stood up, beaming. "You see, Miss Hudson—may I call you Regina? You see, Regina, it's all part of the Plan."

Regina stared. Nelson seemed quite pleased with himself. "I don't expect you to understand all at once. These are profound theological issues. It took *me* a long time to figure them out. But at least you've stopped crying."

Regina didn't dare tell him *why* she'd stopped crying. It was because if she tried to make any sound at all, what would come out would be a scream that wouldn't stop until she'd screamed herself insane.

# CHAPTER THREE

*I should have known better.* Trotter made his way through the building with Petra Hudson's words echoing through his head. Her son had been wild, accusatory, kept from violence only by his inability to decide exactly whom he should be violent to. Rines told the story while a doctor patched up his arm, and ambulance attendants bundled off the dead man. Jimmy Hudson wasn't having any. Not Mr. Nelson. Impossible. They were all plotting against him. Trotter said sure, then ignored him. Irrational people were easy to shrug off.

But Petra Hudson wasn't even angry; she had no blame for anyone, not even herself. *I should have known better.* Than to get into the game in the first place, Trotter supposed. Than to try to change sides and get away with it. Than to have let Trotter talk her into hoping.

When Trotter had worked out some probabilities, and told her it wasn't over yet, she'd just smiled sadly at him. Thanks, but no thanks.

All right, to hell with her. He had work to do. Reports coming back from Rines's men indicated that Nelson was making his way to the back of the building, keeping to open areas as much as possible to avoid having someone jump out from behind a closed door and coldcock him before he could do anything to his hostage. So far, with the FBI and security guards carefully kept away, they'd been through the bullpen of Hudson Features—a thousand desks but no cubicles, and the second-floor cafeteria. The route was identical to the one Regina had taken him through for his Grand Tour of the place when he'd first arrived. That made sense—Regina was undoubtedly the tour guide for this little jaunt, too.

Next, they'd go downstairs to the main entrance hall, then across the catwalk through the pressroom, down again, and out the back. Trotter hoped.

The key thing was the pressroom. Nelson *ought* to love it; visibility all around and nowhere for a sniper to shoot from except the tops of the printing presses. If printing presses were easy to climb, there'd be no need for the catwalk.

To do any good, Trotter had to get there first. Nelson had a head start, but Trotter wasn't dragging a hostage, and he could run through corridors on a more direct route.

There was no one around the catwalk door when he made it there. He opened it just to make sure they hadn't gone ahead of him, but all he could see was the pressroom with everything in readiness for the special issue of *Worldwatch*. Far across the room, he could see the glassed-in control area. The man inside raised his arm and waved and gave him a sign to indicate everything was ready.

The idiot. What if Trotter had come in with Nelson and Regina right behind him? It was gratifying to know that Rines had gotten the doctor off him long enough to make the necessary phone call and that the press operator understood the instructions, but Trotter *had* to go through with this no matter what, and there was no sense taking the risk of the subject's finding out.

The asshole was still waving. Trotter waved back, which seemed to make him happy, then went back through the door. He leaned against it and waited.

And thought. Could he have saved a few lives, kept Regina out of this spot, if he'd been a little less cautious? If he'd jumped up out of his pew the minute the first drops of water hit Elizabeth June Piluski's cute little head, grabbed Nelson by the collar, and hauled him off to be locked in chains while they tossed the parson's house, who would be alive? Who would be safe? A lot more people than were now.

Because Regina or no Regina, Nelson could not be allowed to get away. He hadn't had time to discuss that with Rines, but it was almost as if the Congressman's voice had sounded simultaneously in both their brains. Azrael was not to be allowed to flap his angel's wings and fly away. It wasn't that he'd go back to the Russians, it was that he was simply too goddam sick (and too goddam successful) to be allowed to stay loose. So there was no question about bringing him down; the question was: Could you make him fall without his bringing somebody with him.

Trotter doubted it. This angel would not fall alone. The only thing left in doubt was who with. There was a big FBI ambush waiting at the other end of the building. Trotter had sworn that whatever happened, Regina Hudson would not be part of it. Trotter had gotten her into this; he'd get her out.

But there was more than that at stake. Trotter had sworn long ago to fight Cronus, and to help all his brothers and sisters, those who'd been born to be used. Regina was one of them, and she was the key to her mother's future. The revelations of Petra Hudson could make Cronus too hot to use, but in order to put the message across, Petra Hudson had to have enough interest in life to convince Congress and the Press she didn't doubt the truth of her own story. The Petra Hudson he'd left a few minutes ago, the one who "should have known better," could never pull it off.

Trotter wanted Cronus destroyed; he wanted Regina Hudson to live. The world was a lot easier to care about with his Little Bash in it.

He smiled at the thought. The world with his Little Bash in it was worth dying for.

# CHAPTER FOUR

The man with his back to the door (it had to be Trotter) was smiling.

Roger knew it was a false smile, bravado, designed to upset him. He resolved not to let it.

"Mr. Trotter," he said. "Stand aside, please."

"Let's talk for a minute."

"Stand aside. I don't want to hurt Miss Hudson."

"Damn right, you don't. The second you do, you are ground round. I promise you that personally."

"I have the gun, Mr. Trotter. You seem to be unarmed."

"I don't have a gun. But I'm about the only government employee in this building who doesn't. It's only respect for Miss Hudson that keeps them from killing you now, and that won't last."

"You're talking as if you have a suggestion to make."

"I do. Take me instead."

"Why should I?"

"Better for you. Not to brag, or anything, but I'm important. I assume you know why you were sent to kill Smolinski."

"I know." It had been one of the things Control insisted on telling him. They feared this Trotter. They were afraid to make him angry. If the Russians had so much respect for him, our own government would probably do anything to keep him safe. Much more, in the perverted way Godless governments had of looking at things, than they would to save an innocent girl. Furthermore, it would allow him to risk the life of a spy, whose soul was

205

undoubtedly a *catalog* of sins, rather than Miss Hudson's. It looked like a good offer. It looked *too* good.

"All right," Roger said, "that's why I should do this. Why should you?"

"What do you mean?"

"You know what I mean. Why are you putting your life in danger?"

"It's embarrassing," Trotter said. He sounded apologetic.

Roger had no more time to waste playing games. "If it's too embarrassing, then, never mind. Move aside."

"I'm in love with Miss Hudson. I'm not supposed to leave myself open for emotions like that, but I am. I'd do anything to protect her, it's as corny and as simple as that."

Miss Hudson said, "Allan." It was the first time she had spoken since he'd baptized the dead FBI man.

"And love embarrasses you?" Roger said. He would never understand how these men survived such an evil existence.

"It's against my training," Trotter said.

"Why should I believe you?"

Anger flashed in Trotter's eyes. "Show a little Faith, Reverend."

It was ironic. A man like that reminding Roger to have Faith. He used his faith now, taking a few seconds to think and pray. The Lord gave him a plan.

"Here," he said, "is what I am willing to do. You will stand aside from the door. Miss Hudson will open the door and stand in the open doorway. You will drop to your hands and knees and align yourself in a straight line with her. Miss Hudson will walk backward across the catwalk. You will crawl. I will follow. I will give Miss Hudson a ten- to fifteen-foot head start. When she reaches the door at the other end of the catwalk, she may go through, and go wherever she likes, and I'll proceed with your valuable self, Mr. Trotter. Until the far side of the catwalk, if you attempt to do anything but what I tell you, I will shoot Miss Hudson. If she does anything, I'll shoot you. If anyone else tries to interfere, any of Mr. Rines's men or anyone else, I'll shoot you both. Is that clear?"

Now Trotter was thinking. "It's clear enough," he said. He did not look happy.

"Do you agree, Mr. Trotter?" Roger demanded.

Trotter's face was sour. "I wish I'd gotten to know you better. Why didn't you ring the bell when you dumped Hannah Stein's body in my hallway? Why'd you dump her there at all?"

"Did you baptize her, too?" Regina Hudson asked.

"Of course he did," Trotter said. "That's why everybody's hair was wet. Mr. Nelson wouldn't just kill somebody and leave them naked to the powers of hell. What kind of Christian would that be?"

"A very poor one," Roger said. "She left the house that night specifically to meet me. I was instructing her. She was a good girl. And I left her in your hallway on orders. They wanted to try to tie you up with the police, to distract you until they attained their objective. Apparently, Mrs. Hudson continued to surprise them with her stubbornness, and anyway, the police weren't interested in you. Now, are we done wasting time? Do you accept my offer?"

"What if I don't?"

"If you don't, you stand aside, and I proceed with Miss Hudson. If you refuse to stand aside, I will shoot you dead. Unfortunately, I won't have the chance to baptize you."

"I bet that would just break your heart."

"In spite of your cynicism, Mr. Trotter, it would. I will pray for you and hope some other clergyman can be found to perform the proper rites before your soul is hopelessly lost. Now, for the last time, do you agree?"

By way of an answer, Trotter dropped to his hands and knees. "Do I have to bark?" he asked.

Roger almost smiled in spite of himself. "That won't be necessary, Mr. Trotter. Miss Hudson, open the door, please. Stand there with your back to the catwalk. Right away, please, or I'll have to shoot Mr. Trotter."

"Go ahead, Regina," Trotter said, "do it."

# CHAPTER FIVE

He announced he loved her, then put them in the worst imaginable circumstances, worse than waiting to die under the Kirk River. Here she was, walking backward on a solid catwalk high over the pressroom with a madman's gun aimed at her heart. Every step felt as if it would send her plummeting over the edge of something, so that she would fall the thirty feet or so to the concrete floor below, making a one-point landing on her head, smashing her brain to jelly.

At that, it might be better than letting Nelson kill her, which he assuredly would, as soon as they got to the other end of the catwalk. For all his promises he wasn't going to let her live, especially now that he had the valuable Mr. Trotter.

And the valuable Mr. Trotter was no help, either, talking to her all the time. "Watch the rivet, Regina, about a third of the way there, Regina, chin up, Regina, remember to run like hell when you get through the door on the other side, Regina." Where did all this Regina stuff come from? In the last minutes of her life, when this arrogant and enigmatic bastard she'd lost her heart to had finally said he loved her; when she could *use* a little tenderness before this nut killed them both; it would be all right to use the pet name. In fact, it was rapidly becoming her last wish—to hear him call her Bash one more time.

Though Allan was doing all the talking—the only sounds in the whole pressroom were the humming of the motors of the presses on standby (and why weren't they running? she wondered. It was way past time to roll on *Worldwatch*) and the sound of Allan's voice—he wasn't talking exclusively to her. He was keeping quite a flow of comments addressed to the Reverend Mr. Nelson. Evidently, Mr. Nelson was getting sick of it, or maybe stung by it. He began to answer back.

Allan said, "That's the Old Testament God you work for, right? The one who got mad and slew anybody who crossed him. The New Testament is a little heavier in the Free Will department."

Nelson mumbled something.

Regina wondered how Allan could calmly put his knees down on the pebbled-metal surface of the catwalk without any trace of pain showing in his voice. "Speak up," he snapped. "I can't hear you."

"The Lord," Nelson announced, "is moving and working among us this very day."

"Of course he is, but you're the best. You've got him working for the Russians, the most vicious bunch of sinners in the history of mankind."

For the first time, Regina saw a look of insanity on Nelson's face. "You don't understand the Plan! They were working for *me!*"

Allan stopped and looked up at Nelson over his shoulder. "For *you*," he said. "For *you*. My apologies. I wasn't aware of your promotion."

"What are you talking about? Keep moving."

Allan stayed where he was. Regina could see Nelson's hand tightening on the gun.

"We were talking," Allan said, "about the Lord working for the Russians. You come back with the announcement that *they're* working for *you*. Here I was thinking you were simply Azrael, the Angel of Death—"

Nelson's eyes opened wide. *"How did you know that?"*

Allan ignored him. "—but now it turns out you're God Almighty Himself. If I'd known, I would have worn a cleaner shirt. What are you? The Second Son, or the Second Coming?"

"You mock because you don't understand. God works through me!"

"*Bullshit* works through you. You kill because you like to, pal, and you've come up with the Azrael stuff because your conscience is a coward and needs an out."

Regina was looking at the gun. Nelson's hand was clasped so tightly around it, it trembled, but he didn't fire it or get it in position. It was as if Allan had struck a high-voltage wire in him.

"In fact, if you didn't have that goddam gun, I'd get up and bash your eyes shut. Do you hear me? *Bash!* Your *eyes! Shut! Now!*"

Just as he said *now*, a bell rang. For a crazy second, she thought it was her brain letting her know Allan's message for her, that he had been calling her Regina to get her ready to be called Bash when it counted. That he had a plan, and he wanted her eyes shut when it went into effect.

As she squeezed her eyes closed, she realized what the bell was—it was the warning bell before the presses started up. Just as the bell ended, just before the huge machines would roar to life like waking dragons, Regina heard the crack of bone on bone, followed by grunts and a man's scream. She opened her eyes just in time to see Nelson and Allan go over the railing of the catwalk. Regina opened her mouth to scream. The effort made her lungs hurt, but she could hear nothing in the roar of the presses. Then there was a tearing sound, like a million sails ripping in a hurricane, and the room was filled with a blizzard of torn paper that flew at her, sliced at her. She covered her eyes again, but not before she saw that among the white pieces of flying magazine stock, there were some that were wet, and bright red with blood.

# CHAPTER SIX

When the bell rang, Trotter made his move. He hadn't been sure he would. It's one thing to decide to die for something, it's another to go *do* it. Talking, baiting Nelson, had been his consciousness buying time, begging him to think of something else. There wasn't anything else. He warned Regina, as well as he could, that the air would soon be filled with nastiness, said the magic "Now" before Nelson got tired of the goading and took advantage of one of the extra chances Trotter kept giving him to shoot them both.

Nelson may have been a maniac, but he was still human. He had senses; he had reflexes. Trotter had known the clanging would start, and could be ready for it. Nelson would *have* to be startled. He'd flinch; he'd look around wildly to see where the sound was coming from. It was the only edge Trotter had.

As soon as the ringing started, Trotter heaved up with his arms, bunched his legs beneath him, and jumped blindly, straight back into the man with the gun. There was a loud noise and a pain in his head, and for a second, Trotter was sure he'd been shot. When his brain kept working, he realized what had happened was that he'd rammed the top of his head into the point of Nelson's chin. He didn't know what happened to the gun, and with the noise of the machines, couldn't know. All he could do was to keep his feet churning against the catwalk, keep driving the man back.

Until they both went over the side. Nelson had hold of him by now—he wasn't going to go over alone. That was all right. Trotter had figured that was the way it would be. For a few seconds it was like flying, first with an angel, then, when some jolt on the way down broke them apart, solo. Then the floor came up, and there was nothing.

•   •   •

*Betrayed*, Roger thought as his back leaned against nothing and his feet came up and his head started down. This *spy*, this Satan, had pushed them over the edge.

The joke would be on Trotter, because he would wake up in Hell, tormented forever. Roger, at last, would share the sweet

**210**

reward he'd helped so many others to attain, with the Lord he'd served with all his heart, no matter what words the Devil put in the mouths of his servants—

*Except.*

Except how could this be part of the Plan, how could a Godless killer like Trotter *beat him*, beat Azrael, kill the Angel of Death?

*Suppose.*

Suppose Trotter was *right*, Roger was just a madman, a—a *killer* no better than Trotter himself, because if he *were* an Angel of the Lord, would he be facing death with these damnable doubts? *My God, my God, why have you forsaken*—

*No.*

No, because in the jumble of images that rose around him as he fell, he found his Salvation, a rush of wind that hummed like a song, above the roaring of the gross inventions of man, a shimmering whiteness that was no solid shape, a light to guide him home, and as Roger let go of Satan forever, and reached out to meet the whiteness, he knew everything was going to be all right. He was going home.

•   •   •

The machines stopped roaring. They *gurgled* to a stop, as though they'd been stabbed to death. There were voices now, people running into the pressroom. She took her hands from her eyes. The first thing she saw was blood oozing from the paper cuts on the backs of her hands.

Then she made herself look over the edge of the catwalk and saw all the blood in the world. There was an *ocean* of blood on the floor of the pressroom. With islands floating in it. One of the islands was Allan, lying very still. Another was the right arm, shoulder, chest, and head of the Reverend Mr. Will Nelson, and the last was the rest of him. There was an archipelago of spilled parts scattered among them. Mr. Nelson had come too close to the speeding paper. Allan hadn't. Allan was intact. She'd warned him days ago about the edge of the web. She hadn't told him not to throw himself off the goddam catwalk.

She couldn't look anymore; she turned away and was sick. Each spasm was an expression of hatred for Nelson. That *bastard*, that bastard. He had made a fool of all of them, tormented her whole family, and now his death was so disgusting she couldn't even feel triumph over it.

And Allan. He'd known all along this was going to happen, and he did it, anyway. To save her. All the time she'd spent with him, even when they were making love, she wondered how he felt about her. He'd shown her now, and now it was too late.

Voices from down below. "Hey, look at this." It sounded like Albright.

She looked over the edge and saw Albright and a bandaged Rines standing in the middle of the red ocean, looking at Allan. Rines looked up and said, "Get that thing over here, now."

There was some kind of mumble in response. Regina couldn't make it out, but Albright did. "To *hell* with your shoes," he said, "I'll *feed* you your motherfucking shoes you don't get over here right away. This guy is *alive.*"

Regina felt her legs tremble, but she forced herself steady. This was no time to fall. She started to cry, then she laughed when Albright said it again.

"He's *alive.*"

# EPILOGUE

*Washington, D.C., November*

"I hate this top-secret stuff," Regina said. "I've been camped in that waiting room two weeks."

Trotter smiled at her. It was one of the few movements he could make that didn't hurt. "I've been under anesthesia most of the time," he told her. "I never realized you could break so many bones just by falling thirty feet."

She took hold of the hand that had fingertips sticking out of the cast. She touched the fingers gently. "You were a *mess*. I heard the ambulance guys talking when they took you away. They ought to call *you* Bash. And then they get you stabilized, they immediately jet you down here. We have excellent hospitals in Kirkester, and your credit was good."

"Top-secret stuff. I didn't have much to say about it."

"The secrets are safe. I've got an excuse to be in Washington, keeping my mother company while she testifies before Congress."

"I screwed up *Worldwatch* that week, didn't I?"

"Boy, you *have* been out of it. The issue shipped, only a day late. *Time* and *Newsweek* let us use plants of theirs."

"Journalism lives."

"Especially when you give them a big enough story. It's been amazing. Five prominent women my mother's age have committed suicide since the story broke. Even the big-city liberal papers haven't been able to explain it away, and Mother is keeping the heat on."

"Give them time, they'll think of something. Your mother is a brave woman."

"I guess so. Jimmy's getting treatment, too. It shook him up. I did what Rines asked and sat on the story about Mr. Nelson. We concentrated on Mel Famey—his name was in the stuff they found in Smolinski's place and sort of implied he killed Nelson. I *liked* Mel Famey. I still have trouble believing—"

"He made his choice a long time ago. Anyway, Albright will love you for it."

She nodded. "He called me an angel." They thought about that one for a second. Then Regina said, "Allan?"

"I'm not going anywhere."

"You expected to die, didn't you?"

"I expect everybody to die."

"That's not what I meant. Stop laughing."

"It hurts, anyway."

"Did you mean what you said? About loving me?"

He sighed. "Yes, I did."

"Well, don't sound so miserable about it. I want you to help me run the paper when you get well. Not the day-to-day stuff. Write editorials or something. I—I need you. Mother is going to sort of retire—lecture, do a book, things like that. Everything you suggested."

"I'll think about it, Bash. I—I'm glad you're here. I never said this to anybody before, but I need you, too."

"You're *always* going to need me. When you get out of traction, I'm going to give you an orgasm that will make you blind. Then I will lead you around."

"You can be a wise mouth with me all tied up like this."

A nurse came in and made a hand signal. Trotter lowered and raised his eyelids in acknowledgment. "When can you come back, Bash?"

"Is that a subtle way of telling me I have to go? I can be back whenever. I'll come back tonight about eight, is that okay?"

"It will give me something to dream about during my nap."

"I love you," she said, and kissed him on the forehead.

"I love you, too." He watched her go.

•    •    •

214

Trotter did not go to sleep, at least not immediately. He had another visitor. A tough-looking man pushed the wheelchair in; the shrunken figure in it waved a hand and sent him from the room.

The Congressman worked his mouth. He worked it hard, forcing the living half to do all the work. The Congressman was very good at getting work from the reluctant—the speech was slow and a little slurred, but it was perfectly comprehensible, and undeniably the Congressman.

"You look like hell," he told his son.

Trotter laughed, winced, laughed again. "Whereas you, on the other hand, look great."

"Should have seen me before."

"We did it, Congressman. Saved the Hudson Group, pulled the plug on Cronus."

"*You* did it."

"I had a lot of help."

"You. Key man. You have to run the Agency."

"All right."

The good side of the Congressman's face froze. For a moment, Trotter was afraid he'd given the old man another stroke.

"You heard me," he told his father. "I'll do it until you get well. All my life I've been running from this rotten job, but I don't think I'll be doing much running anymore. Have you seen the X rays of my legs? Don't bother. So you've caught me. Someone's got to do the job."

"Rines isn't up to it."

"He's up to it. My being alive gets in his way, that's all."

"You tried to kill yourself."

"I was ready to die. There's a difference. You trained me. If I'd tried to kill myself, I would be dead."

The old man made a half smile.

"Anyway," Trotter went on, "for the first time ever I think I really want to live. So I'll run your goddam Agency for you. But not from Washington. Good cover jobs are hard to come by, and I'm damned if I'm going to run for Congress. We'll keep Rines on the case down here, and I'll help Regina run the Hudson Group. I'll have Albright with me, and things will be golden. I might even get married."

"Bad idea."

"Maybe so. But if I think it's a *good* idea, then I'll do it. Got that? If I'm running things, I'll make the decisions."

The Congressman showed him another half smile. "Good luck, son," he said. He pressed a button on the side of the wheelchair, and the tough-looking man came and got him.

Trotter let his eyes droop shut. He thought about the long

recuperation ahead of him; he thought about Regina and her happy threat to blind him; he thought about the job ahead. The rotten, corrupting, had-to-be-done job of fighting the rot and corruption of the Russians. He thought about the constant struggle he'd have to fight to keep himself from turning the Hudson Group, whose freedom he'd smashed himself up defending, into another branch of the Agency, without, of course, letting its enormous resources go to waste. He'd think of something. Bash would help, if only by yelling at him.

He settled back against the pillows. For a man whose long-dreaded destiny had caught up with him at last, he didn't feel too bad.

## Moscow

It was deep winter, now, but Borzov had ways to keep warm. His shower had been fixed (at last), and he had begun to let the young yellow-haired Sergeant Maria Malnikova warm his bed and whatever portions of his ancient anatomy happened to get cold.

And when he really wanted heat, he could allow himself to reflect that the Hudson Group failure was the third consecutive time the Congressman had done him down.

The damage was not irreparable. The advantage of a cold war over a hot one was that the damage was never irreparable. When the battleground was the mind of an uncontrolled citizen, and the weapons were history and news, each defeat could become the basis for a new success.

Let the Americans revel in the anti-Soviet feeling this operation had caused. Let them trumpet their triumph and stir up hatred. Borzov would use it, as he would have used the Hudson Group. His plan would continue, and the next American election would tell.

But he owed the Congressman something personal, too, after three reversals, and that account, Borzov knew, would be paid. He might even break the precedent of a lifetime and cross the ocean to see it paid in person. But come another November, Borzov's old American comrade, and this young man who was so like him, would watch their country fulfill the destiny Borzov had designed for it so many years ago, and then they would die.

If Borzov had to tell them himself, they would know who had beaten them.

Because that was something else about a war such as this. As the aggressor, Borzov had all the advantages. The Americans would never know how badly they were losing until long after they had already lost.